Penguin Books

Other People: A Mystery Story

Martin Amis was born in Oxford on 25 August 1949. He was educated in Britain, Spain and the USA, attending over thirteen schools and then a series of crammers in London and Brighton. He gained a formal First in English at Exeter College, Oxford. He has been an editorial assistant on *The Times Literary Supplement* and was Literary Editor of the New Statesman from 1977 until 1979. He now works as a Special Writer on the *Observer*. His other novels are: *The Rachel Papers*, which won the 1974 Somerset Maugham Award, *Dead Babies*, *Success*, *Money* and *Einstein's Monsters*; and a collection of essays, *The Moronic Inferno*. All of these are published in Penguins.

His novels have won widespread acclaim: writing about *Success*, Blake Morrison in *The Times Literary Supplement* said, 'The narrative economy and manipulation of sympathy make this Martin Amis's most assured work so far. The presentation of city life in its sadness is forceful in itself, but what is especially impressive is that all the detail counts in the overall design'; *The Times* wrote of *Dead Babies*, 'It's transfixing . . . At first it's funny. It teases, exaggerates, deliberates. Then it becomes ferocious, stricken, moving . . .'; the *London Review of Books* called *Money* 'one of the key books of the decade' and the *Guardian* thought it 'terribly, terminally funny: laughter in the dark, if ever I heard it'.

Other People
A Mystery Story

— ∿ —

Martin Amis

Penguin Books

PENGUIN BOOKS

Published by the Penguin Group
27 Wrights Lane, London w8 5tz, England
Viking Penguin Inc., 40 West 23rd Street, New York, New York 10010, USA
Penguin Books Australia Ltd, Ringwood, Victoria, Australia
Penguin Books Canada Ltd, 2801 John Street, Markham, Ontario, Canada l3r 1b4
Penguin Books (NZ) Ltd, 182–190 Wairau Road, Auckland 10, New Zealand

Penguin Books Ltd, Registered Offices: Harmondsworth, Middlesex, England

First published in Great Britain by Jonathan Cape 1981
First published in the United States of America by The Viking Press 1981
Published in Penguin Books 1982
Reprinted 1982, 1983, 1986, 1987, 1988

Printed and bound in Great Britain by
Cox & Wyman Ltd, Reading
Filmset in Linotron Plantin by
Rowland Phototypesetting Ltd
Bury St Edmunds, Suffolk

To my mother

Contents

Prologue

This is a confession, but a brief one.

I didn't want to have to do it to her. I would have infinitely preferred some other solution. Still, there we are. It makes sense, really, given the rules of life on earth; and she *asked* for it. I just wish there was another way, something more self-contained, economical, and shapely. But there isn't. That's life, as I say, and my most sacred duty is to make it lifelike. Oh, hell. Let's get it over with.

~ ~ ~

Part One

Part One

I
Special Damage

———— ∼∽∼ ————

Her first feeling, as she smelled the air, was one of intense and helpless gratitude. I'm all right, she thought with a gasp. Time – it's starting again. She tried to blink away all the water in her eyes, but there was too much to deal with and she soon shut them tight.

Someone leaned over her and said with a voice so close that it might have come from within her own head, 'Are you all right now?'

She nodded. 'Yes,' she said.

'I'll leave you then. You're on your own now. Take care. Be good.'

'Thank you,' she said. 'I'm sorry.'

She opened her eyes and sat up. Whoever had spoken was no longer there, but other people were moving about near by, people who for some reason were all there just to help her through. How kind they must be, she thought, how kind they are, to do all this for me.

She was in a white room, lying on a spindly white trolley. She thought about this for a while. It seemed quite an appropriate place to be. She would be all right here, she thought.

Outside, a man in white walked quickly past. He hesitated, then poked his head round the door. His posture suddenly relaxed. 'Come on, get up,' he said wearily, his eyes closed.

'What?'

'*Get up*. It's time. You're all right, come on.' He walked forward, glancing sideways at a low table on which various items were scattered. 'These all your things?' he said.

She looked: a black bag, some scraps of green paper, a small golden cylinder. 'Yes,' she said secretively, 'these all my things.'

'You better be off then.'

13

'Yes all right,' she said. She swung herself over the trolley's side. She stared down at her legs and moaned. The poor flesh was all churned and torn. Reflexively she reached down to touch. Her flesh was whole. The shreds were part of some wispy material laid over her skin. She was all right.

The man snorted. 'Where *you* been,' he said, his voice moistening.

'Can't tell,' she muttered.

He came closer. 'The toilet?' he said loudly. 'You want to go to the *toilet*?'

'Yes please,' she said, without much hope.

He turned, walked towards the door, and turned again. She stood up and tried to follow him. She found that heavy curved extensions had been attached to her feet. The idea was obviously to make movement very difficult, if not actually impossible. With one leg wobbling she came towards him at an angle along the slipped floor.

'Get your *things* then.' He shook his head several times. 'You people . . .'

He led her into the passage. Walking ahead of him now, and feeling his eyes on her back, she looked hastily this way and that. There seemed to be two kinds of people out there. Most of them were the ones in white. The other kind were smaller and bound in variegated robes; they were being carried or led about with expressions of defencelessness and apology. I must be one of them, she thought, as the man urged her down the passage and pointed to a door.

The first hours were the strangest. Where was her sense of things?

In the trickling narrow room, whose porcelain statuary she could not connect with herself, she placed her cheek against the cold wall and looked for clues inside her head. What was in there? Her mind went on for ever but contained nothing, like a dead sky. She was pretty sure this wasn't the case with other people – a thought that produced a sudden spurt of foul-tasting liquid in the back of her throat. She steadied herself and turned to face the room, catching the eye of a shiny square of steel on the wall;

through this bright window she briefly glimpsed a startled figure with thick black hair who looked at her and ducked quickly away. Is everyone frightened, she wondered, or is it just me?

She didn't know how long she was expected to stay where she was. Any minute now the man could come and get her again; alternatively, she might be allowed to hang around in here for as long as she liked, perhaps indefinitely. Then it occurred to her that the world was her idea. But in that case it couldn't be a very good idea, could it, if she sensed such unanimity of threat, such immanence of harm?

The door was a puzzle she speedily solved. The man had gone when the narrow room let her out. Without pausing she moved in the general direction of the white-clad keepers and their slower charges, towards the light which raced in playful eddies along the colourless walls. Abruptly the passage widened into a place where movement ceased and new kinds of people stood about in furtiveness and grief, or lay sweating warily on white-decked tables, or yelled out as the trotting keepers smuggled them away. Someone covered in blood stood hollering spectacularly in the centre of the floor, his hands raised to his eyes. Beyond him open double-doors admitted a cool wash of air and light. She moved forward, careful to skirt the thrashing pockets of confusion and distress. No one had time to prevent her.

She hurried from the indoors. When she tried to accelerate down the glass passage the devices on her feet abruptly checked her with their pain. She bent down to examine them and found, to her pleased surprise, that she could remove them without much difficulty. Two passing men carrying an empty hammock shouted at her and frowned meaningly at the discarded machines on the floor. But she could smell the living air now, and she hurried from the indoors.

At first, outside seemed no more than a change of scale. Everyone was still required to keep on the move, loose herds in the tall spanned passages. Quite a few seemed damaged, but there weren't many to guide or carry them. Those in pressing need of velocity and noise used the trolleys, numberless and variegated, queueing and charging along the wide central lanes in vaporous, indocile packs. The streets were full of display, of symbols whose meaning was coolly denied to her. Through an absence of power or will – or perhaps simply of time – no one bothered to stop her joining the edgy human traffic, though many looked as though they would like to. They stared; they stared at her feet; they had all grown used to their own devices – and where were hers supposed to be? It was her first mistake, she knew: no one was intended to be without them, and she was sorry. But she moved, and kept on moving, because that's what everyone else was required to do.

There were six kinds of people outside. People of the first kind were men. Of all the six kinds they were the most fully represented and also the most varied within their kind. Some went where they had to go in an effaced and gingery shuffle, hoping no one would pick them out: not many of them looked at her, and then only with diffidence and haste. But others moved with a rangy challenge, an almost criminal freedom, their jaws held up to front the air: they certainly looked her way, and with enmity, several of them making sounds of cawing censure with their mouths. People of the second kind were less worrying; they were shrunken, compacted – mysteriously lessened in some vital respect. They limped in pairs, with such awkward caution that they hardly made any progress at all, or else whirled about with a fluttery, burst, directionless verve. Some were so bad now that they had to be wheeled round in covered boxes, protesting piteously to their guides, who were people of the third kind. The third kind resembled the first kind quite closely except at the top and the bottom; their legs were often unprotected, and they skilfully tiptoed on the arched curves of their elaborate devices (I must be one of them, she thought, remembering the narrow room and lifting a hand to her hair). They looked at her for just a moment, then at her numb feet, then turned away in pain. People of the fourth kind were men who couldn't get their hair right, some using hardly any at all, others smothering themselves with the stuff, and still others who actually wore theirs upside down – the matted face climbing towards a great globed chin of naked scalp. *They* seemed to think that this was all right. People of the fifth kind stood apart on corners or edged their way sideways through the guiltily parting crowds; they didn't talk like other people talked; they either muttered darkly to themselves or spun away at an angle to wring their hands and admonish the air. She thought they must be mad. The people of the fifth kind included people of most other kinds. And they were never seen in pairs. People of the sixth kind, of course, were sorrily shod with tangled stockings, and weren't sure who they were supposed to be or where they were going. She thought she saw one or two of these, but on closer inspection they always turned out to be people of some other kind.

No one out there reminded her of anything much. She sensed that she was on the brink of the inscrutable, ecstatic human action, that all she saw was ulterior, having a great and desperate purpose which firmly excluded her. And she still couldn't tell to what extent things were alive.

No change yet, she thought.

Then something terrible started happening slowly.

Not too far above the steep canyons there had hung an imperial backdrop of calm blue distance, in which extravagantly lovely white creatures – fat, sleepy things – hovered, cruised and basked. Carelessly and painlessly lanced by the slow-moving crucifixes of the sky, they moreover owed allegiance to a stormy yellow core of energy, so irresistible that it had the power to hurt your eyes if you dared to look its way. But then this changed. The tufted creatures lost their outlines, drifting upwards at first to form a white shawl over the dome of the air, before melting back into a slope of unbroken grey beneath their master, which lost its power and boiled red with rage – or was it just dying, she thought, as she started to see the terrible changes below. With humiliation, candour and relief, people of all kinds duly began to hasten in hardened fear. Variety grew weary, and its pigments gave up their spirits without struggle, some with stealth, others with hurtful suddenness. Soon the passages and their high glass walls appeared to be changing places – or at least they agreed to share what activity remained: the daredevil roadsters broke in two and raced their ghosts away. Above, the bruised distance seeped ever nearer. Baying in panic with their wheels out, showing their true colours now, the trolleys of the sky warped downwards towards the earth, as further below the people made haste to escape from beneath the falling air.

Where were they all going to hide? Soon there would be no people left and she would be here alone. Someone of the second kind hobbled past, paused and turned, and said shyly,

'You'll catch your death.'

'Will I?' she asked.

She moved on. People lingered in the well-lit places. Sometimes you walked in glazed bleak silence, measuring yourself to the yellow relays of light; then you turned into a buzzing gallery of action and purpose. Alone or in small groups they eventually ducked into the darkness, determined to get somewhere while they still could. They went on staring at her, some of them, but perfunctorily now – at her feet, at her face, and perhaps at her feet again, depending on the kind of people they were.

For a time breakdown arrived on the streets. They teemed with a last, released, galvanic hate. People experimented with their voices, counting the harsh sounds they could make; others dashed headlong into the deepest shadows, as if only they knew a good secret place to hide. It was then that her sense of danger started climbing sharply, in steep swerves. Each turning seemed more likely to deliver its possibilities of hurt and risk; soon, someone or something would feel the need to do her special damage.

Enough of this, she thought, deciding to get these things over with and out of the way.

Not until the world was moving past her at quite a speed did it occur to her that she was running . . . Running pleased her, she realized. It was the first clear and urgent prompting that had come her way. The bricked passages reeled by. Such people that remained turned after her; a few shouted out. For a while one of them lolloped clumsily along in her wake, but she moved clear ahead. She seemed to be able to go just as fast as she liked. She thought that running would save time, that by speeding things up it would inevitably make the next thing happen sooner.

At last she made it to a place where there were no people left. The concrete floor spanned out into another kind of life. This was the end of whatever she was in. Beyond spiked rods green land rose in a calm swell. Overhead, she noticed, the fat creatures had crept back beneath their spangled roof – all heavy and red now, and their deity a sombre silver in the lake of darkness. Suddenly she saw a gap in the cage: a lane fed straight into the green land, with only a horizontal white bar to mark the point. She moved forward, bent herself beneath the bar, then ran as fast as she could up across the soft ground.

She soon found a good place to hide. There was a moist hollow at the foot of a leaning tree. With her breath lurching she lay down and folded herself up. Her body began to quiver: this is it, she thought, this is my death. The pain that she had harboured all day burst from the tight crux of her body. Her face leaked too, and some convulsion within her was squeezing unwanted sounds through her lips. She told herself to be quiet. What was the point of hiding if you made all this noise? The shadows put on weight. The ground gave way to receive her. At the last moment the air seemed to hum with iron and flame as one by one, above the vampire sky, the points of life went out.

2
Everybody's Queer

~~~

Statistical evidence shows fairly conclusively that all 'amnesiacs' are at least partially aware of what they're missing out on. They know that they do not know. They remember that they do not remember, which is a start. But that doesn't apply to *her*, *oh* no.

Of course, the initial stage is always the most difficult in a case like this. I'm pleased, actually. No, I am. We've got phase one over with, and she has survived quite creditably. Between ourselves, this isn't my style at all really. The choice wasn't truly mine, although I naturally exercise a degree of control. It had to be like this. As I said earlier, she *asked* for it.

. . . So what have we here?

A rising stretch of London parkland, a silver birch tree crooked over a shiny hollow, a girl in the recent dew. The time is 7.29 a.m., the temperature 51° Fahrenheit. Over her body the wind-dried leaves click their tongues – and no wonder. What in hell has happened to the girl? Her face is made of hair and mud, her clothes (they are hardly clothes any longer) have found out all the slopes of her body, her bare thighs clutch each other tight in the morning sun. Why, if I didn't know better, I'd say she was a tramp, or a ditched whore, or drunk, or dead (she looks very near to the state of nature: I've seen girls like that). But I know better, and, besides, people usually have a good reason for ending up the way they do. Whatever happened to this one? Something did. Let's move in closer. Let's find out. It's time to wake up.

~~ ~~ ~~

Her eyes opened and she saw the sky. For quite a time her thoughts insisted on being simultaneous. They worked themselves out like this.

At first she didn't know where she was or how she had got there.

She assumed that that was what memory was doing to her, subtracting day after day so that she would always have to start from the beginning, and never get ahead. Then she remembered the day before and (this was probably an earlier thought, the second thought perhaps) the day before reminded her of the idea of memory and the fact that she had lost hers. And she had lost it, she had still lost it, and she still didn't know what exactly this entailed. She sent light out into the corners of her mind . . . but time ended in mist, some time yesterday. She wondered what happened when you lost it, your memory. Where did it go, and was it lost for good or were you meant to be able to find it again? Well, here I still am, she thought finally; at least I haven't died or anything like that. Something about sleep worried her, but she let it pass. And even she could tell it was a beautiful day.

She sat up, testing her wet senses, and blinking at the light that had made the long journey back again while she had slept. Small but influential creatures were screaming at her from above. She looked up – and realized she could name things. It was simple, just a trick of the mind's eye. She knew the name for the birds; she could subdivide them too, to some extent (sparrows, a hooded crow staring at her humourlessly); she could even loosely connect them with memories of the day before: the jumpy, thin-shouldered, frowning, supplicant dogs, a long cat flexing its claws on the glass of a shop window. She wasn't sure how things worked or what they had to do with each other, how alive they all were, or where she fitted in among them. But she could name things, and she was pleased. Perhaps everything was simpler than she thought.

As soon as she stood up she saw them. In the middle distance over the damp green land there was a wasted, scattered area against a line of forgotten buildings. Other people were there, some standing, some still lying flummoxed on the floor, some sitting in a close huddle. For a moment she felt the squeeze of fear and a reflex urged her to hide again; but she was too pleased and too weary, and she had an inkling that nothing mattered anyway, her own thoughts or life itself. She started to move towards them. How bad at walking she was. They seemed to be people of the fifth and second kinds, which was encouraging in its way.

As she limped into the slow range of their sight, one of them turned and seemed to eye her coolly, without surprise. Even at this distance their faces gave off a glow of distemper, suggesting rapid changeability beneath the skin. She was getting nearer. They did not turn to confront her although some knew she was coming.

'Mary had a little lamb,' one of them was saying in a mechanical voice not directed at her, '– its face was white as snow . . .'

She came nearer. They could harm her now if they liked. But nothing had happened yet, and it occurred to her exhaustedly that she could probably walk among them as she pleased (for what it was worth), that indeed she was condemned to move among the living without exciting any notice at all.

Then one of them turned and said, 'Come on, who are you?'

'Mary,' she lied quickly.

'I'm Modo. That's Rosie.'

'Neville,' another said.

'Hopdance,' said the fourth.

'Come on then, come in the warmth.'

With nonchalance, with relief, they included her among themselves. She sat on their square grill, beneath which a vast subterranean machine thrashed itself rhythmically for their heat.

'Here, wet your whistle, Mary. Keep the cold out,' said Neville, handing her a shiny brown bottle. She tasted its spit and fizz before Rosie claimed it.

Neville went on, to no one in particular, 'Twenty-two years of age, I was one of the top six travellers for Littlewoods. My own car, the lot. They wanted to do a, an article on me in the papers. But I said – no, I don't want no publicity.'

'No, you don't want no publicity,' agreed Rosie sternly.

'You can keep your publicity, mate. That's what I told them.'

'Publicity . . .? Hah!' said Hopdance, then shook his head, as if that settled publicity's fate once and for all.

She resolved to be on the lookout for publicity. It was obviously a very bad thing if it was to be so vigilantly shunned even here . . . She peered at them through their hot breath. Their skin was numb and luminous, but all their eyes were ice. I'm one of them, she thought, and perhaps I always have been. And as she looked from face to face, sensing the varieties of damage which each wore, she guessed that there were probably only two kinds of people. There were only two kinds of people: it was just that all kinds of things could happen to them.

⁓ ⁓ ⁓

Correct: but only as far as it goes. (I generally find I've got some explaining to do, particularly during the early stages.) These people are tramps, after all.

You know the kind of people I mean. The reason they are tramps is that they have no money. The reason they have no money is that they won't sell anything, which is what nearly everyone else does. You sell something, don't you, I'm sure? I know I do. Why don't they? Tramps just don't want to sell what other people sell – they just don't want to sell their time.

Selling time, time sold: that's the business we're all in. We sell our time, but they keep theirs, but they don't get any money, but they think about money all the time. It's an odd way of going about things, being a tramp. Tramps like it, though. Being a tramp is increasingly popular, statistics show. There are more and more tramps doing without money all the time.

I'm obliged to deal with these sort of people fairly frequently. In a sense it's inevitable in my line of work. I'd far rather not, of course: they're always wasting my time. I'd avoid them if I were you. You're much better off that way.

⁓ ⁓ ⁓

'I know what you are, Mary,' said Neville, leaning forward to tap her warningly on the thigh. 'You're simple.'

Mary nodded in agreement.

'See?' he said.

It was true. She knew little, and what little she knew she would have to keep to herself. She would have to learn fast, and other people would have to show her how.

'Aren't you a beauty though,' he added slowly. 'Here, isn't she a beauty though, eh?'

Mary hoped he was wrong about this . . . But the accusation clearly wasn't a very serious one; the man's hostility gave out, and he turned away, raising the bottle to his lips. It wasn't too bad

23

here, Mary thought, though she was quite curious about how long it would go on.

'Right, come on love, you're coming with me. On your feet, girl.'

Mary looked up expectantly. It was someone of the third kind – a girl, she thought, one of me. Mary had noticed her before, out on the edge of the other people there, hanging back with a certain sense of her own exclusiveness and drama. She was big, one of the biggest people Mary had ever seen. Her numberless hair was a violent red, trailing from her head in distracted spirals; and her eyes were ice.

Without protest Mary was helped to her feet. As she straightened up, Neville made a cunning but enfeebled lunge towards her. The big girl thumped her great fist down on the back of his neck and then kicked him skilfully, so that he barked his forehead on the metal grill.

'You leave her alone, Neville, you dirty little sod! Ooh, I know you, mate. Yeah, that's *right*! She needs a good friend to look after her, that's what she needs.'

Neville murmured grumblingly as he curled up away from them.

'What? *What?* You want to watch it, mate, or I'll kick your bloody head off. All right? All *right*? . . . Come on, my love. Let's get away from this lot. Scum of the earth, they are – the pits. I mean, some people. Where's the consideration? I mean, where is it?'

With her shoulders working, the big girl marched Mary off towards the pale line of forgotten buildings. As soon as they turned the second corner she halted and looked Mary carefully up and down.

'My name's Sharon. What's yours?'

'Mary,' said Mary.

Sharon looked into Mary's eyes. She frowned. Her broad face seemed to carry an extra layer of flesh, a puffy afterthought grafted on to her natural features. It was a layer of delay; there was a sense of missed time about everything one would get from that face, thought Mary. Something skipped a beat between the face and any feelings that might prompt it.

'Phew, girl. Someone's done you over, haven't they?' She laughed harshly, and started to straighten Mary's clothes. 'We all do it though, don't we? Isn't it a scream? I mean, I like that every now and then myself, providing they're all nice boys of course, and it's just for fun.' She lifted an erect forefinger. 'I won't be peed on though. I just won't stand for it,' she added with considerable hauteur. 'I will *not* be peed on!' She brushed dirt from Mary's shoulder. 'Mm, they could have put you somewhere after though, couldn't they? I mean, a couple of quid for a nice little hotel or something. But you know what men are like? It's silly that we love them so much, isn't it really?'

Mary was ready to agree. Sharon was flouncing on, however, and she followed. Mary was getting worse at walking all the time. She attributed this fact to the knot of mighty pain that had wedged itself somewhere in the plinth of her back. What a pain, what a grabby pain. It hurt her, too, because of its wayward naturalness, its suspended familiarity; it was a simple and unworrying pain, she felt. But it *hurt*. That was the trouble with pain; it wouldn't really bother you much if it weren't so painful sometimes.

'This is where *I* stay when I'm down this way,' said Sharon, leading her past a series of metal traps, behind one or two of which she could see old cars sleeping. 'Not that I'm down here too often, mind you.'

They moved past the flat walls of an empty cave. There was a brackish smell of wetness and age, and a richer smell that was man-made and attacked the juices of the jaw. Someone smothered in clothes looked up sheepishly from the ground. Near him a toppled bottle creaked gently on its axis.

'Don't mind him,' said Sharon briskly. 'That's Impy. His name's Tom really, but I call him Impy because he's . . . important – im*pot*ent. Aren't you, Impy, you little wreck!' She turned to Mary and said conciliatingly, 'You know, I think it's always better to laugh about these things, out in the open, you know. Otherwise he's bound to get a complex about it or something. Eh, Impy? How are you this morning then?'

'I'm cold,' said Tom.

'Well *you* go out and get some then. Don't look at me. Now this is Mary and you keep your bloody hands off her. What's the matter with you, girl? You look like you're giving birth . . . Does, does it hurt?'

Mary nodded in apology.

'Where? Where does it?'

Mary stroked her sides gently.

'Did they do your back in too? What *sort* of pain?'

'Just a simple pain.'

That frown again, and that little click of time as it showed on her face. 'Whew! You *are* simple, aren't you.' She reached for Mary's waist with hands that were less harsh than Mary feared. 'Here,' she said. Mary felt pressure lifting from her middle. 'Everybody's something. That's one thing I've learnt from life. Everybody's something. Don't mind him – you've seen it all before, Impy, haven't you?' Gracefully holding Mary's hand aloft, Sharon helped her step out of the skirt. They both looked down and saw a complicated network of bands and clips. 'You aren't half a mess, my girl. Were you in somewhere? Well take down your knicks! You must have been in somewhere. Over here. Come on then! . . . Gawd, you're helpless, girl. Take some looking after.' Sharon slipped her fingers into the central band. It started to come away quite easily. 'You're pretty though. I always wanted to be dark. It lasts longer. Talks nicely too, doesn't she Imp? That's it, now crouch down. Go *on*, silly. You . . . just let it . . . *That's* it. Ah, don't – no need to cry now. Silly girlie. Everybody does it. Everybody's something. You know what my granny used to say to me? "Everybody's queer dear, except you and me dear, and even you dear look a bit queer dear." We're going to take you away from here, yes we are. We're going to get you fixed up.'

3
Inside
Out

————∽∽————

Mary, of course, had no very clear notion of what being 'fixed up' by Sharon might entail. Fixed, fixed up. But she thought it sounded quite a good idea, and she didn't have a better one.

They headed off together towards the distant, stirring streets. The grass was kind to Mary's feet; Sharon hovered hugely in the corner of her eye. Already she felt less fear about the question of her re-entry into the vociferous, the astronomical present. And she was pleased about everyone being queer. Mary looked up. The corpulent beings of the middle-air were hanging around again, rolling slowly on to their backs to enjoy the sun. She wondered with interest what Sharon had in mind for her.'

'Fuck!' said Sharon suddenly. She halted and placed a hand on Mary's shoulder. 'Scuse my French.' She crooked a leg and groped downwards. '*Hate* walking on the grass in these heels.' Her heels did indeed look particularly vicious, curved on to a thin prong and secured to her ankles with metal clamps. 'God, we've got to get you some shoes as well, girl. I generally keep, you know, a little wardrobe down here but . . . You must be fucking *freezing*. Whoops!' She straightened up with a grunt. 'It's lucky the weather's turned.'

They walked on. The weather had turned. It was lucky. Everything was coming right. Mary now felt inclined to dismiss or at least extenuate the insidious burden of what had happened to her while she slept. Because something had. Boy, something certainly had. Something had come at her in the night, something had mangled her, something had turned her inside out. Whatever it was had hated her life, had wanted to murder her soul. Was this how the past got back at you? Perhaps. It made sense, in a way, for the past to wait until you were asleep before sneaking up on you like that. And the worst thing was that she had wanted that violence done to her. She had brought it about. And she had wanted more.

'You know, Mary,' said Sharon, 'I'm buggered if I – sorry – if I know why I keep coming back here. I don't know for the life of me why I still do. Only for Impy I suppose, soppy old fool that I am. I'm not accustomed to this sort of circle at all really. I'm not like *them*. But, you know, get a couple down you and, *you* know . . . When I wake up I never know how I got here. But we all do it, don't we? Silly really, isn't it?'

'Yes,' said Mary, 'I suppose it is.'

Mary walked the streets again, but with purpose now. Accordingly they seemed rather less effusive to her eye. Sharon knew the way: her progress was bold, even brazen, and yet she saw nothing. The streets did not strike her, nor did the other people and their storms of fortunes.

They walked quickly and Mary was always trying to catch up. The streets Sharon led her down varied in size and demeanour. Some were owned by the raucous cars: these were given over to movement, so that the very air seemed to shoo the people along in its gusts and backwash. When enough people massed on a corner the cars would arrest themselves and wait in lines, rumbling with impatience. Occasionally a man whirled hectically out to dodge across the precipitate passageways, while the snouty cars stuck with menace to their tracks. Other streets were owned, collectively and with civic pride, by their buildings, the houses: these were in the interests of quiet, and their air was still. You hardly ever saw anyone going into the houses and you practically never saw anyone coming out. Anxious to divine the laws of life, Mary assumed that once you got inside you stayed there, avoiding the streets and all their chances. Here, cars nosed about with diffidence or had already come completely to rest, and people could cross more or less as they pleased.

'Money money money money money money money money,' said Sharon. 'You haven't got any, have you?'

'What?'

'Money!'

'I'm not really sure.'

28

'Let's have a look then . . . You must have had a skinful last night, my girl.'

Sharon delved expertly into Mary's black bag, while Mary looked on in wonder. She hadn't given it a thought – and yet the bag had remained at her side, its straps still clinging to her shoulder. Mary almost lost her balance as Sharon's movements suddenly grew driven and frantic, her hands working deeper downwards.

'Hello-ello-ello, what have we here?' In her trembling fingers Sharon held up the two scraps of wrinkled, faintly luminous paper. 'Know what we can get for this?'

'Money,' Mary ventured, but Sharon wasn't listening now. With huge strides she crossed the street. Mary was nearly running again.

'What do you reckon?' panted Sharon. 'Clan Dew? Couple of Specials each? Some nice Port Character?' She slowed down. 'Or what about a bottle of Emva,' she said shrewdly. She halted and looked at Mary with narrowed eyes. 'Or shall we get some spirits . . .'

'Yes,' said Mary, 'let's get some of them.'

'Yes, I think that'd be best,' said Sharon, on the move again. 'You know, this time of the morning, spirits are more . . . refreshing. Don't you think. It's awful really though, isn't it. But we all do it, don't we? Now you wait here, killer. Be back in a sec.'

Sharon made her entrance to the sound of a bell. Mary peered through the glass sheen and discovered she could read. Now this is more like it, she thought. Signs told her in elementary style about money and goods. Whoever drew up the signs kept getting the numbers wrong and was repeatedly obliged to cross them out and put new numbers in their stead. Using a trick of her eyes Mary looked beyond the window through to the gloom within. There were the bottles that the signs had pictured and praised, flamboyantly ranked against the wall. Sharon was inside this complicated grotto, busy doing her deal. The exchange occurred, with the man giving Sharon something extra before she turned and came back through the reflections towards the door.

'Hair of the dog,' said Sharon in the sidestreet near by. The bottle top gave a crack as she twisted it off. 'Your health, my girl.'

Her bulky face, with its puffed layer of time, looked both glazed and intent. She poked the small bottle into the hole in her head – her mouth, that wet and curious private part, a thing that seemed to have no business there, too vital and creaturely against the numb contours of her face. With an unobtrusive movement Mary lifted a hand up and checked. Yes, she had one too. And from the inside she could trace the scalloped bone curved on to the hard inner lips. Was there anywhere else like that in your body, a place you could feel from the inside and outside at the same time? She couldn't feel one; and so she felt mouths must be very important.

'Now that's a bit more bloody like it,' said Sharon. It was Mary's turn. 'Go on then,' said Sharon, 'down the hatch.' Mary opened her mouth and poured.

'I've never seen anything like it,' said Sharon a few minutes later. 'What the hell's the matter with you? You must be in a shocking state, my girl. Nice little drop of brandy and you cough yourself inside out. I mean, it's not natural, is it?'

'I'm sorry,' said Mary.

Sharon drank. 'It's all very well being *sorry*. You *spilt* half of it!' Sharon drank. 'I mean, brandy's supposed to do you *good*.' Sharon drank.

'I'm sorry,' said Mary.

Sharon dropped the dead bottle to the ground. She stared at Mary sharply. 'I'm not an alcoholic, you know.'

Mary stared back. Oh yes you are, she thought. Oh I bet you are.

~ ~ ~

Sharon *is* an alcoholic, of course (among many other accomplishments) . . . Alcoholics: you know what *they're* like, don't you. Certainly you do. Chances are, you know one or two personally, or you know someone who does. Think about it. How many do you know? There are an awful lot of drunks about these days. It wouldn't really surprise me if you turned out to be one yourself. Are you?

Drunks are people who can't stay sober. They would rather be drunk. They can't bear being themselves. They have a point. It is harder being yourself than it is being drunk.

Drunks aren't themselves: they're drunks. They aren't like other people, though they used to be before they started being drunks. People are various: drunks aren't.

When drunk, drunks all think, feel and behave in exactly the same way. When sober, drunks just think about drink, all the time. They do. That's what they're thinking about. If you ever wonder what they're thinking about when they're not being drunk, that's what they're thinking about: being drunk.

Most of them know some things about why they can't bear being themselves, and some of them know a lot. But they all think they know things that other drunks don't know, and they think they are special. They are wrong about that. They aren't special: they're drunks, and all drunks know the same things. It seems sadder and more interesting from their end. It is, too, in a sense. They all have their reasons, and some of their reasons are good. I don't blame anybody for being one.

It's my theory that everybody would be a drunk if they could bear to get that way. We'd all feel so much better if we were drunk all the time. But it's very hard going, getting to be a drunk. Only drunks seem to be able to manage it.

I'm forever having to cope with these rather puzzling and regrettable people. You'll be running into a few more of them too. But all under my control, of course, all under my protection and control.

～ ～ ～

Sharon was telling Mary why she liked a few drinks every now and then – it was because of her nerves, she explained, together with her partiality to a good time – when without much warning the buildings dropped back to reveal a great breezy rift in the stacked and staggered city. Only a few arched, magical streets had been selected to ride this swathe of air. It made Mary's body hum; she would have turned and tried to run again but Sharon urged her on, unterrified. As they walked up the wide entrance to the sky Mary looked downwards and saw that the turbid tract beneath them was in fact alive, boiling, throwing bits of itself restlessly in the air, as if to catch the screaming birds that swerved and hovered just above its surface, taunting, enraged.

'It's too big,' said Mary.

'Pardon? I love the river. Go quietly, sweet Thames. We're going to the other side,' she explained, nodding towards the hulked structures gaping like battlements on the far shore. 'We're going home first, then I'm taking you up the pub.'

Mary wondered what these places would be like as she speeded up and followed Sharon south.

'We're home!' shouted Sharon.

Mary stood behind her in the cuboid vestibule. So this was what it was like on the inside: they were home. Everything was padded or reinforced, and it was hotter than she had thought it would be.

Immediately a half-glass door flew open further up the passage. A man who combined the attributes of being very small and very big peered out, let his head jerk back in consternation, then came bowling down the passage towards them.

'No you don't, my girl,' he said rumblingly. 'Come on – out, out, out!'

'Ah come on, don't be so *mean*,' cried Sharon as the man began to crowd her back towards Mary and the door.

'You don't belong here!'

'But this is my bloody *home*.'

Although Sharon was far more redoubtable than the man with whom she clumsily grappled, it was clear that all strength and stubbornness were melting from her face. Sharon looked like somebody who had yet to do all the things that Sharon had done. We're going to get put outside again, thought Mary – no question. But then Sharon's features twisted back through their layer of time, and as if in response her shoulders performed a similar convulsion, causing the little round man to give a harsh shout and lie down very quickly on the floor.

'See? See?' he said.

'Oh Dad, get off, I didn't touch you!' As she leant over him, with every appearance of solicitude, a leg shot out from beneath her and suddenly the two of them had formed a thrashing tangle at Mary's feet.

'Mother!' he yelled. 'Lord help me somebody!'

'What's happening *now*,' said a voice full of exhausted compliance. A woman appeared at the doorway and limped speedily into the light. 'Murdering her own father now, is she? I see,' she said in the same tone.

A pudgy hand slithered free of the panting combatants on the floor. The new arrival took the opportunity of stomping on it with her right foot. Her shoe, Mary noticed, was grotesquely enlarged, sporting a brick-like extension on its sole – perhaps for this very purpose.

'That's my hand you're treading on, Mother,' the man pointed out. 'Get her by the hair.'

'Bloody Ada. Give us a hand then,' the woman said to Mary. 'Gavin! Gavin!'

Before Mary had time to comply with such a doubtful request, Gavin strolled down the stairs and sighingly extricated the people below. Mary watched this spirited reunion with a feeling of provisional panic. (She knew the *streets* were full of traps and pits and nets . . .) It made no sense to her, but perhaps it did to them.

So it proved.

Very soon Sharon and her Mum and Dad were squabbling companionably in the comfort of the lounge, a cramped inner chamber whose prisms were much too various for Mary to begin to break them down with her eyes. Time passed – lots of it passed. Far from demanding an explanation of her presence, or ignoring her altogether, Mr and Mrs Botham appealed constantly to Mary for corroboration and support in their cheerful denunciations of their daughter. Mary didn't know why she was expected to know anything that they didn't know already. And although she was quite reassured by the way they kept calling her Mary, she couldn't help wondering what they wanted from her or what they were using her for. I must be pretty amazing, she thought, a girl with bare feet who has lost her mind. But they didn't seem to think so at all. Either this was because they were related in some way (a fact indignantly emphasized with phrases like 'his own daughter' and 'her own father' and 'your own mother'), or else everybody was even queerer than Sharon had let on.

Yet how dismal if this was all there was. She wouldn't admit that it could be so. Gavin sat beside her. Throughout he had been marked by his own air of cool exemption, and he was without that aura, that drift of lost time. Mary was particularly impressed by his eyes. Apart from their abundance of colour and light, they seemed to know things that nobody else's eyes had so far known. They knew things not contained here.

He turned to her and said, 'Are you one of them too?'

'One of what?' said Mary.

'Another lush-artist.' His eyes flicked towards the other three. 'They're at it all the time,' he said. 'They never know what the hell's going on.'

'Do you?'

'Do I what?'

'. . . Know what's going on?'

'Now if you'll excuse us,' said Sharon loudly, 'I think what my friend Mary would like is a nice hot bath.'

'Yes of course she would, the poor little thing,' said Mrs Botham. 'However did she get like that?'

'Oh,' said Sharon, 'she just had a little accident.'

As soon as they were safely locked in with the bathroom's porcelain and steel, Sharon threw open a cupboard and started rummaging inside it. She did this with the same edge of frenzy that she had shown when looking for money in Mary's bag. And sure enough she met with the same reward.

'Now you're talking,' said Sharon, uncapping a brown bottle and drinking from it freely.

'Gavin – what's he like?'

'Gavin? You can forget *him*. He's queer. Can't you tell? You see all that shit on his eyes?'

'Yes I see,' said Mary, giving up hope for the time being.

'God he's handsome though. *Now* my girl. We don't really want a proper bath, do we. Do we? We'll just give you a nice stand-up wash, you know, just do your underarms and your love-pot. Mind your legs. Because they'll be opening soon, won't they?' she added ominously. 'Pull it over your head. That's it. Now let's have a little think. You can have my white boots for a start. What size are you? And Mum's red crimplene'll be nice on you. Bit mini on you, mind, but there's no harm in that, is there? Eh? Sorry, does that tickle? I'm awful, I am. I am, I know. Lift up your arms. Mm, you

34

can have my white polo-neck, show off your little titties. You'll knock them dead, girl.' She went away but she soon came back again. 'You know, Mary – sit down there. You know, Mary, I'll be surprised if we aren't a couple of bob to the good by the time tonight's over. Oof! They're a bit loose, but there it is. I know Whitey will do his nut when he sees you – if he's there of course. He'll jump on you like a *kangaroo*. No, just slip into it. You don't want any knicks or anything, this time of year. I don't believe I've got a clean pair myself. Still, *they* won't mind that, will they. Eh? Eh? Let's just tuck it in. I tell you, they'll think it's Christmas when you walk in there. Right. Let's have a look at you.'

Sharon swung open the cupboard door again and Mary saw herself. She turned away quickly.

'What's the matter? Go on, look. En*joy . . . That*'s it. Don't say I don't look after you. You look a real cracker, you do. A real dish. I tell you, when we get you down the pub, they're going to *eat you alive*.'

It hadn't been easy getting into the house, and it wasn't easy getting out again.

Sharon told Mary to be prepared to leave in a hurry. When they came down the stairs Mr Botham was already standing by the front door, his arms folded.

'You're not going anywhere, young lady,' he said. 'You're stopping home.'

A half-hearted scuffle took place, and Mrs Botham limped down the passage to make her scandalized contribution. Mr Botham vowed that Sharon would not go through that door unless she stepped over his dead body. She went through it anyway, and Mary went with her.

'Don't go, Mary, for the love of God,' cried Mrs Botham. 'Don't go with her! You'll regret it . . .'

Mary was pretty sure Mrs Botham was right. It all confirmed her suspicions about houses and homes. They were hard to get into; and once you were inside, it probably wasn't a good idea to go out again.

4
Bad
Language

~~~~~~~~

The pub was a public house, one of those rare places where people could go without being asked. Appropriate care had therefore been taken to make things as hard on the senses as possible – or else everybody would come here, or else none of them would ever leave. There was a stale, malty, sawdust heat, and an elusive device to hurt the ears; the wall of sound came and went at you very cleverly, with deceptively brief intervals, never giving you time to rearrange your thoughts. Everything clamoured for exchange – the multi-coloured glass banked up high over its trench, the boxy machines with their clicking trapdoors, their conditions and demands. Even the air stung the eyes and made them cry. It had been full in there for quite a time but no one was ever turned away. In the tall and endlessly proliferating room people formed in laps and circles of power and exclusivity, sometimes opening to let another in and sometimes closing to let another out. They were all playing with what Mary knew to be *fire*.

'Of course, I'm not a nymphomaniac or anything like that, you know,' Sharon assured her, looking towards the door. 'I think that's such a silly word, don't you? . . . Where *are* they? I mean, I just like a good *time*.'

Time – she needed more and more of it as time went by. Sharon was known, valued and believed in here: she had credit. A few minutes of coy pleading at the bar secured her a Stingo every time. Mary was given one too, a fizzy black liquid so candidly hostile to the palate that after a few cautious sips she put it back on the table and left it alone. But Sharon couldn't get enough of it; she seemed to like the way it slowed her down, and closed her eyes off behind their layer of time.

'It puts me in the mood,' she said. 'No harm in that, is there? Jolly good luck to you, that's what I say.'

Mary found Sharon's remarks more compelling than might be

supposed. Harm, luck and time were precisely the sort of things she was keen to know more about. Sharon's references to them were of course too intimate to be of much help, but they told Mary that language was out there somewhere, waiting to be discovered and used by her. Each word she recognized gave her the sense of being restored, minutely solidified, as if damaged tissue were being welded back on to her like honey-cells. Even now she knew that language would stand for or even contain some order, an order that could not possibly subsist in anything she had come across so far – that shadow driving across a colourless wall, cars queueing in their tracks, the haphazard murmur of the air which gave pain when you tried to follow it with your mind . . . *Reading* might well hold the key to any order the world disclosed, Mary felt; and she was keen to exercise this new skill of hers. There wasn't much to read in the public house. Only a few stark announcements of exchangeability, and one or two things like 'YOU don't *have* to be MAD to work here – *but* it HELPS!' and 'ALL RIGHT, so *you're difficult.* WITH *a little effort*, you could be IMPOSSIBLE!'

'*Fuck.* Whoops!' said Sharon. 'Beg pardon. Gone on my *dress.* Don't usually use bad language. We all do it though, don't we. We do, don't we.'

Sharon went to the bar again. She was gone quite a long time, but she came back without a new Stingo. She sat down heavily. 'Fuck,' she repeated. After a while, and with an expression of dignified appraisal, she began to contemplate Mary's unattended glass. Her hand moved across the table. 'I don't know why it's so dead in here,' she said.

Mary looked briefly round the room and listened to it. She wondered why people kept using that word *fuck* and its cognates quite so often. It wasn't like all the other words, although the people who used it pretended that it was. And they used it so often that the air seemed to quack. In the centre of the room two men were pushing one another while several onlookers shouted encouragingly. But you could hardly hear them anyway. Mary thought: If this is what it's like when it's dead, what's it going to be like when it's *alive*?

'I mean, but with some blokes,' Sharon went on sadly, 'well – it's like electricity, isn't it? Bigger than both of you, *you* know. I get that electricity thing with quite a few blokes. With most blokes, actually. Just lucky, I suppose. I –' A harsh shout jumped from between Sharon's lips. She had clamped a hand over her mouth, but just a second too late. 'Ooh . . . Excuse me. I mean, I just like a good *time*. No harm in it. But they're buggers sometimes, aren't they Mary? The trouble is, and I've been with an awful lot of blokes, is that if you go with a lot of them they give you these diseases. You're supposed to stop then. My trouble is – I can't! Why should I? I mean I'm a healthy young *girl*!' Tears began to run unhindered down her cheeks. Mary wondered whether other people often just melted like this. Sharon sniffed and said, 'When I was little I was going to be a nun when I grew up. My mum said I'd look lovely in a nun's veil. I can, I mean it's still – never too late, is it Mary? It's never too late to change. And then you have all those years of happiness to look forward to, don't you? Father Hoolihan was the only man who ever really understood me. I'm going to go and – There they are! Yoo-hoo, Jock! Jock, we're over here!'

Two men joined them, and Mary saw that she was in quite serious trouble. For one thing, it was instantly clear that Sharon was no longer on her side, if indeed she had ever been. Sharon had brought her as far as she was going to bring her, and now Mary was on her own again. Sharon wasn't on Mary's side any more. Sharon was on the other side.

Not that the men weren't sufficiently alarming in their own right. Lumpy Jock was tall and slow and much too big. His black hair was coated with wet light. Even though he said little, his mouth remained open at all times, the tongue idling on the lower teeth. It was hard to tell how much danger Jock contained. His companion, who went by the name of Trev, was an altogether more effective-looking unit. He was small and hard, packed tight into his clothes; he gave off a freckled, caramel sheen all over his body, a sheen just like his smell; and his hair was dirty orange with a nimbus of yellow where it caught the light. Trev was much closer to Mary than Jock was, and seemed intent on getting closer still. They both had an air of defiant self-neglect. And all their eyes were like Sharon's eyes.

'Where'd you get this one?' said Trev, his breath playing on

38

Mary's cheek. His voice had a special upward lilt, not unpleasant in itself.

'On the site,' said Sharon.

'Where she from?' he pursued.

'Yeah, where you from, Mary!' said Sharon.

Mary felt heat scatter across her face. She wished she knew whether it was safer to reveal her fear or to keep it hidden.

'See?' said Sharon. 'She doesn't bloody know! You're *simple*, aren't you love?'

Mary looked up. Sharon's face was expanding with new men and new drink. This was her victory. Mary knew she would get no help from her now.

'Look at her,' said Trev seriously. He paused. 'Look at her. She's like a fucking film star.'

'See?' said Sharon. 'She's worth a tenner of anybody's money. Go on, Trev. I've cleaned her up and everything for you. You said you would last time. With Janice you said you would.'

'Don't start talking to me about no tenners, Shar,' said Trev. 'Don't talk to me about no tenners.'

'Janice was a right slag,' said Jock in his gurgly voice.

'That's what I mean!' said Sharon. 'Mary, now she's something special. Say something, Mary. Go on, say something for the boys.'

'Does she fuck?' said Jock.

Sharon's head jerked round towards him. (Do I fuck? thought Mary. Well, *do* I?) 'Of course she does!' said Sharon indignantly. Mary was quite pleased that Sharon was still sticking up for her. But then Sharon leaned forward and said to Trev. 'She's simple. She won't mind. You can do what you like with *her*.'

Mary felt Trev's breath veer closer again – ripe moist breath almost condensing on her cheek, its questions forming like sticky droplets.

'What's your name?'

'Mary.'

'How old are you?'

'Young.'

'Where you living?'

'There.'

'Oh you're living there, are you. And what day of the week is it?'

Mary smiled.

'What's two and two?'

Mary smiled.

'And you got no man to look after you?'

'I –'

'You fucking beautiful, you know that? Hey Jock,' he said, without redirecting his voice or his eyes, 'I said she fucking beautiful, Sharon you can pick them I tell you that. Listen Mary now. We have some whisky and they shut here and we go to Jock's and I fuck you to kingdom come. What a that?'

Mary shrugged and said yes. Behind her, in paroxysms of authentic disgust, a machine hawked money into its metal trough. 'Time,' shouted an old man wearily, gathering glasses as he moved among them. 'Time. Time.'

～ ～ ～

Trev and Jock are criminals, I'm afraid. They make their living by doing things so risky and depressing that hardly anyone else can bear to do them. It's all about money, of course, like so much else. Mary doesn't really know about money yet.

Jock, for instance, had worked out as a lad that the best way of getting money was to attack weak people who already had some. Which weak people? He divided them into four categories: weak young men, weak young girls, weak old men and weak old ladies. After a few outings he satisfied himself that old ladies were the weakest and therefore the best people to attack. (They seemed to mind less too, probably because they hardly ever had any money.) His police record soon became a sorrily monotonous rollcall of decked grannies. Jock would run up to these people, hit them as hard as he could, and try to run away again with their money. The trouble was that even the oldest of them seemed determined not to part with their handbags; Jock hated the way he had to fidget through the leathery crevices with their sparkling dead make-up while the old ladies shrieked at him in that self-satisfied way they had. Sometimes he just hit them as hard as he dared and, breathing very sharply, hung around until he felt it was all right to run away – which he did with great skill, running really very fast. He *was* good at that bit. When times were low and Jock was recalling his few successes in life, his eyes would often fill with tears of pride at the thought of his swiftness at such moments.

Trev is different, his twin passions being drink and fighting. He doesn't know why he keeps doing all the terrible things he keeps doing. Sometimes he attributes it to the coruscating hatred he feels for everyone he doesn't know. But he hates everyone he does know too, so it can't just be that. Like all true heroes Trev has a tragic flaw: he isn't especially good at fighting, whereas he affirms and in fact believes that the opposite is the case. Accordingly, he keeps starting fights, fights that other people keep finishing. But he wins the fights he has with women, and he has quite a few of those.

I hope Mary will be all right. It's a great shame, to say the least, that she had to get taken up by such people at this early stage. She just isn't equipped to deal with them yet. Furthermore, show me criminals, and I'll show you policemen, not far behind. And the last thing we want is to have Mary tangle with *them*.

With Jock squiring Sharon, and with Trev at Mary's side, they walked up a steep passage, so narrow that the buildings on either side seemed to be brushing foreheads to keep each other up. Mary was surprised by the way they had paired off. She thought they would be paired in colours. Sharon and Trev were the same ginger, after all, and Mary was as dark as Jock. But they had been paired by size, and Trev was small and firm, like herself. Sharon and Jock were brushing foreheads too; they explored the deep shadows together while, a little way back, Mary walked with ginger Trev's ginger arm pressed tight over her dark shoulders. He was making sure she wouldn't get away. At one point Jock and Sharon twirled off further into the night (raising their voices together in a weird wail so that the others could keep track) and Trev slammed Mary up against a wall and tried to cover her mouth with his. Mouths again, you see. His was as private as hers; it contained much wetness and bad air. *Her* mouth, all on its own, made several attempts to slide out from under his, causing Trev's arms to tighten round the back of her neck. And his mouth, which was alive, kept sliding after hers. Mary was getting the idea now;

but she still wasn't sure about the kind of harm Trev intended to do to her.

'Don't say I don't look after you,' said Sharon haughtily, glancing back as she descended some crackly stone steps.

Mary – who, incidentally, was going to say no such thing – stood and blinked at the sunken building. Abruptly she saw herself, behind a hurriedly shut door, crying naked on her knees. She felt Trev's urging pressure on her shoulders. He almost had her where he wanted her now.

'Come on, Mary,' he said. 'This is it.'

Mary bent her head and continued down the steps.

Later, when she tried to reassemble the parts of that stretched night, she found that it came back to her in hot thudding pockets of image and heartbeat . . . A dark and rancid room with a square veil of milky light on the wall. Heavy brown bottles swilled from hand to hand and white nuts that the others swallowed. Sharon standing up, falling over, hopping on one foot, pulling clothes over her head with an electric crackle, subsiding again in careless laughter with Jock behind a screen. Then Trev's slow attack. She couldn't tell what he wanted, she couldn't work out what he wanted. 'Loosen up. *I said loosen up,*' he said. He was testing, testing, probing her skin in search of its openings. If she had known what he wanted she might have struggled less. He hit her twice across the mouth early on. She thought that was part of it. She heard the methodical grunting from behind the screen. She tried to drain her body of all its powers of resistance. She started to understand. His two wet red points wanted to get as close as they could to her, to get inside. His two tongues wanted her two mouths. I can bear this, she thought; but there was more. He spread her a different way, on her side with her legs splayed. He started preparing something very complicated in the nexus of her body. She bit her hand to put the pain off centre. This was new all right, this was more. It reminded her of something, even then; squatting on the garage floor, a bottle still creaking on its axis, Impy looking on and Sharon saying that everybody did it. Trev laughed and said, 'You dirty bitch, you've done this before, ooh you've done this *before.*' Mary couldn't believe she had done this before: she knew she never wanted to do it again. Suddenly his body snapped tight and she felt a foul snarl over her shoulder. Then he sank down sideways, out and away from her. 'Wake me in an hour,' he said. 'With your tongue.'

Mary didn't stir for some time. I'm dead she thought. He's killed me. Why? How did he dare? And soon he's going to kill me again. So when she heard Trev start to cough himself awake, the idea came to her as if it were the most obvious thing in the world. She thought, no, not me: *him*, kill *him*. Quickly she groped among the plentiful rubble on the floor. She found a wedge-shaped brick; it was sharp and heavy. She hit him twice and there was a double-crack each time. She hit him in the mouth, of course. Where else?

She was ready when the others woke up. She had slept a little too – and the past had come and mangled her again while she was inert and helpless. She sat hugging her knees against the wall. In the far corner, buckled and wheezing on the floor, lay ginger Trev. Mary had inspected his face coldly – bottom half in red tatters – and turned it away so that it nestled against the stone corner of the disused fireplace. She waited. At length, Sharon and Jock came alive again on the floor, creaking apart from each other, letting out muffled moans of painful reproach.

Then Jock was standing in the centre of the room, stripped raw and panting faintly. 'My God. Trev took a knock then,' he said.

'I'm sorry,' said Mary, who was about to explain what she had done and why.

'Is not *your* fault.' He went closer. 'Fucking madman in his drink, Trev,' He knelt. 'Bloody hell, he broke his *mouth*,' he said, turning to Mary with slow bafflement.

'Go on, Mary,' said Sharon from the floor. Sharon looked at Mary palely. Sharon was gone. Sharon was on the other side.

Mary hurried up into the air. The light was still squeezing her eyes when a hard hand clamped down on her shoulder and she was being rushed out into the street, with someone's chest pressing flat against her back. Mary thought – naturally enough – that she was going to get fucked again.

'Just routine, my love,' said an indifferent male voice. 'Just

43

relax and there'll be no grief. We'll have you sorted out in no time at all.'

Under a slackening grip he led her towards a black bus on whose haunches two men in silver-studded blue suits nonchalantly lounged. The bus opened up to let her in.

'She was on her way out, sir. Come on, my angel, up you get.'

Mary did as she was told. The doors closed again. She sat down on the narrow ledge and scratched her hair. A bank of sun beamed in at her through the caged windows. It was a few dizzy seconds before Mary realized she was not alone. She felt his breath before she saw him, a square figure hunched on the facing ledge. She had to hold a hand over her eyes before she could see his – greenly glinting in the negative shadow.

'Name,' he said.

'– Name what?'

'You. What's your name?'

'Mary.'

He sighed. 'What's your other name, Mary?'

'Mary Lamb.' Mary Lamb: sounds good, thought Mary.

'Sounds good,' he said. 'Sounds innocent anyway. I've seen you before, haven't I. I know you.'

'I haven't seen you before,' said Mary. There was a long silence. Mary's blood was beginning to climb down again.

'What brings you along this way, young Mary Lamb? These people aren't your kind, are they?'

'No, I don't think they can be.'

'Stay with your own kind then. Listen. If I see you again there'll be trouble. Lots of it. Okay? Off you go then.'

'Thank you.'

He kicked open the door. 'Let her go, Dave,' he said. 'She's not one of them.'

Mary walked erectly down the street, a fire of eyes prickling on her back. Once she had turned the second corner, she leaned against a wall and pressed a hand to her forehead. The strangest thing about him was his breath. Its smell chimed with her earliest memory – two days ago, waking in that white room. She remembered now. Someone had been with her when she woke up; someone had asked if she was all right and told her to be good . . .

Well, I'll try my best, she thought, and started to walk again.

There was something else about his breath. Everyone else's breath was alive. His wasn't. His breath was dead.

Part Two

Part Two

5
Gaining
Ground

———～～———

'More tea, love?'

'Yes please,' said Mary.

'How you getting on then?'

'Fine, fine. I feel better all the time.'

'Coming back to you, is it dear?'

'Well – a little,' Mary lied.

'It's just a matter of time,' said Mrs Botham thoughtfully, '– purely a matter of time.'

Watched and smiled at by Mary, Mrs Botham limped back to her seat – her inviolable armchair, wedged into the corner by the fire with toy flames. *Limp* hardly did justice (Mary coolly reflected) to the spectacular unevenness of Mrs Botham's gait: she walked like a clockwork hurdler. Mary attributed this to the fact that one of Mrs Botham's legs was roughly twice the length of the other. The standard limb sported its special extension, like a black brick; but that scarcely made up the disparity; and her longer leg seemed embarrassed by its own profligacy, bending outwards in a sympathetic arc. Mr Botham – and Gavin, too, naturally – spoke of something going wrong with Mrs Botham's leg a long time ago in her life. Something with a dark name had come and stretched it for her. No one said how or why.

'I knew a lady from the clinic,' said Mrs Botham, her head angled solicitously, 'she took a knock on the head one night, said that she couldn't remember, you know, hardly anything.'

'She was probably pissed,' said Gavin, who sat nearby on the couch, gazing, as was his habit, at a magazine full of glaring, near-naked men. They had all built their own bodies, and had all made a terrible mess of it.

Mrs Botham's head twisted round towards her son. 'She was *not* pissed, Gavin! I mean drunk,' she added, returning to Mary with her smile. 'She had *amnesia*. Her mind was a complete blank! In the morning she couldn't recognize a soul, not even her own husband who was cradling her in his arms or even her own little children, Melanie and Sue.'

'That's not amnesia, Ma,' said Gavin.

Mrs Botham's features, which until that moment seemed poised for resigned and melancholy sleep, hardened watchfully. '. . . What is it then?' she asked.

'It's called a hangover,' said Gavin, without looking up.

'Why do you behave in this way to your own mother, Gavin? Why? Please tell me why, Gavin.'

Gavin turned another page of his magazine, and another tiny head beamed out from its fortress. 'Because you're an alcoholic, Ma,' he said.

'No she's not,' said Mr Botham, who as usual had been sitting in cheerful silence at the table. 'She's an ex-alcoholic.'

'Ah, no, my dear,' said Mrs Botham, her face all abrim again, 'now that is where *you* are wrong. There is no such thing as an ex-alcoholic . . .'

'Only an alcoholic.'

'Only an alcoholic.'

'Only an alcoholic,' they all said at once.

'And she was an *amnesiac*!' Mrs Botham told her son. '. . . And you're just a queer anyway.'

'That's right, Ma,' said Gavin, and turned a page.

'You see, Mary,' said Mrs Botham: 'once an alcoholic, always an alcoholic. Oh, if I could've just got Sharon to come to Al Anon! But she'd never come. She was too drunk all the time. Do you know, Mary, that the true alcoholic' – and here she closed her eyes – 'they fear nothing. Nothing. Oh, I've had the lot, I admit it, Mary. Methylated spirits. Turpentine. After-shave. The lot. Silver-polish. Weed-killer. Paint-remover. Washing-up liquid. Everything. Disinfectant. 4711. Cough-mixture. Nasal deconges- tant. Windowlene. Optrex. I've had them all. You see, Mary, that was before I came to value my sobriety above all things. I *treasure* my sobriety. Have you ever looked up *sobriety* in the dictionary, Mary? Have you? You see, it doesn't only mean not being drunk. It means honesty, quietude, moderation, tranquillity, sanity, dignity, temperance, modesty, honesty . . .'

Mary settled herself more comfortably. Mrs Botham had already explained to Mary about sobriety, half an hour ago; but Mrs Botham was so drunk by now that she either couldn't remember or perhaps didn't care anyway. Mary wasn't about to mind. She fixed her eyes on Mrs Botham's lost numb face, seeing Sharon everywhere, and employed a skill she had learnt to perfect over the past few days. When Mrs Botham was talking to you, you just looked her way without really listening. Mrs Botham wasn't about to mind. As far as she was concerned, talking was the main thing. It wasn't really to do with you: it was to do with her. Mrs Botham acknowledged as much, quite frequently. She kept saying how nice Mary was to talk to. She said that was what she really liked – someone to talk to.

Mary even glanced around the room from time to time, or she sent her restless senses out on their patrol. There on the table was the empty blue plate, the teapot and its family. At nine o'clock every night Mrs Botham would lollop into the kitchen and shut the door behind her. She said she hated the Nine o'Clock News. Mary didn't blame her. Mary feared the television too. It was a window with everything happening on the other side – it was too much and Mary tried to keep it all out. At half-past nine Mrs Botham would emerge in processional triumph, bearing the small metropolis on her tray: the twin stacks of toast woozy with butter, the boiling pink tea so powerful that it made the mouth cry, the fanned brown biscuits like the sleeping dogs on the tin from which they came. According to Gavin, Mrs Botham always got drunk again while she was in the kitchen alone. Mary believed him. Mrs Botham was certainly very anxious to talk about sobriety on her return. But Mary didn't mind. She was very grateful to Mrs Botham for everything she had done in making her so welcome here.

'Don't worry,' Gavin told Mary on the first night. 'I'm queer.'

They were to share a room and a bed. Mary was still terrified, seeing no good reason why she shouldn't get fucked again.

'What does that mean exactly?' she asked.

'It means I like men. I don't like women.'

'I'm sorry,' said Mary.

'Don't worry,' he said again, looking at her with his knowledge-able eyes. 'I like *you*. I just don't want to fuck you or anything.'

'That's good,' said Mary to herself.

'It's a drag actually,' said Gavin, taking off his shirt. He had built his own body too, but he hadn't done it quite so badly as the people in his magazines. 'It's supposed to be okay liking men. I don't like it. I don't like liking men.'

'Why don't you stop?'

'Good thinking, Mary. I'll pack it in tomorrow.' He sighed and said, 'I know a man who's queerer than me. He only likes Spanish waiters. Only them. I mean he doesn't even like Italian waiters. I said, "That's funny. I like all sorts." He said – then you're very lucky. But I'm not lucky. I'm just not as unlucky as him. Do you, can you remember who you like?'

'No,' said Mary.

'That'll be interesting, won't it.'

'Perhaps I'll like men too.'

'That won't make you queer.'

'Won't it?'

'We'll see. Good night, Mary.'

'I hope so,' she said.

Queers like men more than women because they liked their mothers more than their dads. That's one theory. Here is another: queers like men more than women because men are less deman-ding, more companionable and above all cheaper than women are. Queers, they just want shelter from the lunar tempest. But *you* know what queers are like.

Soon, Mary will know too. She will learn fast here, I'm sure. The Bothams were just what she needed. She isn't alarmed by them and, more importantly, they aren't alarmed by her.

Mrs Botham is in fact alone in her conviction that Mary is an amnesiac – hence her constant spearheading of this unpopular view. Gavin, who spends more time with her than the others, has vaguely formed the opinion that she must be somehow retarded: Mary had the mind, he thought, of an unusually bright, curious and systematic twelve-year-old (she would be very clever when she grew up, he often found himself thinking). Mr Botham, finally, and for various potent reasons of his own, is secretly under the apprehension that Mary is quite normal in every respect. Granted, Mr Botham is something of an enigma. A lot of people – neighbours and so on, Mary, perhaps you yourself – assume that he must be a man of spectacularly low intelligence. How else has he managed to live with an alcoholic for thirty years? The answer is that Mr Botham himself has been an alcoholic for twenty-nine of them. *That's* why he has stuck to Mrs Botham's side during all these years when she's been drunk all the time: *he's* been drunk all the time.

But Mary will gain ground fast now. If you ever make a film of her sinister mystery, you'll need lots of progress-music to help underscore her renovation at the Bothams' hands . . . Ironically, she enjoys certain advantages over other people. Not yet stretched by time, her perceptions are without seriality: they are multiform, instantaneous and random, like the present itself. She can do some things that you can't do. Glance sideways down an unknown street and what do you see: an aggregate of shapes, figures and light, and the presence or absence of movement? Mary sees a window and a face behind it, the grid of the paving-stones and the rake of the drainpipes, the way the distribution of the shadows answers to the skyscape above. When you look at your palm you see its five or six central grooves and their major tributaries, but Mary sees the numberless scratched contours and knows each of them as well as you know the crenellations of your own teeth. She knows how many times she has looked at her hands – a hundred and thirteen at the left, ninety-seven at the right. She can compare a veil of smoke sliding out of a doorway with a particular flourish of the blanket as she strips her bed. This makes a kind of sense to her. When the past is forgotten, the present is unforgettable.

Mary always knows what time it is without having to look. And yet she knows hardly anything about time or other people.

‿ ⌣ ‿

But she was gaining ground fast now.

She got to know her body and its hilly topography – the seven rivers, the four forests, the atonal music of her insides. By watching Mr Botham, who did it often and expressively, she learned to blow her nose. Her body ceased to surprise her. Even the first glimpse of lunar blood left her unharrowed. Mrs Botham talked constantly about these things and Mary was prepared for almost any disaster. (Mrs Botham was obsessed by her grisly torments during what she ominously called 'the Change'. The Change didn't sound worth having to Mary and she hoped it wouldn't get round to her for a long time to come.) She told Mrs Botham about the blood, and Mrs Botham, in her unembarrassable way, told Mary what she had to do about it. It seemed an ingenious solution. On the whole, yes, Mary was quite pleased with her body. Gavin himself, who was a body-culture expert, announced that she had a good one, apart from her triceps. Conversely Mary didn't think that Gavin's body was all it was built up to be – Gavin, with his dumb-bells, his twanging chest-flexers and his stinking singlets. But she assumed he must know what he was talking about. There were many really bad bodies round where they lived, with bits missing or added, or twisted or stretched. So Mary was pleased with hers; and it was certainly all very interesting.

She started reading in earnest.

At first she was inhibited by not knowing how private reading was. She kept an eye on all the things the others read and secretly read them too.

Mr Botham read a dirty sheath of smudged grey paper that came and went every day. It was never called the same thing twice. There were pictures of naked women in it; and on the back pages men but not women could be bought or sold: they cost lots of money. In the centre pages someone called Stan spoke of the battle between cancer and his wife Mildred. Cancer won in the end, but heroism such as Stan and Mildred's knows no defeat. It was all about other places, some of them (perhaps) not too far away. It told of atrocious disparities of fortune, of deaths, cataclysms, jackpots. And it was very hard to read, because the words could never come to an agreement about the size or shape they wanted to be. Mrs Botham read pamphlets sent to her by Al Anon, of whom she always spoke most warmly. The pamphlets were all about

54

alcoholics and sounded just like Mrs Botham did. They had scales and graphs of what alcoholics got up to: they drank alone, they lied and stole things, they trembled and had visions of mice and shellfish. Then they forgot everything. Then they died. But if you put your faith in A.A. and God, it would all turn out right in the end.

Gavin spent a lot of time gazing disdainfully through his slippery magazines, but he had some other things in a cupboard in his room which he would occasionally consult or sort through. They were books, and books turned out to be where language was kept. Some were from school; others were acquired for a night course that Gavin had got too disheartened to complete; still others had been pressed on him by a friend of his, a poet, a dreamer. Mary was rather dashed to discover that Gavin had gone to school for eleven years and yet even now considered himself to be lamentably ill-educated. She never knew there was so much to know. Gavin said she could help herself to his books, and so, slackly prompted by his nods and scowls, Mary got started straight away.

Books were difficult. She read *The Major Tragedies of William Shakespeare*. It was about four men made up of power, mellifluousness and hysteria; they lived in big bare places that frightened them into speech; they were all cleverly murdered by women, who used an onion, a riddle, a handkerchief and a button. She read *A Dickens Omnibus*. It was about parts of London she had not yet seen. In each story a nice young man and a nice young woman weaved through a gallery of grimacing villains, deformed wags and rigid patriarchs until, after an illness or a separation or a long sea-voyage, they came together again and lived happily ever after. She read *Rhyme and Reason: An Introduction to English Poetry*. It was about an elongated world of elusive vividness and symmetry; there was a layer, a casing on it that she found nowhere else and knew she would never fully penetrate; the words marched to the end of their rank, sounded a chime, darted back again, and marched forward cheerfully, with renewed zest, completely reconciled to whatever it was that determined their role. She read *The Jane Austen Gift-Pack*. The six stories it contained spoke more directly to her than anything else had done. The same thing happened in every book: the girl liked a bad man who seemed good, then liked a good man who had seemed bad, whom she duly married. What was wrong with the bad men who seemed good? They were unmanly, and lacked candour, and, in at least two clear instances, fucked other people. Mary re-read one of these stories and was anxious that things would turn out the same way as they had before. They did, and she found this very comforting. She read *The Rainbow*, *What Maisie Knew*, and two fat shiny works about natural disaster and group jeopardy . . . At one point it occurred to her that books weren't about other places: they were about other times, the past and the future. But she looked again and saw that Shakespeare's book, for instance, was much newer than Lawrence's, and that couldn't be right. No. Books were about other places.

Where were they? How far did life stretch? It might go on for ever, or it might just stop dead a few corners away. There was a place across the river called the World's End. For a long while in Mary's mind this was the limit of life. (Similarly she once half-heard from the television that there was fighting in Kentish Town – with machine-guns and tanks. When she discovered that the fighting was actually taking place in Kurdistan, she didn't know how relieved to be about this.) She wondered where the end of the world was and what the world ended with – with mists, high barriers, or just the absence of everything. Would you die if you went there? Often she nauseated herself by sending her mind into the sky, past the bloated nursery-toys of the middle-air, ever upwards into the infinite limey blue. She knew a little about death now. She knew that it happened to other people, to every last one of them. It was a bad thing, obviously, and no one liked it; but no one knew how much it hurt, how long it lasted, whether it was the end of everything or the start of something else. It couldn't be that bad, Mary thought, if people did it all the time.

With Gavin, with Mrs Botham, and sometimes alone, Mary walked the streets of London, London South, as far up as the River, as far down as the Common, carving a track of familiarity from the grid of ramshackle streets, eviscerated building-sites, and the caged sections of high-wire concrete. You needed to walk through somewhere seven times before it ceased to be frightening. Knowing other people helped, and Mary was getting to know quite a few of them these days. They waved at her as she moved past them in the streets, or talked in her direction when she went to the shops and exchanged money for goods under Mrs Botham's stern-eyed but unsystematic tutelage. Mary invested inordinate emotion in these routine sallies. A courtly particularity from the greengrocer could make her smile all afternoon; an unreturned glance from the milkman could bring the beginnings of tears to her eyes and sink the whole day in mist. At the newsagent's one morning Mary got briefly excited by all the magazines called things like *People*, *Life*, *Woman* and *Time*. But they weren't what she had hoped for. They were still all about other places instead.

In shops everyone talked about money. Money had recently done something unforgiveable: no one seemed to be able to forgive money for what it had done. Mary secretly forgave money, however. It appeared to be good stuff to her. She liked the way you could save money as you spent it. Mary developed a good eye for bargains, especially in the supermarket where they openly encouraged you to do this anyway. Mrs Botham was always saying how much money Mary saved her. Pretty good going, she thought, considering that all she ever did was spend it. But Mrs Botham still couldn't find it in her heart to forgive money. She hated money; she really had it in for money. She would repetitively abuse money all day long.

So on top of all this and one way or another, Mary learned a little about glass, desire, voodoo, peace, lotteries, libraries, labyrinths, revenge, fruit, kings, laughter, despair, drums, difference, castles, change, trials, America, childhood, cement, gas, whales, whirlwinds, rubber, oblivion, uncles, control, autumn, music, enmity, time.

Life was good, life was interesting. Only one thing worried her, and that was sleep.

'Good night,' said Gavin, still panting rhythmically from the fifty press-ups he always did last thing.

'I hope so,' said Mary.

'You – why do you always say that? I hope so,'

'Well I do. I hope they're going to be all right. They haven't been good so far.'

'What, you have nightmares, do you?'

'Yes, I think that's what I have.'

She had expected sleep to be ordered and monotone. It wasn't. She lived through the days on tracks because that was what other people did. But her nights were random, and full of terror.

Mary knew other people had bad dreams but she was pretty certain they weren't as bad as hers. Incredible things happened to her while she was asleep. For hours in the darkness her mind struggled fiercely to keep the dreams away, when Mary would as soon have given up and let the dreams begin. But her mind wouldn't listen to her: it thrummed on its own fever, dealing her half-images of graphic sadness and fluorescent chaos, setting her hurtful tasks of crisis and desire, trailing before her that toy alphabet with its poisonous ps and qs. And then the dreams came and she must suffer them without will.

She felt that the dreams came from the past. She had never seen a red beach bubbled with sandpools under a furious and unstable sun. She had never felt a sensation of speed so intense that her nose could remember the tang of smouldering air. And the dreams always ended by mangling her; they came down like black smoke and plucked her apart nerve by nerve.

And she asked for it, and wanted more.

6
Law's
Eyes

'Moderation,' said Mrs Botham. 'Temperance. Calmness. Reserve. Not being drunk all the time. *That's* what sobriety means, Mary! And if you lose your sobriety you lose everything. I admit it, oh, I admit it, Mary! Shoe-polish, shampoo, Pledge, Brobat, Right-Guard, Radox, Sanflush, Harpic . . .'

The air tasted sweetly of toast and tea. The television flashed and rumbled about other places, wryly monitored by Mr Botham. Gavin sat beside Mary with a magazine on his lap. The splayed glistening pages depicted a new kind of person, a man with hair all over his body. Judging by the man's expression, people of this kind were very exalted and rare, and generally much prized. Gavin's forearm rested limply on Mary's lap. She liked it being there. She liked Mr and Mrs Botham being where they were too. She liked the fire whose flames did not burn. She smelled the air and liked its taste. I'm all right, she thought. She looked at the hump-backed teapot and her dutiful children; she looked at the high shoulders of the comical armchairs, spreading out their wings in gestures of arthritic welcome. This is enough, thought Mary – and why should it end?

Here's why.

One hundred yards away down the stone terrace, in a three-walled wasteland peopled by destitute furniture and mangled prams, Jock and Trev crouch opposite one another, panting with cunning and gurgling with adrenalin and drink. Their eyes confer about when to make their move. Gradually Trev starts sniggering in the dark . . .

It is indeed a noble dream: to come running into the Botham home, to do it and its occupants as much harm as they reasonably can in the few noisy minutes they have earmarked for the occasion

– and to inflict on Mary, our Mary, that special damage which she had feared. Possibly they will be obliged to take Mary with them when they leave. Trev, for example, has quite a few things that he wants to do to Mary, and he is counting on time and leisure to do all that needs to be done.

'You get him and her. I'll get the queer,' ginger Trev had panted to his friend a few seconds earlier. Big Jock, who actually has little taste for the venture, heard Trev out with considerable relief. 'Him and her' meant Mr and Mrs Botham, and Mr and Mrs Botham were old people. Jock is quite good with old people. He has a way with old people. Jock is only doing this because Trev wants him to so much. Being Trev, Trev thinks that Jock wants to do this as much as he himself wants to, and he wants to do it very much indeed.

. . . Uselessly, like a sick old seal, Trev's tongue flaps round among the rockpools and barnacles of his mouth. He remembers that night, what he did to her and what she did to him. Ever since, his mouth has throbbed and roared, a hellish reef of flayed roots and frayed nerves. Trev isn't quite sure what Mary did to him, but he remains entirely clear about what he's going to do to her. He's going to turn her inside out. 'Let's go,' said Trev.

Time is a race, a race that gets faster all the time. If you listen hard you can hear each second gasping with the strain of keeping up. Do it! *Listen.* Time is a relay, sixty after sixty, each moment passing on its baton and dropping back exhausted, its race run. Time will end too, one day. Time will end too, one day, you know, thank God. Everything, your bones, the air itself, all of it will end in time.

⌒ ⌒ ⌒

The moment she heard the door make its signal, Mary felt the tranquil advance of change. It was late. Mr and Mrs Botham straightened their backs in unison, and Gavin stirred gruffly, lifting his eyes from the page. To Mary's eyes the room became stark and exemplary, fugitive and yet eternalized in her gaze. She knew that she had lost it then, the room and all it contained.

'If that's that Sharon . . .' said Mrs Botham tightly as her husband rose to his feet. 'I'll bloody murder her, so help me God.'

Mr Botham moved past Mary towards the door. It was clear from his face that he had nothing on his mind. He walked slowly down the passage. He knew he would get there in time . . . They heard the door open. They heard Mr Botham's smothered rising shout, and then a double-thud, a thud in two stages, the second somehow more abrupt than the first. There was only time for Mrs Botham to start screaming before the men were in the room.

Mary saw it all.

To his palpable confusion and distress, Jock found himself in the lead. Trev had lingered to do some more loud stomping in the hall. Egged on by time, Jock dashed miserably across the room and started doing one or two things to Mrs Botham. Instantly and galvanically her reinforced foot shot up in hair-trigger self-protection, catching Jock a mighty blow between the legs with its heavy black brick. Jock gasped, clutched himself, and wandered dreamily away before subsiding slowly to his knees. By this time Trev himself stood in the doorway, already past his best, half-winded by all that stomping. But then he saw Mary and lumbered hungrily forward, seeming to have no time for Gavin, who stood up and with a short arc of the arm drove a muscular fist into the lower half of Trev's face. Trev paused, glanced sideways with a vexed, put-upon expression, before being snatched backwards flailing through the air to land upside down and motionless by the passage doorway. Jock, meanwhile, was on his hands and knees, vomiting (by some last courteous reflex) into the ornamental coal-scuttle. Mrs Botham screamed so much the louder. Gavin rubbed his knuckles, frowning, and stepped over Trev into the passage.

Mary never moved.

She did the next day: she had to – there was no choice. The next day she found herself alone again. Mary always knew a thing like this would happen to her some time.

'I said if I saw you again there'd be trouble. Didn't I.'

'Yes you did,' said Mary.

'And now I'm seeing you again.'

'That's right.'

'And there's trouble.'

'I know.'

'How old are you . . . Mary Lamb? Do your parents know what you get up to?'

'I'm in my twenty-fifth year,' said Mary carefully. 'My parents died.'

'Of what?'

Mary hesitated. 'One of consumption,' she said, 'the other of a broken heart.'

'People don't die of those things any more. Well they do, but we call it something else these days . . . What did they die of, Mary – if of course this isn't too *painful*?'

But it was. More out of a desire to change the subject than from any real indignation, Mary said, 'I'm not sure you're allowed to talk to me like this.'

'Oh I am, I am. You ought to know that I am.'

'Why?'

'You've broken the law.'

Mary didn't know what this meant. Her first instinct, under-standable in the circumstances, was to ask if the law would ever get better again. But she said, 'I'm sorry. I didn't know. What do you get when you break the law?'

'Time,' he said.

His room was like his breath; it had that dead, hospitalic tang. There was something extra, something acrid, in its taste, the taste of headaches and wax.

'I see,' said Mary.

'Don't worry.'

'Why not?'

'You haven't done anything that serious yet, not in the eyes of the law.'

Mary turned away from him. His eyes terrified her: they knew too much. They were a feminine green, narrow and oddly curved at the outside edges. Instead of light they contained only a glint of yellow, a bad yellow, the yellow of urine and fever. Or were these just law's eyes, she wondered, the eyes of authority and change? He stood up. He was shaped into his clothes with the obedient indifference of a shopwindow dummy. Who had put him together, who had dreamed him, the thin wedge of the nose, the perfectly horizontal mouth, the short but innumerable hair? He took out a white handkerchief and waved it lightly.

'You're crying,' he said.

'I'm sorry. Thank you,' said Mary.

'Listen to me. You've started badly. You're going to have to cut away from that kind of life, that kind of people. You don't belong there and they'll just spit you out every time. You'll need a job. You'll need a place. Hang on.' He leaned over his desk and started writing something, very fast. 'You can stay here for a while. I'll call them. If you need help you know where I am. My name's John Prince. I'll put it here.' He straightened up. He held Mary's eye for several seconds. She didn't think that face could ever look puzzled, but that's what it looked. She could tell he was trying to place her in his mind.

'You're trying to place me, aren't you,' she said in fear.

He laughed and said, 'I've got a lot of time for you, Mary.'

Mary and Gavin went back on the Underground. Gavin had made a statement, but didn't want to talk about it. Mary had never travelled on the Underground before, though she'd used the red buses once or twice with Mrs Botham in the past. Gavin gave her laconic warning, and Mary was grateful. He didn't want to talk much on the way back and neither did Mary.

When you considered this world – people winched up and lowered down into the earth in steel cages and speed-fed through the tunnels, with doors cracking shut everywhere, and arctic winds mingling with dusty gasps of fire from the planet's core – it was hard to believe how delicate life was, how breakable things were. Things were easy to break; things were terribly delicate. Evidently Mary had broken the law now, just as the night before she had broken Mr Botham's back. Yes she had – crack, she had broken it for him. It wouldn't have broken if it hadn't been for her. Trev would get time for this, but so would Mary in her way. Mr Botham's condition was 'most serious', everyone said. Mary agreed, but she thought it could have been more serious: she could have broken his heart or his nerve, and people died of that. But it was still very serious indeed. Mary had heard from Gavin that Mr

Botham was a carpet-layer when he could find work. Well, he wouldn't be able to find it now; he wouldn't even be able to look. No one knew if his back would get better again. And he was old, which made it even more serious.

The small house was well aware that things had changed; it didn't like being looked over at a time like this. The expression it wore was vulnerable and strained. There was no one inside, of course. Mrs Botham was at the hospital day and night, by her husband's side; she was drinking more heavily now, or more openly anyway. Mary couldn't stay – really there was nothing to stay with – but she said,

'Why can't you and I stay here and hope they come back?'

He looked at her with reluctance – and with scorn. She knew she shouldn't have said it. 'Be *serious*,' he said. 'We can't afford to have you here. We never could. We're not – there's no leeway here. Don't you *understand*?'

'I'm sorry.'

He said, 'Where will you go?'

'Here.' She took out the piece of paper she had been given.

'Christ,' he said.

'He said he'd call them. He said it would be all right.'

Gavin looked away. 'I suppose it'll be all right for a while,' he said. 'But I'm not going to like thinking of you in there.'

Together they packed Mary a suitcase; there were some clothes of Sharon's, and some of Mrs Botham's that were more or less Mary's by now. Mary would have liked to take along a book or two, but she didn't want to risk asking. He told her how to get there on the Underground. He gave her four pounds: it was all he could spare. He embraced her quite tightly at the front door but Mary could tell he was already on the other side; she broke away quickly and hurried down the steps.

Mary didn't want to go underground again.

She walked. The suitcase was light at first but became steadily heavier as the day closed in. She asked other people the way, holding up the small sheet of paper. They read the address and did what they could. Some were no help; some were so bad at talking that they couldn't have told her anyway; some found the piece of

64

paper distasteful in itself and moved on without answering. She got there in the end. It didn't take too long.

On the way she had her first memory. It made her stand still and put the case down and lift her hands to her hair. She heard a child shout and turned round shyly; she was in a quiet street, one marked by an air of prettiness and poverty; its small houses were clubbed together with their doors and windows open, and the staggered gardens displayed the family clothes. She was in a quiet street – but then, nowhere was a quiet place for Mary. She wanted to be somewhere the same size as herself and indolently dark, a place where she could shut out the clamorous present. But Mary stood where she was, her hands on her hair, and remembered.

She remembered how as someone young she had wanted to shine a light through other people's windows, to see into other people's houses . . . She was standing on the grey brow of a terraced hill at evening. The spiked gates of the city park have just been shut; the keeper walks back into the distance, glancing sideways and pocketing his keys. The boys have all gone home. They are all safe and having tea in other people's houses, behind other people's windows. Turning her head, she could look down the hill and into the square. Here in all their rooms they were shoring up against the darkness. She wanted to see them, to shine a light, to sense the careless ripples of their carpets, the unregarded cracks in their papered walls, the shadows on their stairs. She knew it was impossible – she would never be let inside. She turned and ran wherever she was supposed to go.

Mary dropped her hands to her side. That was all: she could follow herself no further. She looked up. Immediately, the street – the air, the incorrigible present – seemed a little less bright and unanimous to her eyes. She picked up her suitcase and walked on, quicker than before, anxious to find her place. She knew now that she would find it in time.

7
Don't
Break

~~

The young women at the Church-Army Hostel for Young Women have all taken smashes recently. They have all taken big ones. Some have broken. (Some are not so young either.) They have all gone out too deep in life.

They have all done too many things too many times with too many men, done it this way, that way, with him, with him. They are all inside here because they have all used everything up on the outside – used up money, friends, chances, all their good luck. They have all taken a smash and turned a corner. Some are trying to turn back. Some have stopped trying. They are fallen women.

Their position is shameful, or could be considered so. But *shame* is not the word for what they feel. That's fine by me. But what are they supposed to feel instead? Who did this to them? How would *you* feel?

. . . Have you ever taken a smash in your time? What, a big one? Will you get better again? If you see a smash coming, and you can't keep out of the way, the important thing is – don't break. Don't break! . . . Can you see another smash coming? How big will it be? If you see a smash coming and can't keep out of the way – don't break. Because if you do, nothing will ever put you back together again. I've taken a big one and I know. Nothing. Ever.

~ ~ ~

So now Mary started living by the rules.

She awoke in the basement with her two room-mates at six-thirty sharp, to the sound of a bell. She always woke up in fright, quickly gathering her scattered senses. She got dressed at the same time as Trudy, a shrill-faced, chain-smoking divorcee, and together they joined the queue outside the bathroom while Honey, an apathetic young Swede, was left to linger moaning in bed before

66

rejoining them later for breakfast in the dining-room upstairs, among all the other girls. There they would be stared at with cursory severity by Mrs Pilkington, the Sri Lankan co-superintendent who ate alone at a table set apart. Her husband, lean Mr Pilkington, the other co-superintendent, would already be thrashing flusteredly through the day's paperwork in his hot office near the front door. Any trouble and the girls were out. Breakfast cost sixty pence, so Mary just drank her tea.

'You'll go blind, you will, girl,' said Trudy.

'No blind,' said Honey, blinking.

'You will, you know. You can't leave yourself alone, can you? She can't. Knowing you, you'll probably nip down for another one, won't you, before clear-out. Just a quick one, just in case.'

'Is good, it says.'

'What *says*? All those pussy cookbooks you read?'

'Is not cookbook. It say is good to touch yourself.'

'Oh yeah?'

'Is good for tension.'

'What's so tense about you, brilliant? What have *you* got tension for. All you do is lie around wanking all day.'

'I want a job,' said Mary. 'How do you get one?'

'Oh you want a job, do you,' said Trudy, turning to Mary and nodding slowly. Beneath the table she waggled a crossed leg. '*I* see. Well what's your *calling*, Madame? What sort of thing have you *done before*?'

'I don't know yet,' said Mary, who often wondered what sort of things she had done before, before she broke her memory.

'You people . . .' said Trudy. Trudy disliked Mary's good looks. She did: Mary could tell. She disliked Mary's looks because they were better than hers. On her bad looks Trudy blamed all her bad luck. Mary used to watch her staring out of the bedroom window, at nothing at all, with her stretched, smarting face. Mary knew what she was thinking. She was thinking: If I could have just traded in some of my good brains for some good looks. Boy, could I have done with some good looks . . . Mary thought that people were probably quite right to go on complaining in their minds about this sort of thing. But she wasn't sure. *Were* things changeable? They had to be. People couldn't just be wasting their time.

Honey was quite good-looking too, so when she said, 'I go down now', and began to move away with her cup and saucer, Trudy called out loudly, 'Off for another quickie, are you? You'll get dishmaid's hand, you will, Honeychile. Dumb split,' she added to Mary. 'She's amazing, that girl. Wanked to a frazzle. I mean, she's just all *wanked out*.'

'I want a job,' said Mary. 'I want to make some money.'

'Hang on, girl,' said Trudy. She looked at Mary narrowly. 'Jobs – they take time, you know.'

'I know they do,' said Mary.

You had to be out by nine. You couldn't come back until twelve. Time was slow on the streets when you had no money. Time took for ever. Through diamond-wire Mary watched children playing in the sun. Children gave off noise and motion helplessly all the time. She watched the tublike housewives plod from shop to shop. Housewives accumulated goods grimly until they could hardly walk, martyrs to their carrier-bags. She watched the men idling in loose knots outside the turf accountants' or on the corners by the closed pubs. Men moved their heads around in the wind and gestured freely, having for the time being nothing that they needed to do. A big dog lay panting in the parched gutter. Ants weaved up from the cracks and over the planes of the uneven pavement. The fat white creatures of the sky loved it on days like this. They were all there. Not one of them had been left behind.

Mary was looking for a job. She didn't know whether you found them by moving or by staying still. Where were they? Who gave them away? She had all this time to sell, but didn't know who might want to buy it. She thought about the jobs she had seen other people doing, and the special kinds of time they had to sell. They were all the masters of their conspiratorial skills. The grocer with his lumpy racks, the adroit swivel of his paper bag, the jerking, centipedic apparatus that dealt him money: but he had food to sell (layered like ammunition in a cave), as well as time. The bus-conductor, clambering through the day with his expert handholds, yelling news about his progress, unravelling his costly paper from the machine beside his moneybag: but as well as time he had the bus he shared with the man in front, and the travel they sold. Who paid the roadsweeper for his buckled back, the gladiatorial dustmen with their poles and shields, the policeman and his lucrative swagger? They all got paid by someone. It was only tramps who chose to waste their valuable time . . . When she walked the streets Mary often looked up at the spangled canyons and saw with a sense of glazed exclusion the people up there behind the high windows, all intent about the sky's business.

Mary had lunch because lunch was what everybody had at that time. In the afternoons you could stay in the common-room so long as you stayed quiet. Girls wrote letters hunched over the table, or knitted things, or sat watching dust move. The day was already getting to them, reducing them to themselves, prying at their emptinesses . . . You could read the books in the cupboard if you put them back. Mary read them all. The girls in the books in the cupboard were taunting parodies of the girls condemned to read them. Will Alexandra marry elderly Lord Brett or the young but unreliable Sir Julian? When Bettina goes to stay at Farnsworth, all the Boyd-Partingtons except Jeremy treat her shabbily until she saves little Oliver from drowning and turns out to be an heiress after all. Lonely lodges, postillions, horses ridden to death, forests, vows, tears, kisses, broken hearts, rowing-boats in the moonlight, happiness ever after. Like many stories, they ended when marriage came; but they couldn't make you care. They made you sure of something that other books made you only indifferently suspect: that stories were lies, imagined for money, time sold.

Then at evening the girls gathered here and on the stairs and in their rooms. The talk was all about good luck and how they had never been given any. The talk was low. If only I hadn't, if they just didn't, if it only would. Some of them had been given babies by men and then had them taken away again by somebody else. They talked all the time about these babies who had passed through their hands, and about how, if they ever got them back or were given another one, they would treat them properly this time and never neglect them or have fights with them again. Some girls kept having fights with their men, and always losing. They bore the marks. Why would a man fight a woman? wondered Mary. He would always win; he wasn't fighting – he was just doing harm, doing damage. The girls talked about the men they had fought, some with fear and great hatred, some with languor, some with haggard wistfulness for this inconvenient but at least unmistakable form of attention, as if a black eye were a valued emblem among the spoken-for. Some were prostitutes, or were trying to be. Most of them weren't very good at it, apparently. They were prepared to offer their bodies to men for a certain price; but the men never thought the price was worth it. So they offered their bodies for nothing instead. Mary watched them closely, these adepts of men, acquiescence and time. They talked about the things that money could buy as if money were a game, a trick, a word. Some girls were drunks. They talked about . . . well, Mary already knew what drunks talked about. She knew about drunks. She knew what drunks did.

But she really didn't know whether she would ever get away from these people, these people who went out too deep in life and then swam up at you through the fathoms, trying to tug you under to where you would choke or drown. Would she ever get to the other side, the side that Prince had hinted at, the place where money didn't matter and time passed coolly? She looked at the girls and she knew there would always be these other people out there, always out there and always wanting her back, the lost, the ruined, the broken, the effaced. She thought: I mustn't go out too deep in life. I must stay in the shallows. I must keep to the surface. It's too easy to go under, and too hard to get up again.

At night after lights-out Mary listened with a sense of deliverance to Honey's routine and low-IQ yodels of abandonment and release. 'I finish soon!' she would plead in response to Trudy's unpredictably vehement rebukes. Honey's pleasure was real, and Mary approved of that pleasure. But it worried her too. Secretly Mary had tried the technique herself, without success. She couldn't find anything to catch her mind on to. Her mind had nothing to do, so it thought about other things.

'What do you think about when you do it?' she once asked Honey.

'Nice men,' said Honey with a delighted glare. Her smile had an almost celestial vapidity at such moments. 'Nice big men.'

'Oh I see,' said Mary.

That night Mary tried to think about Gavin and Mr Botham. It didn't work. And she kept unwillingly thinking about Trev, which was no help either. That was it: you couldn't seem to control what you were thinking about. The whole activity was clearly among the strangest things that other people did.

'What is it you think about the nice men when you're doing it?' she asked Honey the next day.

'I think of Keith. He's my most favourite. And of Helmut. They whip me,' said Honey, beaming furtively, 'and make me do all these terrible things. Keith get me from the back and Helmut put his –'

'Oh I see.'

Honey looked up at her meekly and said, 'I do it to you if you wish?'

'No, it's all right,' said Mary. 'But that's very kind of you.'

'It's okay, don't mention it,' said Honey.

As soon as she was alone in the bedroom Mary glanced through Honey's pamphlets – *Love Yourself, To Be A Woman, Female Erotic Fantasies*. She understood quickly: it was a memory game. Now she knew why she couldn't play.

Mary wondered whether she had ever done the thing before, when she was alive. Had she gone into a room somewhere, and taken off all her clothes, and made herself so open like that? Had she *wanted* to? And who else had been there at the time? She couldn't remember: it might have been anybody. Trev said she had 'done this before'. Trev had meant it too – Mary never doubted that. But it was still hard to believe that she would ever want to do it again

It was on the seventh day that the letter came.

'It's for you,' said Trudy.

Mary was sitting over her morning tea. She looked at the white envelope, at the name and the address. Yes, Trudy was right. It was for her.

'Is from a *man*?' said Honey.

'Course it's from a *man*,' said Trudy. 'Look on the back.'

Prompted by their eyes. Mary turned the letter over. Small black letters said. 'Be alone when you open this.'

'Told you,' said Trudy bitterly.

Mary went downstairs and sat on her bed. As she waited for her breathing to subside she inspected the envelope – quite calmly, she thought. She had seen other people opening letters but it turned out to be far more difficult than it looked. The envelope would jump and twirl from her hands, and kept incurring subtle rips whenever she tried to prize the letter free. Then she lost her nerve and brutally yanked it out.

The letter tore, right across the middle. Mary knew she had done a terrible thing. With a moan she squared up the two scraps of pink paper and flattened them out on the blanket. The letter didn't say much. It said:

Dear Miss Lamb,

Is it all right if I call you that? I mean – is it *accurate*? I said I'd seen you before, didn't I? Don't you remember?

Of course I could be mistaken. But stick around while I look into this. I'll be in touch.

Yours sincerely,
John Prince

Mary read the letter several times. It still made no sense to her. On an impulse she flipped over the bottom half of the pink sheet. There were more words. They described a girl called Amy Hide (26, 5′ 7″, Dark, Brit., None), who had recently become a missing person. The police thought she had been murdered, but they didn't seem to be absolutely sure.

Mary picked up the top half of the letter. She turned it over. There was a photograph of a girl. It was Mary.

8
Stopped
Dead

———◠◠———

It was Mary. Was it? Yes . . . it was Mary. How could it be?

Late at night in the basement bathroom when all the lights were meant to be out, Mary stood in front of the mirror and held up the pink letter beside her face. Above her a bare lightbulb burned in its dust.

It was Mary. But it was *older* than Mary . . . The face looked out at her defiantly, with perhaps even the beginnings of a sneer or a snicker in the raised left-hand side of the mouth. The mouth itself was looser than Mary's, more crinkled along its parting line. The mole beneath her right temple was there, but on the wrong side. And the eyes – they weren't her eyes. The eyes were dead, they were knowing, they were incurious, they were old. Mary stared. The half-smile in the photograph seemed momentarily to broaden, to become the real smile, to admit Mary. She blinked and looked again. The smile had gone but the eyes now held triumph. Quickly she dropped the letter and turned away with a hand to her head. She knew what the real difference was. Mary's face – Mary believed, Mary liked to think – was a good face, the face of somebody good. But the face of the girl in the photograph –

'Oh God, what have I done in my life?' said Mary.

All day nausea had tried to climb the rope-ladder in her chest. Now, with relief, with humiliation, with terror, she knelt on the bathroom floor and was convulsively and disgustedly sick, sick inside out, just sick to death. She couldn't get rid of enough of herself. She was sick for so long she was afraid her heart might fall out, might fall out and break.

Now she waited each morning for more news about herself but no news came. No news came and nothing happened.

Time was passing so slowly. She had no money left to help time on its way. You needed money to make time pass: that was how money got its own back on time. And time was taking for ever.

Mary read all the books again. She read the devotional literature splayed out on the hall table. Its general drift, in common with Mrs Botham's pamphlets from Al Anon, was that everything turned out right in the end, whether it seemed that way or not. We all had a second chance in life and could probably be redeemed quite easily. It had always been this way since the Fall of Man, when man fell and broke. But you shouldn't worry. God would handle everything. The girls talked about God quite a lot, or at least they referred to Him frequently, and to His son, Jesus Christ. And it didn't seem to be doing them much good at all.

'I don't know what you girls are thinking of half the time,' said Mrs Pilkington. 'You lose everything, you come here, you have nothing.'

Mary agreed with her, in detail.

'You say you don't know your National Insurance number.'

'That's true.'

'You have no idea whether your contributions are up to date.'

'I don't, no.'

'Where on earth *are* your records?'

'I give up,' said Mary without thinking, '– where are they?'

'Now don't you be cheeky to me. You say you want a job, it will take you a long time to get a job. First you must do all this.' She tapped the stack of forms with a warning finger, 'Here. Fill them all in.' She returned to her work. She added without looking up. 'You're only allowed to stay here three months, you know.'

'Three *months?*' said Mary.

Mary sat outside in tears on the windy bench. She spent quite a lot of time doing this nowadays. She dropped the last of the forms on to her lap. She couldn't read them. She could read *Timon*, but she couldn't read *them*. Even if she slowed down, and followed the phrases in a moronic lip-mime like Honey frowning over *Love Yourself*, the words were giving nothing away, smug, sated, chockful of good things sneeringly denied to her. Mary wanted to get out of here and on to another plane of life; but these words weren't going to help her out. They had been put together with only one thing in mind: to lock her in.

★

No news came. Mary looked for news in the mirror. She played the mirror game. Mary Lamb was getting to know Amy Hide quite well now.

Was Mary Amy, or had she at some point been Amy, and to what extent? Amy had done things. To what extent, and how automatically, had Mary done them too? Did it matter? What authority was there? God? Prince? Who minded?

Mary did. She minded. She locked herself in the bathroom and looked into the mirror. She wanted to be good, and she didn't believe that Amy could have been all bad if Mary had in some sense come out of her. Perhaps every girl was really two girls . . . Mary looked into the mirror. She didn't look too bad. On the contrary, she looked quite good. Look at the whites of her eyes, like whites of egg, the true angle of her nose; the teeth gave occasional refuge to small pockets of discoloration but the intimate pink of the gums was smooth and whole; and the line of her lips shaped well with the oval evenness of her chin . . . As she turned away from the mirror she saw the ghost of a smile from the knowing genius that lived behind the glass. The image flickered: there was chaos in there somewhere. Mary stared on. Her eyes fought with all their light until they had subdued whatever hid behind the glass. But as she turned away she knew that whatever was hiding there would now coolly reassemble and go on waiting for whatever it was waiting for.

Her dreams changed. Her dreams ceased, or at least she thought they had. Dreams were about variety, and her dreams were no longer various. The nights were all the same now, like the days.

For the first hours she lay back and let her head boil with the opposite of sleep, wild thoughts, wounding thoughts, thoughts that did not mind whether or not she could bear them. Then sleep began and it was always the same.

Amy was running across a black sky. Amy was flying: she could go where she wanted just as fast as she wanted to go. She was unterrified by her pursuer; she even turned sometimes and gave a shout of excited, taunting laughter. The pursuer was the beast. It was black, naturally – a panther, perhaps, but with the yellow tusks and top-heavy square head of a hog. Amy would often let her pursuer come quite close before veering off delightedly, with such airy sharpness that the beast would hurtle on into the distance, make a great trundling arc, then straighten out along her track, its mechanical, unvarying tread picking up through the darkness behind her. She swerved again but this time the beast flashed past only inches away and she felt the hot rush of goaded rage and the smell of inflamed saliva and gums. Now she was Mary and now she was food. Suddenly the black terrain was a tight tunnel, and she was running with such desperate speed that she seemed about to overtake herself, her limbs like golden cartwheels, her hair like a mane of nerves. The beast followed in extravagant bounds. At any moment she expected to feel its grip and its headlong weight on her back, riding her to the ground and washing its hands in her face. So she slowed down to make it happen quicker, she stopped dead to make the next thing happen faster, and the beast veered up and, with dispatch, with contempt, swiped her body into flames of blood. Then she awoke to a brain already boiling again with thoughts that did not mind whether or not she could bear them. It happened every night, every night. – Why?

Because this is one of the ways the past gets back to you, the thwarting, indefatigable past.

You know, don't you, that your forgotten wrongs will never cease to caffeinate your thoughts? . . . How is your sleep? Can you trust it? Is everything reasonably quiet down there? Or is it swelling – will it burst? Is it all coming out to get you?

Oh man . . . sometimes I wake up at night and there's nothing. I am a dead tooth in the jaws of the living world. My mind just isn't on my side any more. It's on the other side. It is the prince of the other side . . . Mary: get it right next time, be good next time. Oh Mary – heal me, dear.

I used to think there was no time like the present. I used to think there was no time *but* the present. Now I know better – or different, anyway. In the end, the past will always be there. The past is all there is: the present never sticks around for long enough, and the future is anybody's guess. In time, you always have to hand it to the past. It always gets you in the end.

All the girls, the fallen girls – they just wanted a second chance, they were just looking for a break. That was what Mary was looking for too. And then she found one.

It was midday. She was walking the streets with a kind of half-studied aimlessness, with no conscious prejudice other than avoiding her familiar pathways, her known handholds on the city grid. She wandered into a busy, sheltered area of ramshackle houses and cavernous shops. Buckled men and women were arraying their belongings on bare racks in the road, and passers-by added their voices to the sound of junior commerce and informal exchange. Overhead, a stilted street climbed up into the cold morning lucency like a newly-opened gangway to the sky. Even the fat white layabouts of the middle-air dipped down closer to see what was going on . . . Yes, of course it is, thought Mary, and I must never forget it: life is interesting, life is good, everything you look at is secretly full of the real stuff. She turned another corner and saw a wide dark window: the window held a message for her but at that moment a speeding van played a trick with the sun and the words were erased in a bank of light. She waited, and the message reappeared, with belittled yet insistent clarity. It was a sign. It said: 'WAITRESS WANTED'.

'By the police?' said Mary, thinking of Prince and his room.

She moved closer. It said: 'WAITRESS WANTED – Help needed. Inquire within.'

Mary inquired within. Before her eyes had grown used to the gloom a yawning young man had looked her up and down, leant back in his chair to exchange nods with a woman behind the counter, and asked Mary if she could start tomorrow. Mary said she could and turned to leave before anything had a chance to go wrong.

'Wait!' he called. 'You don't want to know about anything else? Money? Time?'

'Oh, yes please,' said Mary.

'Eight to seven with Sundays off.'

'. . . And money?'

'We talk about that in the morning. My name is Antonio but you can call me Mr Garcia. What's your name?'

'Mary Lamb.'

77

'Okay, Mary. In the morning – eight sharp.'

'I haven't got an Insurance number or anything,' she added quickly.

'So what?' said Mr Garcia, and yawned again. 'We don't care about that shit.'

Mary walked down the street again. She was very optimistic. She knew what waitresses did, and she knew she could do that shit as well as anyone else.

9
Force
Field

Pallid Alan sat in his little office beyond the kitchen, gazing out of the window and worrying about going bald.

Mary watched him carefully. It was very interesting. Every ten or twelve seconds. Alan's right hand would slip off the desk and – jerkily, gingerly, as if only nominally under its master's control – snake upwards to take a bite out of Alan's hair. Next, and with an expression of shrewd annoyance, he would inspect the contents of his palm, with a quiet tightening of the pale lips; then he shook it all away in a bedraggled gesture and flapped his hand down again on the desk. Ten or twelve seconds passed, and then it all happened again.

Covertly, not for the first time, and out of unadorned curiosity, Mary did to her hair what Alan kept doing to his. Her hand disclosed the odd twanging wisp of light, which she duly flicked to the kitchen floor. But it didn't bother Mary like it bothered pallid Alan. So far as Mary was concerned, there was always plenty more where that came from. Mary's hair, in addition, was clearly good stuff, clearly worth having. Alan's wasn't. It was churned, parched, like failing corn – and in relatively short supply. In Mary's view, the sooner Alan's hair was all gone or used up the better things would be. He wouldn't have to keep wrenching it out. And after all you didn't *need* hair, did you? Plenty of people got along fine without it. Alan didn't see it this way, though, and Mary watched his sufferings with comparable pangs of her own. She wanted to tell him to stop pulling it out if he prized it so much. But she didn't. She knew that pallid Alan was terrified of talking about anything to do with hair.

'Hey, Baldie!'

Mary felt the thud of air from the swing-doors and heard the comical death-rattle of the dirty plates. She turned, and Russ sauntered into the kitchen – loose-shouldered, sidling Russ, with

79

his glamorous black T-shirt, his chunky blue jeans, and his extraordinary shoes, which resembled a pair of squashed rats. To Mary's eyes, these rats were far from satisfied with their role in life and always seemed to be resentfully contemplating their comeback.

'I said – hey, Baldie!'

'*Yes*,' said Alan, tensed down over his desk.

Russ surged up behind Mary, so close that she could feel the pleasant hum of his force field, and, extending one arm artistically, toppled a skeleton of white plates into her sink. Mary turned to him and smiled. Mary had never met anyone quite like Russ before. But then Mary had never met anyone quite like anyone before.

'Well looky here,' murmured Russ, applying his fat lips to Mary's bare neck. In the kitchen she wore her hair up, on old Mrs Garcia's disdainful advice. Abruptly Russ backed off, dropping his head and raising his arms like someone embarrassed by a round of unwarranted applause.

'No. No,' he said. 'I mustn't get your hopes up. I've caused enough artbreak in my time to know better than that.' He came forward again, rubbing an erect forefinger behind his ear. 'You see, girl, I'm not sure you're good-looking enough for my taste. On the whole, I like um a bit better-looking than you. Oh God, don't cry, Mary! Oh God, please don't cry!' Mary nearly always did want to cry when he told her not to. He said it so seriously. 'Hang on, though, eh girl? No arm in hoping, is there? You never know your luck, if the weather stays this hot. Here, I'll tell you something: I wouldn't mind murdering you. You're well worth murdering, I'll give you that.'

Mary didn't say anything. You didn't have to. Russ talked about murdering girls quite often, and so casually that Mary was beginning to wonder whether it was such a serious business after all. In Russ's scale of things, it was better for a girl to be worth murdering than not worth murdering. 'Not even worth murdering' was the worst you could possibly say about a girl, and Mary was relieved that she wasn't thought to be *that* bad.

Russ wheeled out into the centre of the room. '*Fuck off, darling*,' he yelled, addressing the air now and deftly removing a comb from the seat of his jeans, *'you only look like Brigitte Bardot!'* He arched backwards in front of the dusty mirror on the wall – then buckled and jumped away as if invisible hands were snatching at his belt. 'Leave it out, Sophia,' he said in hardened warning. He straightened up. 'Aah!' He buckled again. He clawed at the phantom that was riding on his back. 'Aah! Raquel! Will you – get off my – bloody –' He flipped the phantom over his shoulder and on to the floor, where he gave it a good jabbing with his foot. Mollified, he corrected the shape of his jeans and leant back in front of the mirror again. 'Gor, all this *air*,' he said, patting and teasing it with both hands. 'Where's it all *come* from is what I want to know. You know,' he said, turning to Mary and wagging the comb at her, 'you know what's really crippling me? You know where all my money goes? Onna haircuts! It does, I swear. Cheryl says let it grow but Farrah says she likes it short. What you reckon, Mary?'

'Russ,' said Alan.

Russ went on combing his hair. 'What can I do for you, Baldie?'

'I'm going to bloody murder you one of these days,' said Alan in his cracked, uncertain voice. He added nervously, 'You fat swine.'

'Oh don't do that, Al. Don't murder me, please. Old me up, somebody,' he drawled, 'me knees are quaking. Fat? *Fat?*' He sprang backwards, his hands flat on his stomach. 'There's not an *ounce* of surplus weight on this superb specimen. If I'm so fat, ow come all these film stars are after me? Eh? Eh? They're not after *you*, are they, oh no. You know why? *Because baldness disgusts them.* That's why.'

'Russ,' said Alan, and shut his eyes.

'Hang on though, Al, you've got a point. My dick. Now my dick *is* a bit on the fat side. No go on, I admit it. The film stars, they're always saying to me – Russ baby, I'm crazy bout you Big Boy, but your –'

'*Russ,*' said Alan. 'What you want. Eh?'

Russ glanced at Alan, who now stood palely in his alcove doorway, and then at the clock above Mary's head. It was ten to six. 'Oh yeah,' said Russ. 'Old Pedro Paella out there says he wants the invoices in early tonight.'

'By when?'

'Before six, I think he said.'

'Bloody *hell Russ*,' said Alan as he ducked back to his desk.

Whistling piercingly and straightening the waistband of his jeans, Russ strolled back to Mary's side. He fell silent. Slowly he curled an arm round her waist. Nodding to himself, he watched as Mary cleaned a plate, and another, and another. 'Here, are you still taking me for a drink Saturday night?' he whispered hoarsely.

Mary nodded.

'I must have your solemn promise: you're not going to try and get me drunk or anything, are you. You're not going to try nothing.'

'I promise.'

'That's my good girl. Here.' He placed a finger under her chin and swivelled her head round to face his. He looked at her for a long time with a humourless, evaluating frown. 'You know, maybe you *are* good-looking enough for me. Maybe I *would* look good on you. Maybe you *are* in my class . . .' He went on staring at her for a few more seconds, then closed his eyes and shook his head. 'No,' he said. 'You're not. You're not.'

Russ walked out through the blatting swing-doors. Mary got back to her washing-up. Alan worked in quiet frenzy over his desk for nine minutes, then trotted out himself. Soon he returned. Mary didn't have to look around to know it was Alan. His force field was quite different from Russ's human heat. It was made up of yearning and apology and vast tentativeness. For a moment she felt the air move behind her, as if Alan now writhed in elaborate gestures, gestures of beckoning and supplication but she knew it was just his eyes all swarming across her back.

⌒　⌒　⌒

After fifty hours of her presence Alan has fallen in love with Mary. I'm afraid. I'm sorry to say it, but it's true. Well, it is. Russ is harder to fathom. His force field gives off more opposition every way. But Alan has fallen. He thinks about Mary all the time. Everything she does hurts his heart.

If you asked him when it happened, he'd say it happened at first sight. At first sight he loved her face, the squashy pinkness of her lips, the volume of her brilliant black hair, the eyes and their flicker of sensitive expectancy. He loved the way she stood nodding with her arms folded, and kept saying yes to old Mr Garcia, and really didn't mind about all the washing-up. He loved the way she set to work without giving Russ much of her time – he was capering about as usual . . . Alan has fallen. Even the grim psycho-drama of hair-loss has become a mere subplot in the heroic poem of his thoughts (Can Mary Love A Completely Bald Man?). He thinks about Mary all the time. Time and Mary are the same thing. She hurts his heart. He fears she may be out of his class: he may be right. Pallid Alan is very, very worried.

And so am I. Love. In love. Falling in love with other people. Are you in love, is it love, are you falling? If you fall, you might take a smash, you might break. Fall, but don't smash. Don't break! And don't listen to the word – just don't *fall* for it. Love is only the most you can feel, that's all love is. Never let anyone tell you that what you feel isn't love (don't fall for *that* one) if it's the most you can feel. Love is nothing by itself. Love is nothing without you there to feel it.

You know what I wish? I wish Mary knew more about *sex*. Why? Because it takes time to learn. It's the one thing you can't learn without time.

～ ～ ～

Mary loved her job.

She loved the way everybody knew everybody else, the familiar acknowledgements of morning and evening, the sense of inclusion and with it the sense of time made lighter, the summer angles of the sun on the wiped dishes.

'Now here is my Mary,' old Mr Garcia would say in the cramped cloakroom by the front door. Old Mr Garcia was so bad at talking that he often seemed to say things like 'Ow are you to die?' or 'What has Mary got to sigh'; but he meant her no harm. On the contrary, he would often gently reassure her by stroking her hips and backside or by meditatively massaging her breasts with the palms of his hands. He did this in a stooped, incurious fashion, chuckling contentedly to himself, and Mary always smiled at him most warmly before hastening into the low hall of the café.

Old Mrs Garcia would already be busy behind her counter, while languid Antonio was invariably dozing or actually asleep in some shadowed nook he had curled himself up in. Sometimes he slept on a line of chairs or, more candidly, flat out like a child on one of the tables in the back. Today he stood slumped over the pie-warmer, rubbing his eyes with his fists. He looked at her with a sly smile. Mary wondered why Mr Garcia and young Antonio liked looking at her so much. They liked looking at her so much that they even liked looking at her when she was in the lavatory. They had a tiny hole in the wall which both of them used. Mary was intrigued that they should both like looking at her during such unsavoury and generally rather regrettable moments. One day, on consecutive visits, she said hello and addressed them by name. They stopped looking at her then. After that, they didn't like looking at her at all, not for a while anyway. But they were getting friendlier now, and getting to like looking at her again.

'Eh Mary, *puta tonta – vente a cocina, eh!*' shouted the colourful Mrs Garcia, busy as she was, and Mary hurried eagerly past.

Then she would slide through the slack swing-doors, into her place – and there would be Alan, flinching over the desk in his alcove, and there would be Russ, sprawled in extravagant indolence on his chair by the sink.

'Morning Mary,' Alan would lean back and say, peering up at her through his wan lashes, and giving the words equal weight, as if they were interchangeable, a secret shared by only Alan and her.

'"La Lollo" they call her,' Russ would then fairly typically begin. 'I don't blame them either. She lalolloed me flat last night. "Gina," I kept saying. "Not again, eh? Do us a favour? Three o'clock I'm due up Park Lane. The Dunaway bitch." But she wouldn't listen, not her. No don't touch me Mary! Not yet!'

At the stroke of eight Russ would slide up from his chair and enter the inner sanctum of the scullery, with its sizzling terrors of rayburn and microwave. Old Mr Garcia stuck his head through the hatch and started calling out the first orders of the day. Mary ferried the slippery plates from Russ's counter to Mr Garcia's tray, and took the rubbled returns back to her own waiting sink. Mr Garcia trundled back and forth unsmilingly into the growing rumours of the café. Sometimes he would say, 'Mary, the bacon toast – you bring it', or 'You bring the steak salad, Mary', or 'You bring it, Mary – the treacle custard', and Mary would bring it, straightening her apron and patting her hair before moving out into the café's noisy limelight. Nearly all her hours were spent over the sink, erasing from white plates the many kinds of blood lost by food. After the breakfast clamour subsided into mid-morning, Russ would come from his cauldron to help her with the drying-up. And after the two-hour panic of lunch even Alan would leave his pads and clips and spikes to stand beside her rolling up his sleeves. That was the pinnacle of Mary's day, when the three of them were round her sink. Sociable flies weaved their fishing-nets in the air. 'Jesus, these fucking *flies*,' Russ would complain, dancing backwards from the sink and uselessly batting the air. 'What's the bloody *point* of them, that's what I want to know.' Mary, who moreover knew several of them by sight, wasn't worried by flies. She knew what the point of flies was.

How readily the world had spanned out to accommodate her. Really the main thing about life was its superabundance: there was so much of it, and always room for more inside. The girls of the exhausted Hostel, even the ones with jobs or men, suffered bitterly at the hands of boredom. They said that life itself was boring, life was dead. But surely the terror lay the other way, the loosening of the mind at the thought of all that life contained.

And when the present became too populous you could always look to the skies and their more idealized fortunes. There variety itself was abstract. On the way to work in the morning, the sky looked like heaven. On the way back to the Hostel in the evening, the sky looked like hell. At morning the white beings rode the blue vault in yachts and galleons, showing all their sail, or they smugly sunbathed with their arms tucked behind their heads, in heavenly peace and freedom. Later, and obedient to the iconography of evening, they lost their outlines in the hellish cliff face of the west, forming a steep red fault into the chaotic night.

This was on good days, of course. On bad days Mary felt saddened and battered by the thought of the things she might have done in her life – and anyway the clouds came then, and you couldn't see the creatures at all.

10
Good
Elf

————~~~————

One morning Mary carried a trayful of heaped plates to the quartet of incredibly old cabbies who always liked to sit by the window near the door. They were nice to her, these old men, they were nice; not bad going, Mary thought, to be nice after forty years of boxed rage. Also to their credit, she supposed, was the fact that they all still looked like men. Women of this age didn't look like women. Women of this age looked like men: they had given up the ghosts of their femininity. Perhaps life was just extra hard on women, or perhaps being a man was the more natural state, to which women were obliged to revert in the end, despite all their struggles.

It was a good morning. It was payday. Tonight she would go out drinking with the boys. Something else pleased her even more. The previous afternoon she had finally managed to ask the boys if they had any books she could borrow and read. '*Books*?' they said in startled unison, and Mary thought she had made a mistake. They went on muttering about it all afternoon – 'books . . . books! . . . books . . .' But this morning they had come with books, three each, and they said Mary could have them for as long as she liked. Alan had brought her *Life at the Top*, *Kon-Tiki* and *Management: An Introduction*. Russ had brought her *Sex in the Cinema*, *Inside Linda Lovelace* and *Britt*. Tomorrow was Sunday, and she would have time to start reading them.

As Mary did her automatic half-curtsy and began to slide the dishes on to the table, she heard, from behind,

'Hello, Mary.'

Unable to turn, Mary hesitated. One of the cabbies reached for his plate and said. 'That's me, my love.' Many people called her Mary by now. But she knew who this was.

'It's not far enough, Mary,' he said.

She turned. It was Prince. He was sitting there with his chair leaning backwards against the wall. She noticed again how effortless and alert he was, compared to all these other people, how in control, how in tune, with his newspaper, his cup of coffee, his cigarette.

'Hello. What's not far enough?' said Mary.

'Me? I didn't say anything,' he said.

'Yes you did. You said it's not far enough. I heard you.'

'You've got big ears, haven't you Mary,' said Prince interestedly.

'What?' said Mary, blushing.

'And you're nosey too.'

'Well you've got a completely square head.'

'Don't be cheeky.'

'What?' said Mary, lifting a hand to her face. Her cheek was certainly very warm.

'You're all lip, you are.'

'What?'

'All mouth.'

' . . . Well I'm sorry.'

'Don't cry, you fathead.'

'I've got a *thin* head,' said Mary.

He laughed and said, 'Oh boy – I'm going to have a lot of fun with you, I really am.'

'Mary!' called Mr Garcia. 'I say *bring* the poached egg toast!'

Mary was about to hurry away but Prince reached out and took her by the wrist. Mr Garcia saw him then and said quickly.

'It's okay. It's okay, Mary.'

'Sit down,' said Prince. 'Mary, Mary Lamb – that name kills me.'

'What do you want from me?'

'Who you are – that's the first thing I want to find out. Who are you? Eh? Eh? Are you Amy Hide?'

'I don't know,' said Mary.

'She was quite a girl, Amy.'

Mary looked down. 'Oh God, I hope it isn't true,' she said.

'The things she did.'

'I, I want forgiveness.'

'I beg your pardon?'

'That's right.'

'Sorry?'

'*Yes*.'

He laughed again. 'I can't get enough of this,' he said. 'But let's be serious for a while. I'm in a hell of a position actually. And so are you. You be straight with me and I'll be straight with you. Let's get our story straight. Okay?'

'Okay,' said Mary.

'Now. Some people have been working on the assumption that Amy Hide came to a sticky end.'

'Did she?'

'Apparently very sticky, yes. Mind you, she was cruising for a bruising all along. And yet, and yet – here you still are.'

'If it's me.'

'If it's you.' He took a piece of paper from the inside pocket of his overcoat. 'I've got something for you, an address.

'Home, perhaps,' he said, and stood up. Cigarette smoke came like spectral tusks from his nostrils. 'Why don't you go and find out, Mary?' he said.

Mary looked down at the address – Mr and Mrs Hide and where they lived.

'Be in touch,' he said.

Mary watched him amble out into the street. A black car swooped down and he got into it. 'He knows about me,' Mary murmured as she walked up the vault of the crowded café.

'Is the feeling of self-loavin I can't bear. Inna mornins. *Used* again. I'm just a bloody pushover, I am. I'm just bloody anybody's – providing they're film stars, I'm a cinch. Open me eyes, and there'll be Mia or Lisa or Bo or Elke, Nastassia, Sigourney, Imogen, or *Ju*lie or *Tues*day or *Cher*yl or *Mer*yl. Hah! It's not my mind they're after – I know that, mate, don't worry! Take you now, Mary –'

'Ah fuck off, Russ,' drawled Alan. They had both got much worse at talking over the half-hour.

'No, come on. This is *serious*. Mary. You see someone like me, dirty great unk like me, the tight T-shirt and the jeans and all, all the equipment. It says only one thing to you now dunnit? S, E, X. Come on, it does dunnit?'

'Russ,' said Alan.

'Is true! Admit it, goo on. Here all right darlin, here's to you. Your good elf.'

'Yeah cheers,' said Alan, raising his glass.

'Tell you what, girl,' said Russ, 'you really livened the place up, you have. Strew. The one we had before was a right dog. A right old poodle.'

'No,' said Alan, 'strew. That's right.'

'No,' said Russ, 'you have.'

'No,' said Alan, 'this is it.'

'I'll tell you what and all. The voice on her. She talks like a *fuckin* princess, she does.'

'Strew. Like a *fuckin* duchess, mate.'

'Like a *fuckin emp*ress mate! She does. I could listen to her all day and all night. Here's to you Mary! Your good elf!'

You see? she wanted to say. I'm *good* – I *am*.

Mary looked round the public house. Though only mildly furious in its pattern of exchange, the room was as crowded and cacophonous as the place she remembered from her second day – when she had been with Sharon, and with Jock and Trev. But how much less loud and various things seemed to her now. Oh, it was still interesting all right, interesting, interesting: did you see the way that woman looked up from her evening paper and towards the stained window with a ragged gasp, or the way that man tried to suppress a beam of love at his patient dog, lying under the table with its nose on its paws? Yes, but it's not enough to fill my thoughts, even here with friends, spending money earned from time sold. She thought, I'm becoming like other people. I'm getting fear and letting the present dim.

~ ~ ~

But it had to happen, Mary.

Life is made of fear. Some people eat fear soup three times a day. Some people eat fear soup all the meals there are. I eat it some-times. When they bring me fear soup to eat, I try not to eat it, I try to send it back. But sometimes I'm too afraid to and have to eat it anyway.

Don't eat fear soup. Send it back.

Some people have fear but some have confidence instead. Which do you have? You're not confident, I know that. I know that, because actually no one has confidence. The most confident men and women you know – they haven't got confidence. No one has. Everyone has fear instead. (Unless they have that third thing, which men call madness.)

They fear they are a secret which other people will one day discover. They fear they are a joke which other people will one day see, which other people will one day *get*.

Do you know, for instance, what little Alan is afraid of now? He is afraid that Russ and Mary will shortly go off together somewhere for a protracted session of hysterical sex. He is. He can see Mary unfurling her immaculate white panties, glancing shyly over her shoulder, while the mightily hung Russ lolls smiling on the bed. And Alan can see himself, Alan, watching the whole spectacle from some abstract vantage, silent, unblinking, and perfectly bald, like a being from the future. Russ, on the other hand, is afraid that Alan will tell Mary, or that Mary will inadvertently discover, that he, Russ, can neither read nor write. (Russ has a further heroic foible: he refuses to believe that he has an unusually small penis. He is wrong about this; he ought to stop refusing to believe it; he does in fact have an unusually small one.) Whereas Mary is afraid of the address in her bag. She is afraid of Prince and what he knows. She is afraid that her life has in some crucial sense already run its course, that the life she moves through now is nothing more than another life's reflection, its mirror, its shadow. Everything she sees has an edge on it, like prisms in petrol, like faces in fire, like other people hurrying through changing light – visions that we sense ought to reveal something, or will soon reveal something, or have already revealed something that we have missed and will never see again.

⁓ ⁓ ⁓

'Time,' said the man behind the bar, 'time, gentlemen, please. Alan sprang up guiltily, barking his kneecap on the table and toppling an empty glass. As it fell, Russ tried to catch it, but only slapped the glass still faster to the floor. It didn't smash or break. It rose up to live again on the wet tabletop.

'Here, let's uh – we'll walk you home,' said Alan quickly.

'Yeah, where d'you live?' said Russ.

'Near here. With some girls,' said Mary.

'I'm not coming,' said Russ. 'I can't risk it.'

But Russ risked it. They all did. They all walked through the shouts and shadows of the night. For every slammed car door a light went out. This was the week ending with a nervous sigh, and getting ready to start all over again.

'You'll have a word with them, won't you, on my behalf,' said Russ. 'Explain and that.'

'If you like,' said Mary. 'I don't think you'll see them. You can't come in.'

'It's one of those places, is it?' said Alan. 'Landlady on the stairs, no radios, no cats.'

'And no film stars,' said Russ. 'That's the big itch.'

'It's not really like that,' said Mary.

They came to Mary's place. Two girls were sitting smoking on the steps. The girls gazed out blankly for a few seconds, then went on talking. Mary could read the smoke coming in thin wafts from their mouths. They weren't talking about anything much. Through the open door you could see the old green passage, and the notice-board breathing softly.

Alan swung his head round at her. 'You don't live *there*, do you Mary?' he said in a stretched, pleading voice.

'Yes,' said Mary, 'I do, I'm afraid.'

'How'd you end up *here*, girl,' said Russ.

'There was nowhere else.'

'Can't have this,' said Russ gravely.

'What happened to you?' said Alan, with his beseeching eyes. 'I mean – haven't you got any family or anything?'

Mary couldn't answer. She didn't know what to say any more. Now Mrs Pilkington loomed in the doorway, the ring of keys in her hand. The girls stood up and flicked their cigarettes into the air, then turned with their heads bowed. Mary moved forward. There was nothing to say. On the steps she turned and waved. The boys looked on, their hands in their pockets, then they too turned and started off down the long defile of the street.

'This is you,' said the driver.

And what have *you* done in your life, thought Mary, as she lowered herself from the hungry red bus. The driver watched her, breathing through his mouth. He was big and fat and red like the bus he drove. She returned his stare, or she let it bounce back off her, as if she were no more than the mirror of his gaze. Obediently the red bus lay there, breathing through its mouth, panting to be off again. The door slid shut, and with a snorting shudder they rode away.

Mary started walking. Grey, bookish, moss-scrawled houses with many windows stood stoically back from the road, beyond shallow stretches of grass where water-machines washed the transient rainbows of the air. In the treacly shadows beneath the garden walls confetti butterflies and corpulent bees flew in their haze . . . All this Mary saw in the Sunday morning light. There was a time when she would have let her senses out to play in the voluptuous present, but now her mind was hot and ragged. She had lost the knack of choosing what she wanted to think about; it seemed she could no longer call her thoughts her own.

Clearing her throat, straightening her shirt, needlessly clicking her handbag, Mary asked other people the way. There weren't many of them about – men carrying bales of newspapers, women pushing prams, children, the old – but asking the way was a sound method of getting to other places. It always worked in time.

She had found the street and was counting numbers, missing a beat, missing a beat, when she halted and lifted a hand to her mouth, and another memory came her way . . . Not now, not now, she thought, and remembered how as someone young she had had to leave her own room and enter a different room containing other people. She was putting on a pink dress, a dress her skin loved. Its pink was not the pastel that little girls ought to wear; it contained tenderness but also blood, the colour of gums and the most intimate flesh. She lifted the dress and blinked as its shadow slipped past her eyes. She smoothed the material out along her hips as if it were the same colour and texture as her soul. She glanced swiftly round her room – her room, which again was no more than a setting for herself – then opened the door and moved down the passage to that other door with its voices and its eyes.

Will it open? thought Mary, stalled on the silent street, her hands on her hair. Well, now I'll find out.

11
Whose Baby?

The door opened. It revealed a woman in black.

Mary tried to begin but couldn't.

'Why, Baby,' said the woman, with worry or concern in her voice.

Mary's teeth shivered. 'Baby?' she said.

The woman leaned forward, her eyes flickering in simple puzzlement. 'Oh I do beg your pardon. Goodness!' She stepped back with a hand on her heart. 'Don't take any notice of me. Can I help you, dear?' she added matter-of-factly.

'Oh I see. I'm sorry, I'm . . .'

'I say, are you all right, dear? You look quite . . . take my . . . *George*!'

Five minutes later Mary sat drinking a cup of tea in the sun-washed kitchen. Like the woman in black, Mary held her cup with both hands. She thought, I'm a girl, so I drink hot drinks with both hands. Girls always do that for some reason. Why? George uses only one. Men use only one hand, although their hands aren't nearly so steady as ours. Perhaps girls' hands are just colder hands. The kitchen, the passage, the house, meant nothing to her, nothing.

'It must be the heat,' said the woman in black. 'And I probably gave you a turn. I thought she was Baby, George. I could have sworn for a moment she was Baby come to see us. Don't you think she looks like Baby, George?'

'Not really,' said George.

'I'm sorry – whose baby?' said Mary.

'Baby's the youngest. She's called Lucinda really, but we always called her Baby. I'm sorry, what did you say your name was, dear?' she asked in her other, more neutral voice.

'Mary Lamb. I came here to ask about Amy Hide.'

The effect of the name was immediate – what a strong name,

94

Mary thought with a wince, oh what a powerful name. The woman in black stared at her shrilly in surprised anger, and George turned away, seeming to give in the middle, his head ducking slightly on his neck. Mary sometimes had the same reflex when she thought about what she had done to Mr Botham.

'Well the least said about her the better,' said the woman with finality. George grunted in agreement, and reached for his pipe.

Mary said quickly, as she had half-planned to say, 'I'm sorry. I knew her a long time ago, before she . . . I know it's very sad, what happened.'

The woman then did something that Mary had only ever read about. She gave a bitter laugh. So that's what a bitter laugh is, Mary thought. It wasn't a laugh at all, she realized: it was just a noise people made to conjure a unanimity of dislike.

'Sad?' she said. 'It isn't *sad*. Nothing about that girl was *sad*.'

Mary was desolated. She said, 'Well it's sad for me.'

'Oh I'm sorry – of course it is, dear. Are you feeling better now? Have another cup, dear,' she said, standing up and reaching for the pot.

'No thank you,' said Mary.

'No, it's just when I think of the pain she caused her poor parents. I swear her mother died of a broken heart over that girl. Ooh, I could . . .'

'Marge,' said George.

Marge sat down suddenly. She lifted both hands to her forehead, the fingertips spread along the pierced tender lines of the brow. Mary was appalled to see brilliantly clear and icy tears jump on to her cheeks.

'Marge,' said George.

'I – I'm sorry. I'll be myself again in a minute.'

'I'm sorry,' said Mary. Everyone was so sorry.

'Isn't it funny? She can still do this to us even now.'

Mary began crying too. She could feel the tears tiptoe down her face but she couldn't reach up and wipe them away.

'Oh Lord, you've started too.'

George ambled to the sink, returning with a large scroll of paper. He tore off sections and handed them out. He kept one for himself, into which he explosively blew his nose. Then, as if it

95

were the natural thing, the three of them laughed softly, with weariness and relief.

Mary said, 'One more thing. I'm sorry, I'm very sorry. I really never meant to cause you pain . . . Can I see her room, Amy's room? It would mean a great deal to me.'

Or it might, she thought. It might.

They moved in file down the first-floor passage. If Mary had had time, she would have wondered why people needed so much space and so many things to put in it. There was so much space in between things. But she was numb, she was raw, she just wanted the next thing to happen quickly.

'Here we are,' said Marge.

Mary felt another gust of heat in her head. Marge hesitated, and George came up close behind Mary, bringing the smell of earth and the sound of his slow breath.

'Of course it's all changed,' said Marge, her hand idling on the white doorknob. 'She hasn't, Amy's not been back here for, let me see, ooh it must be eight or nine years. It's a visitors' room now. But some of it is still the same.'

The door opened, let them in, and closed again.

The room looked Mary up and down. It was a normal room and it looked Mary up and down with intense suspicion. The white-clothed table basking in front of the window held her gaze for a few seconds, then glanced downwards and became itself again. The thin bed cowered in the corner, with its head covered in cushions. On the four walls the romping sprites and goblins of the paper pattern must have once provided food for tenacious nightmares but they held no message for her now. The elderly, slow-ticking clock on the dressing-table would not show its face and had turned its back on her in disdain, as if its arms were folded and its foot tapping with impatience. Mary caught her own eye in the mirror, and the mirror told her plainly that it did not know whether she belonged here, and that, besides, whatever soul the room once held had disappeared or died a long time ago.

'What's that?' said Mary to hide her panic.

Splayed photographs in steel wallets lined the mantel-piece. Mary and Marge approached and ran their gaze together along the shelf. There were people in scattered groups, waving or beckoning. There was a dog standing in a bar of sunlight, panting happily, perhaps hoping that the camera might turn out to be food. There was one of George and Marge themselves, cheek to cheek and looking pretty well stuck with each other. There was a larger and less formal study of a man, a woman and a young girl, standing in a field against a warlike sky. The man was tall and angular with starry grey hair, his narrow face half-averted in a forgetful smile; the woman – lean and dark, old but still a woman, still with the feminine light in the points of her face – reached up a hand to his shoulder, her face full of gentle insistence; and between them, encircled by their lines, stood the young girl.

'*That*'s Baby,' said Marge. 'Years ago, of course.'

'Yes, and who are they?'

'That's the Professor,' she said with a warm gulp, 'and Mrs Hide.'

Mary turned to her and said, 'Aren't you Mrs Hide?'

'What? Good Lord no dear! Goodness me. We just, you know, we're just keeping house while the Professor's away.'

'Oh I see.'

'Mrs Hide . . .' Her face stiffened. She placed a hand on the black bosom of her dress. 'I'm not wearing black for *Amy*, you know,' she said.

'I'm sorry.' So she *did* break her heart, thought Mary. Amy did break it.

Marge looked back towards the shelf. The last photograph contained a smartly posed young man, his chin on his knuckles, gazing out at them with patient, serious eyes.

'That's Michael,' said Marge huskily. 'He's famous now of course. He phoned the Professor, you know, when he heard. Such a thoughtful boy.' Her eyes slipped away. 'None of Amy,' she added quietly.

Mary spent the rest of this day of heat sitting on a bench in the nearby park, watching the families play. They spread blankets, and hunched down on them in clumps. The whirring children cried and complained, spilt things and ran away. Most of them got beaten at some point or another, often hard and nastily. Their tall keepers were often quite unpleasant to each other too, or just frazzled by heat and dislike. In fact there were several families in which no one seemed to have any time whatever for anyone else, no time at all, just no time. But at the pall of the day when the light was used up the families always went home together, usually in pairs, the big holding hands with the small, and the old, too, edging along behind.

The next day when she went back to work it seemed that everything had changed.

Even the flies shunned her – even the flies had found her out.

Russ worked grimly behind his counter. As he handed her the plates he declined to meet her eye. It was difficult that way. Mary dropped one – a writhing egg flapping helplessly in a tempest of tomato blood and chipped plate. As she was clearing it up she glimpsed Russ's reflection in the glass panel – a vindictive grin splitting his fat-nosed face. Even Alan had greeted her coolly. She no longer felt him gently beaming her with his eyes, and when she turned to him nervously he was always looking the other way, seeming to snigger in silence at her and her losses. I can't bear it, thought Mary. It's unbearable. What do you do when you can't bear something like this?

At mid-morning Mary still trembled alone over the dishes in the smoked and yellowed kitchen. Her mind, too, churned and splashed in the villainous water. Why did they hate her? She thought it must be the Hostel. Was it so bad to be there? Did that part of you seep into all the other parts? Or was it the books! When she returned to the Hostel the night before she found that Mrs Pilkington had confiscated four of the boys' books, without explanation. Two remained: *Britt* and *Management: An Introduction*. Mary did not know how serious this was or what she was going to do about it. Then she had a thought that made her whole body fuss with heat. Was it out? Did everybody know about her now? I'm sorry, I'm sorry, I'm sorry, she chanted to herself, and worked on. The flies still circled her, in widening arcs of anxiety. Oh, how vile you must be now, she thought. How vile you must be, when even the flies shun you.

Just after noon the telephone rang in Alan's cubicle. She heard him croak out a few words of muffled thanks. Mary sensed the lull next door in the scullery. She turned and saw that Russ was peering out eagerly at Alan, who stood in his doorway with a shame-faced smile.

'It's all all right,' said Alan. 'There's a room at our place if you want it. You only pay your share of the rates, and it's furnished. You can move in any time. It's sort of an attic.'

'An *attic*?' said Russ. 'That's a studio, mate – that's a bloody *pent*house that is.'

'Well,' said Alan. 'Do you want it?'

'Yes please,' said Mary and started to cry, out of relief but also because she knew for certain now that something had gone wrong with the way she saw other people.

'Here come the waterworks,' said Russ. 'Listen to her owl!'

Alan and Russ moved towards her at the same time. Alan checked himself, and so had to watch Russ take Mary confidently in his arms.

'Come on, Mary,' he remonstrated with his soft breath. 'No *grief*. I always keep a couple of rooms free for my girls. When a new one comes along – you, for instance – I kick an old one out, don't I. Guess whose turn it was for the chop this time? Ekberg. She was getting a bit scuffed-up anyway.'

'Actually it's technically a squat,' said Alan quaveringly. 'But it's an organized squat.'

'No, it's nice there,' breathed Russ. 'Come on, Mary. You'll be miles better off with us.'

～　～　～

Will she be? Do you really think so?

Squats are rich people's houses where poor people come and live when the rich people aren't looking. Some squats are hippie hells, but some squats are nice – if you can cope with the ghastly uncertainty of it all. Some squats are practically legal. People are serious about living together.

But things are always happening there and no one has the power to stop them happening. Downstairs people are arguing about half-bottles of milk and bathroom rosters and utility bills, just like anywhere else; but upstairs, through a different window, there'll be someone staked out on a bed, panting, boiling, coruscating, and one night soon the house will be full of screams. They just can't stop things, they just can't keep things out. And they too might go bad at any minute, because it is easy to go bad when you live on the breaking line.

I want Mary out of all this. I want her out of this whole risk-area of clinks and clinics and soup-queues, of hostels and borstals and homes full of mad women. I want her away from all these deep-divers. She might go bad herself: it happens. She might smash. I see her as a crystal glass that someone has tapped too hard with his knife; she sings along her breaking line.

The breaking line is where I walk, or where I sometimes think I do. On the breaking line you can hear things getting ready to crack, the ground, the walls of air, the sealing sky. Other people walk here but I don't see them. The lines are always somewhere else, they never cross. No lines cross, no figures loom, all are alone on the breaking line.

I've done things to her, I know, I admit it. But look what she's done to me.

Look what she's *done* to me.

12
Poor
Ghost

That night the boys moved Mary out of the Hostel and into the squat.

That night the Hostel was hushed and rumbling. It was always that way when something had happened to someone. Something happened to someone pretty often in the Hostel, about every three nights. It had happened to Trudy this time. She had fought with a man and she had lost. It had been no contest, as usual. The man had broken her nose and two front teeth, whereas Trudy hadn't succeeded in breaking anything of his. She lay on her bed, in a turban of gauze, while Mary packed her case. Trudy would have to be moving on too: any trouble and the girls were out. Trudy didn't know where. It seemed a sensible rule, to make girls leave for trouble. They would never have come here if it hadn't been for trouble. And they could never leave trouble until they left here.

'It'll be better somewhere else,' Mary told her.

'Oh yeah? How the fuck do you know, Mary?'

'This is the worst place, isn't it?'

Trudy didn't answer.

'Well I hope you'll be all right,' said Mary.

'Do you?'

'Yes I do.'

'Yeah,' said Trudy.

Mary might have said something else, but she could tell by the way Trudy looked at her that she was already on the other side.

Honey accompanied her upstairs. Mary had to say goodbye to Mrs Pilkington and give her a fixed address. Russ and Alan were hovering uneasily about in the hall. Neither of them liked it here – that was obvious. And Russ liked it less than Alan. Mary tried to be as quick as she could.

'Well, good luck,' said Mrs Pilkington gloomily. 'There's some money outstanding but I expect your gentleman friend will deal with that.'

'Who's my gentleman friend?' asked Mary, really wanting to know.

'The man who pays for your upkeep! This place doesn't run on buttons, you know.'

'But who is he?'

'How many men have you got who pay you money? You girls . . . He's called – Mr Prince. Does that ring any bells for you, Mary?'

Mary said goodbye to Honey in the hall. Honey told Russ that he had nice eyes and Russ fanned her away playfully. He took Mary's case.

'You very lucky, Mary,' said Honey, 'to have this nice strong man to live with.'

'See?' said Russ. 'See? See?'

Mary was pleased that Honey had said this. It gave them – or Russ – something to talk about as they walked to the squat. She herself didn't mind the routine, exitless, snow-blind silences that quite often opened up when she was with Russ and Alan, but Russ and Alan seemed to mind them, particularly Alan. Silences sometimes made Alan's throat swell into speech, any old words, and he would then have a few contorted minutes trying to tame them back to sense. Mary preferred it when he just relaxed and went back to worrying about his hair, and when Russ quietly continued worrying about whatever it was he continually worried about.

'It's going to be a new life for you, girl,' said Russ. 'I've been thinking about it and, well – if you're good, you might even get a little nibble of the big one.'

'*Russ*,' said Alan, and gave a tug at his hair. 'No,' he added croakily, 'it'll be nice with you there.'

And it was nice.

The squat was a spindly house in a dead-ended play road: cars could be parked there but they came and went with diffidence, knowing very well that the peremptorily hollering children were the true celebrities of the street. The house was full of ordinary people – but then, ordinary people are really terribly strange, deep with dreams and infamies, or so Mary thought. You only have to listen: they'll tell you everything if you give them time. In the basement lived artful, buck-toothed Vera, a young Irish girl with a loose swing in her movements, an actress who seldom found anything to act in; her ambition was to become famous and make lots of money. Next door lived Charlie, a twinkly old Australian who prided himself on not being ashamed of his conviction for child-molesting seven years previously; he kept boasting that he would never molest any children again, and now had thoughts only for tuning his motorbike, which was already so fast that he hardly dared ride about on it. And Russ himself had his room down in the basement too.

The ground floor was communal except for the spacious bedsitter which Norman had allotted himself – fat, pale, floppy-jeaned Norman, who was generally revered as the brains behind the squat. His life had so far been a running battle with what he called a serious weight problem; he hadn't solved it either, not yet, since the slightest variance from a starvation diet rendered him helplessly obese more or less overnight; and he was already incredibly fat as it was. Up on the second floor lived an entire three-strong family, Alfred, a sullen business flop from the Midlands who was ransacking the city for business opportunities and not finding any, Wendy, his broad-shouldered but sickly wife who spent all day in her dressing-gown, and their eight-year-old son Jeremy, who was too frightened to talk much about what he wanted or feared.

Alan lived on the second storey, next to the room shared by two black men, Ray and Paris. They spent the money they earned at Battersea Funfair on the horses or the dogs; but they never had any horses or dogs, or any money either. Together they nursed a dream of becoming professional footballers (and could often be seen perfecting their skills out in the street), Ray intending one day to represent Leyton Orient, Paris shoring up all his hopes with Manchester United. They were both thirty years old and alike in several other respects.

Alone in the attic was Mary.

Her room had a soul, the vestiges of a presence fraily lingering. But the presence moved over with good grace, and the room let Mary in. She had one bed, two sheets, three blankets, one window divided into four, two tables, one high, one low, one lamp, one basin, two taps, three shelves, one cupboard, two drawers, four walls, six coat-hangers, and fourteen sunlit floorboards. It was ideal. With the money she had earned from time sold (and with some pressed on her by Alan: his time was more valuable than hers, though he didn't seem to want the money it realized) Mary bought some Imperial Leather, some Antique Gold, some Cracker Pink, some Honey Beige, some Scotties, some Corgis, some Panthers, some Penguins. When she got back from work she would always run upstairs to see that her room was still there and still all right, still ideal. And later she would lie on her bed and read unquenchably into the night.

She read *The Nice and the Good*, *The Long and the Tall*, *The Quick and the Dead*, *The Beautiful and Damned*. She read *The Real Life of Sebastian Knight*, *A Temporary Life*, *The Life to Come and Other Stories*, *Life Studies*, *A Sort of Life* and *If Life's a Bowl of Cherries, What Am I Doing in the Pits?* She read *Dreams of the Dead*, *Dead Man Leading*, *Die, Darling, Die*, *From a View to a Death*, and *The Death of Ivan Ilych and Other Stories*. She read *Labyrinths*, *Scruples*, *America*, *Sadness*, *Despair*, *Night*, *Love*, *Living*. She soon learned that titles were often deceptive. A few of the books were dead – they were empty, there was really nothing inside. But some were alive: they spanned out at you seeming to contain all things, like oracles, like alephs. And when she geared herself to wake early they were still open on the table, well aware of their power, coolly waiting.

One thing the books couldn't do, though: they couldn't make her start dreaming again or otherwise subdue her sleep.

Nor did they quite explain how you lived with other people.

All week three things hovered – the thought of Amy and what she had done, the thought of Prince and what he might do, and Alan. Alan was the third thing that hovered. Pallid Alan hovered on the staircase when she left her room each morning. He loitered there like an aimless phantom, condemned always to wait on the wrong side of the doors of the living. You'd think he had been there all night from the way he quavered. 'Morning, Mary', as if without constant practice his voice was cracking up altogether. He hovered on the steps of the squat, waiting for Mary and shouting down to the deep sleeping Russ, who valued a few extra minutes in bed more than the elementary breakfast which Alan and Mary usually ate with Charlie, Alfred, Vera, Jeremy and Paris.

Alan hovered behind her at work, using his eyes. He sent his eyes out from the small cubicle to stand guard behind her at the sink, and Mary could feel them smoothing along her back. He hovered outside the cloakroom when it was time to go home, and she felt his force field throughout the evening, in the communal sitting-room where the television played, even when she went out alone into the small garden where you were also welcome provided you took care about other people's flowers, vegetables, weeds and stinging-nettles. And he hovered last thing at night as Mary climbed her own stretch of stairs, saying the words 'Good night, Mary' or 'Sleep well' or 'God bless, Mary' as if they sealed a day of vain but honourable striving in a cause that would now have to wait until dawn, finding him once more on the stairs again. Alas, poor ghost, thought Mary.

He never did or said anything. It was Russ who was always doing and saying things. Old Mr Garcia was more affectionate and demonstrative than Alan was – and even the languorous Antonio openly favoured her with his yawning caresses. But Alan did nothing. Russ gave her painful tweaks on her bottom, tickled her chin, kissed her throat and licked her ears, and talked obsessively and bewilderingly about his elaborate plans for her, or hers for him.

'I don't know when I can fit you in, girl,' he would say, 'but it *could be soon*. I generally make it a rule not to go all the way onna first night. But you know me. Get a couple of Scotches down me and I go all giggly – I'll be putty in your ands!'

'Russ,' Alan would say; but that was all Alan said.

Mary didn't understand. Perhaps none of it mattered that much anyway. She just hoped that Alan would be all right, that he wouldn't break anything.

Early on Friday evening, Mary was ominously summoned into Norman's room to receive a call on the pay-telephone. Norman gestured towards the instrument with a flourish that almost bowled him over and then wobbled from the room, closing the door behind him. Mary had watched people use the telephone several times and was pretty confident that she could handle it. The bandy, glistening dumb-bell was heavier than she had expected. But she had expected the call: she knew who this must be.

'Yes?' said Mary.

A thin voice started talking. Telephones were clearly less efficient instruments of communication than people let on. For instance, you could hardly hear the other person and they could hardly hear you.

'I can't hear. What?' said Mary.

Then she heard, in an angry whine, '*I said turn it the other way up.*'

Mary blushed, and did as she was told.

'Boy, you're a real woman of the world, aren't you,' said Prince.

'I'm sorry,' said Mary.

'Ah forget it. No, actually, you'd better not, come to think of it. Christ.'

'How did you know where to find me?'

'It's the sort of thing I know. Now listen, Mary – did you go there?'

'Yes, I went there.'

'Any joy?'

'No, it was very sad.'

'It didn't take you back.'

'No, I'm still here. It's all changed there.'

'What? No, I mean did you have any *luck*?'

'Well, I've this room now.'

'Jesus.' She heard him stifle a snort of laughter. 'Better pick my words here. Did you *remember* anything, Mary.'

'Only the dress.'

'The address?'

'No, I didn't remember anything.'

He paused. 'Damn,' he said. 'Hell. Hey look, why don't you come out on the town with me tomorrow night?'

'Because I don't want to,' said Mary.

'You're interesting, Mary, I'll say that for you. I'll give you that: you're interesting. I'm afraid I've got to insist about this. Tomorrow. I'll pick you up at work.'

'What do you want from me?'

'I just want to show you the sights, that's all.'

'What sights?'

'You'll see. Goodbye, Mary.'

'Goodbye,' said Mary.

She rejoined Alan on the front steps. They were watching the children play, or Mary was. Alan was too busy trembling and pulling his hair out to have much attention to spare, Mary reckoned. The boys swirled up and down the road in the patterns determined by their energy, watched by the girls from the thrones of the facing garden walls. Cruelty came easily to the boys and found its salute in the girls also. Mary had once seen tiny, stammering Jeremy flattened up against a car by one of these callous-bodied young champions; Jeremy's face was sick and smiling as the boy held him and turned, looking to the girls for their worship or their signal.

'Mary?' said Alan, when his trembling had subsided.

'Yes?' said Mary, and turned to him. She was sorry she was doing all this to Alan. She knew she had given him his new numb-eyed look, his untrustworthy hands, his Jeremy smile. He had given Mary her room and she had given him all this. She had shown him a chaos inside himself which she didn't understand. It wasn't fair, and she was sorry.

'Who was that on the phone?'

'Just a man I know.'

'Ah.' Alan received the remark as if it were a light but expertly stinging rebuke, and one that he moreover richly deserved. 'Mary?'

'Yes?'

'What you like doing best in the evenings?'

'Reading in my room.'

'Ah. Good one,' said Alan. His waved hand suddenly bunched in front of his mouth as, without warning, his laugh convulsed into a cough. 'No. I meant, you know, weekends, evenings out.'

'Oh,' said Mary cautiously.

'Because I was wondering. Say no and everything if you can't or something, but. But I was just wondering if you'd come out with me. Tomorrow. Night.'

'I'm seeing a man tomorrow night,' said Mary.

Alan took his lower lip between his teeth, raised his eyebrows, and nodded twelve times.

Just then Russ came jogging up the basement steps. When he saw Mary he jerked to a halt, as if he'd never encountered her before. Reaching out an experimental forefinger, he lifted her chin. He kissed her, urging his mouth right into hers so that his lips tickled her teeth. Mary thought that if Russ wanted to do this, it was really quite a pleasant and reassuring thing to do; so she opened her mouth wider and put an arm round the back of his head to steady herself. This went on for a long time. Then Russ withdrew his lips with a sudden pop, eyed her judiciously for several seconds, shook his head with pitying sternness, and moved past her up the steps. Alan wrenched a handful of hair from his crown with a faint whimper and got to his feet. Then he raced off down the road, so fast that even the whirling boys hesitated and stood back catching their breath to watch his speed.

~ ~ ~

Boy. Have you ever had it as bad as Alan had it the next day? Do you know that kind of pain? It's a really bad kind, isn't it, right up there in the top two or three? That kind of pain isn't very popular these days and some people pretend not to feel it. But don't fall for that one. The trouble with pain is that it hurts. *Ow*. Ow! ow! ow! Pain hurts! It *hurts*. If love is the most you can feel, then this is the worst. But pain is what can happen when you fall in love with other people.

Boy, Alan has it bad today. Boy. Alan is hurting bad today. When you're in love and trying to make someone love you back, you can hear the texture of your own footfalls, the whistling passage of your breath. Invisible eyes monitor you constantly: even at night something presides over the shape of your sleep. Every thought carries a tick or a cross.

But then failure falls and you feel its weight. You see the stark facts of your loathsomeness. This is what pallid Alan is going through now, in the hunched hell of his cubicle. He is locked in punishment park. Each flicker of his hands, each muffled cough, each falling hair is radiant with his hideousness – and he *is* hideous, he is, because love renders you hideous when the weight of failure falls.

Now his ears have started joining in the terrible fun: they are having hallucinations. Alan doesn't need this. Things were quite bad enough already. And he daren't turn round to see if what he hears is true. A gentle plop of water in the sink is a kiss exchanged by Russ and Mary; a ruffle of the dishcloth is the slide of his hand along her dress; each silence is their joyful shared peace, together among those sentinels of light and all their secrets. With Russ, or with somebody else – it doesn't matter. The whole world is feasting on her, and she *loves* it. Alan's thoughts are riding shotgun, his body is a rodeo, a riot. Each breath is fire. Boy, is he suffering. Boy, is he having a bad time. Boy, does pain hurt in love when the weight of failure falls.

Mary felt the crackle of Alan's radioactivity, his wrecked force field, like the sky at night after the death of kings, all lightning-flashes and hysterias of blazing meteorites. But she couldn't understand it, she couldn't understand its inordinateness. Her instinct was straightforward enough: to help, to be kind. But every word or gesture she offered him was instantly mangled by this new power of hers. What was this power? It was the power to make feel bad. Mary's smiles weren't smiles any more, not to Alan.

Perhaps there just wasn't any way to make other people feel better at such times. Would talking about it help? Russ talked about it.

'What the fuck's the matter with you today?' he asked Alan disgustedly as the three of them ate their quick meal during the afternoon lull. 'Look at his hands! Look at them!' Russ leaned back and put his arm round Mary's shoulders. 'You know what he's got, don't you, darlin. Wanker's lurgy! *Eur*. Look at him. Creeping wanker's lurgy is what he's got. You'll have to cut down, my son – onna andjobs. Look, fuck off, Al, and deal with it, will you? Who needs you here looking like that.'

That didn't help. That didn't help one bit.

At seven o'clock they trooped through the empty café. Russ ducked off to the lavatory – and for the first time that day Mary and Alan were alone. Losing no time, Mary took Alan's hand and squeezed it. He turned to her with his eyes closed in pain. I've done the wrong thing, she thought, but I'll do the next thing anyway. She leaned towards him and said, as meaningly as she could.

'*Yes*.'

His eyes opened. But then they both saw the black car pull up, and Prince sliding out; he rested his shoulder against the door, smiling calmly with his head at an angle.

They moved uncertainly towards the door, and now Russ came trotting after them. Once in the street, Mary hesitated briefly, but of course she knew she had no choice.

'Who's *this* dude?' said Russ as Mary walked away.

'Come on, Russ,' said Alan.

Russ lingered and stared for a few seconds, then hurried on beside his friend.

13
Live
Action

'Look,' said Prince as Mary approached him. He turned. He pointed with a finger, and flattened his forearms on the roof of the car, glancing sleepily at his watch. Mary came up beside him and looked.

Through a half-open doorway across the street a man lurched clattering out on to the pavement. He tensed to start forward headlong but before he could straighten out along the line of his speed a half-clad woman came after him and with a leap, an inhuman or animal leap, was on his back, seeming to ride him to the ground. As he wrenched himself clear his jacket tore audibly in her hands. They were both shouting, the woman continuously and on a higher plane of sound. The man bundled her back towards the doorway, where a second woman appeared, and reaching out in assistance or betrayal held her shoulders until the man had slapped himself free. He jogged off, glancing back twice. The women now embraced, though one still wailed. It was a greedy, tethered sound, growing louder on itself; they heard it even after the women had gone back inside and the door slammed shut behind them.

'Strange things,' said Prince lightly. 'This place is full of strange things if you know where to look. Weird things. Come on.'

He opened the door and watched Mary climb into the car – she did it awkwardly, feet first.

'Mind your hands,' he said.

The door closed with a thud of air and Prince's shadow moved round outside behind her head. He slipped in beside her and twisted the key in its lock. Mary looked out of her window; the café dropped back, averting its dark face. The machine put its head down and started lapping up distance. They climbed quickly on to the concrete beams that meshed the city, the car plunging forward with all its might, trying to get to the head of the herd.

'Of course. You've never been in a car before, have you.'

'Oh I think I must have been some time,' said Mary to the windowpane. She turned sharply.

Prince was smiling at the ravelling road. 'I've got lots of time for you, Mary,' he said. 'I told you that before. Lots of time.'

Life nearly overloaded Mary that night. She had never guessed at the city's abysmal divides and atrocious energies, its furniture, hardware, power and glut. And there could be no doubting Prince any more. He knew about her. He knew about everything.

'Look,' he said in the bar on the forty-fourth floor. Mary turned to see a red-haired girl in a pink dress, laughing on the arm of a fat man with one dead eye. The pink of the girl's dress was childish but her hair was as red as meat. 'He paid an agency fifty pounds to bring her here tonight. She will keep five, perhaps less. Five pounds, for going out with fat guys. Later they will make a deal. He will give her a hundred pounds, maybe a hundred and fifty. She will spend four or five hours of her time in his hotel, then go home to her children and her husband, who doesn't mind, who can't afford to mind.

'Look,' he said in the dungeon beneath the streets. He had pulled up under a bridge and opened a door in the ground with his keys. He had dozens of keys on his ring, keys for all things, perhaps, or just jailer's keys. 'This is where the lines of the city's power run. These are the copper veins that keep things working – water, electricity, gas.

'Look,' he said in the chaotic dormitory of a guarded compound near the airport, where the black hulks of planes screamed plangently overhead, their lights wired to the dark air. Mary turned to see an ochre-faced woman walking from bed to bed with a bundle of sticks and a shrieking baby in her arms. 'The sweeper-woman pinches the boy to make him cry louder for money. But she pinches him also to punish him for his sins in previous lives. He must have been a very bad boy to be born the son of a sweeper-woman. That's assuming there's life after death – natch.

'Look,' said Prince. Mary looked through the windscreen but

she still couldn't believe it. A man standing in the middle of the dark street, peeled raw naked, weeping – and burning money. He had a lighter, and a handful of notes. Other people had gathered to watch. 'Now he looks really well-adjusted. But then, what is there to be adjusted to? Oh *man* . . . what brought you to this? What made *this* seem like the next thing to do? That's it – run! Go on. Run, pal!'

They ate in a cavernous restaurant spanning a city block of festering Chinatown. Thousands of Chinese ate with them. Until then Mary had thought it no more remarkable that people were from Sweden or Sri Lanka than if they had long legs or short hair or were in luck or were out of it. Now she saw that it mattered where you came from, not just to you but to the greater balance. Other peoples . . . dish-faced sprites with their numb glow . . . Prince used his knitting needles skilfully on the sweet food. Mary was too full to eat, though she had eaten little that day. Not only foods fills you up. Sometimes the present is more than enough; sometimes the present is more than you can keep down. She drank the tea and tried to prepare herself.

'Shall we begin?' he said.

Mary nodded.

'How much do you know about Amy Hide?'

'Enough. The photograph was enough.'

'Well we know a little. We know the sort of things she did, the sort of people she was with. One night she went too far. Something happened. We're not sure what. You know what murder is, don't you?'

'I think so, yes.'

'Usually we find a body and have to look for a murderer. With Amy Hide we find a murderer and have to look for a body. We don't find it. We've got a confession, a guy in a cell saying what he did and why. But we haven't got a body. Where is Amy Hide? Then you come along. Show me your teeth.'

Mary made a rictus of her mouth. It felt like someone else doing it for her.

'Mm, pretty teeth. No help though. It seems that Amy never had any trouble that way – anyhow we can't find any records. Ditto with the doc. So it's a hell of a fix.'

'Is it a crime to be murdered?' Mary asked.

'What?' Mary thought that nothing could startle Prince; but this startled him. 'Why did you say that?'

'I just wanted to know. *Is* it a crime? Can you be punished for it?'

'Well it's a strange way to break the law. You see, the thing . . .' He hesitated and wiped his forehead with his palm. 'No. You needn't know that yet. That'll come later.'

'What will?'

'You'll see.' He was calmer again now, and amusement re-appeared in the line of his lips.

Mary said, 'What do you get if you break the law?'

'Time,' he said.

'What do you get if you murder someone?'

'Life.'

'What's life like?'

'Murder.'

'Is it?'

'Hell,' he said and laughed. 'Don't ever try it. Hey, Mary.'

'What?'

'Are you good or are you bad?'

' . . . I'm *good*. I *am*.'

' . . . Are you?'

She made her eyes contest him with all their light. She said, 'Have you ever done a terrible thing in a dream, and then woken up still believing it was true?'

'Yeah,' he said.

'I feel like that all the time. All the time.'

'Poor Mary,' he said, 'poor ghost. Come on. I'm afraid there's one more thing you must see tonight.'

They drove in silence. Prince was no longer disposed to talk and made some show of intentness at the controls. Mary watched the way they came with care. The river again, writhing and orderless in the lunar night, the plumed snout of a still-rumbling factory, warehouses that marched past slowly on either side and seemed to glance back over their shoulders at the car, a stretch of black grass in which an elliptical pond glinted and winked. Then the streetlights snuffed out, and she could see only the smoky beams thrust forward by the black car.

They got out and walked. Mary felt the massed volume of nearby water. Was this another river, or had the river that she and Sharon crossed subtly curled round to head them off again? There was a smell of vegetable dampness and a feeling of liquid in the air. Water dripped and trickled musically. She noticed that dark faces with white eyes watched like masks from misty doorways. Feeble, threadbare dogs – more like recently promoted rats – stared up from a split bagful of rubbish they were eating and barked weakly. The dogs looked bashful about their sudden elevation within the chain of being – as if they wished they hadn't excelled quite so brilliantly in the rodent kingdom and could quietly go back to being rats again. One limped up to sniff at Mary's feet, then tiptoed off again.

'The dog doesn't wag its tail,' said Mary nervously.

'Probably scared it'll drop off,' said Prince.

A heavy bird flapped overhead, and they could hear the hum its wings made against the damp air. Mary thought of the photograph she had once seen of an American eagle, its oriental trousers, the old eyes and their faith in the power of the ripping beak. Mary hurried on. They turned into an alley, and immediately Prince ducked through a low door, beckoning her to follow. She went in after him. The darkness and its dust made a connection with something in her head or throat, a tickle in the veins that feed the nose, the movement of a familiar but disused vent in the track of her blood. Ringed by candles, his face seemingly eyeless in their light, an old black man sat at a table by the inner door. He saw Prince and got to his feet with a sigh. Gingerly he slipped the bolt, stepping back to let Prince in. Prince could go anywhere. Everywhere had to let Prince in. Mournful, embarrassed music timed their ascent on the mis-angled staircase. Through a hole in its floor they came up into the arching shadows of the long room.

This is a slower world, thought Mary, where cause and effect never need to come around. Here people try to live on fever and magic; they can't, but they try. She looked about, then stared at the black floorboards, letting Prince guide her by the arm. There were twenty or thirty people there, perhaps many more. In a far corner film flashed. The talk was low and drowsy with all the fever in the air.

'Don't worry,' said Prince, leading her towards the music and the floppy, clumping dancers, miming chaos against the dusty lights. 'It's a quiet night tonight. Nothing live.' They sat down on bendy chairs round a small square table. An old man sidled up and banged a bottle and two glasses down in front of them. 'Christ, I hate this place,' he said, leaning forward and starting to drink quickly.

Mary watched the dancers. There were only two couples on the floor. An eerily tall black man shuffled slumped over a little ruined blonde. His eyes were quite dead. The girl seemed to be supporting all his weight, hauling him as if in eternal punishment round the littered floor.

'You know what they do here, Mary? Do you?'

'No,' said Mary exhaustedly. 'What do they do here.'

'All the usual things, all the trite things. You'd think people with these needs would pay other people to have them on their behalf, and just sit back and watch. Really this is the last place of boredom. When the world has bored you flat, you come to this place and have it bore you here. Remember?'

Mary watched the dancers. The second couple was different: it still harboured energy. They swayed together with the remains of method, the man forming elaborate patterns on the girl's back with his tensed claws, trailing them up the knobbed curve of her spine and down past the underhang of her breasts. As they worked round the floor the girl stood facing Mary, treading air for several slow beats. She smiled. One of her eyes was puffed and purple; her hollow mouth fell open slackly with silent laughter. In her face was all the relief of having no further to fall. The man jerked her head up to his and they kissed. The girl's good eye still held Mary – see? See? it seemed to say. I'm lost at last, lost.

'Amy used to get down here pretty often, I think,' said Prince.

'Did she?' said Mary.

'That's right, that's right. Amy used to like it best when they had live action here.' His voice moved closer. 'Don't you remember? Are you finding this *boring*? But vice is – it *is*. What's your special interest, Mary? Voodoo, video, violence, vagrants, vandals, vampires? What's your *interest*, Mary, what's your special *interest*?'

Mary turned away. She couldn't deal with the agitation of his tone. It wasn't anger but perhaps the eagerness of woken despair.

'Then they find people who already know what a few teeth are worth. And after they've been roughed up and batted about and peed on, then you get to go up on stage and kick them about a bit yourself. The kickbags get paid – oh good, good. It's fine, fine. Don't you *remember*? Don't you?'

Mary said nothing. The dancers were still kissing, with redoubled violence, as if eating each other's tongues. The man was urging her to the corner where the room was darkest. Wait – there was a door there, a low door almost consumed by shadow. Still kissing, still dancing, still urging, he steered her to the door. Suddenly the girl's head snapped back; she had seen the door and seen it open. Yes, this was further, this was a lot further, this was more, this was a whole new ledge on the way down. But she laughed and stretched her shoulders as if they were wings for flight. They were through and on the other side. The door swung shut behind them.

Mary turned to Prince. She could tell that he had been staring at her for a long time.

'What's behind that door?' said Mary, as they drove back.

'I've been behind the door once. You have too, I believe.'

'Stop playing with me. Why don't you leave me alone? Whatever I was I am *me* now.'

'That's my Amy,' said Prince. 'That's the opposition talking.'

'Stop it. Leave me alone. I'm not doing anyone any harm. And I can't have been murdered, can I, because *here I am.*'

Prince laughed. After a while he said. 'Is there life after death? Who knows. Actually I wouldn't put it past life, would you? That would be just *like* life, to have a trick in its tail . . . Okay. Okay. We'll let you be for a while. In fact, the only thing behind the door these days is a mattress or two, as far as I know. For fucking on. You know about all that, Mary?'

'A bit.'

'Oh well done.'

117

Mary said, 'You know I'm living in a squat now. I suppose you'll disapprove of that too.'

'Me? Not really. Some squats are nice. Some are even legal. People are serious about living together. Whoops,' he said, as the car in front seemed about to wobble free from its tracks.

'It's –'

'I know where it is.'

The car sniffed its way up the play street. Now all the children were sleeping. The garden walls looked frozen in the moon's light, the ghostly court where the young girls sat and watched.

'Mary – two things.' Prince got out of the car so quickly that when Mary opened her door his hand was already there, outstretched and waiting. He straightened her up and said,

'The photographs on the mantelpiece in your old room. Think about them. Try to – see if you can't follow yourself back a little way. Your past is still out there. Somebody has to deal with it.' He paused and turned his head up to the sky. 'Look,' he said.

Spanned out to mist, to white smoke, a lone lost white creature, separated from its flock, curled like a genie round the silver fire of the half-moon. It didn't look worried; it looked pleased to be left alone to its night game.

'They're not alive, you know,' said Prince. 'They're just clouds, air, gas.'

His breath came near her lips for an instant – that median breath – then passed across her cheek. She was walking towards the steps when she heard the door slam and the car start up again.

Mary climbed through the sleeping house. She could be quite silent when she wanted to be. She glided up through the house to the room she loved. Her stairs were there. All things are alive, even these seven stairs, she thought. Everything is alive, everything has something to be said for it.

She paused on the last step. She knew beyond doubt that there was someone in her room, someone waiting behind the door. Never stop now, she thought, and pushed the door open. Someone was sitting in the dark. It was Alan. He didn't even dare take his hands from his face. His arms were as stiff and brittle as thin wood. He couldn't stop crying. Mary undressed. She got into bed and told him to come too. He came. He wanted to get inside her – but not to hurt her, as Trev had wanted to do. Alan only wanted to hide there for a while. She let him in, she helped him in. It was all over after a minute. Mary just hoped he wouldn't break anything. But she thought he probably had.

— ⌣ ⌣ ⌣

Is there life after death? Well, *is* there?

If there is, it will probably be hell. (If there is, it will probably be murder.)

If there is, it will probably be very like life, because only in life is there variety. There will have to be many versions of death, to answer all the versions of life.

There will have to be a hell for each of us, a hell for you and a hell for me. Don't you think? And we will all have to suffer it alone.

14
Sadly
Waiting

———~~———

Alan and Mary . . . 'Alan and Mary'. *Alan and Mary* – as a team.
Well, how would *you* rate their chances? Personally (and it's just
my opinion), I don't think this hook-up is a good idea for either of
them, not really. Love is blind, you might point out. But where
can the blind lead the blind? Down blind alleys, down unknown
paths, with faces shuddering. And then there are other people to
consider too.

Russ, for instance, is *terribly angry*. Alan is in *terrible trouble* with
him about this. Here's a secret that will help explain why. Until
very recently Russ was in the habit of spending three or four nights
a week in the bed of thieving, unemployable Vera down in the
basement (this is actually the extent of his connection with stars of
stage and screen). But last night he strolled in there as usual – to
find the glistening Paris staked out complacently on her bed,
coolly reading the *New Standard*. The next thing he knows, Alan
and Mary are coming down to breakfast hand in hand.

Well, a major rethink seemed inevitable; and once he started
thinking, fresh doubts assailed him on every score. As an illiterate,
Russ is covertly very impressed by many of Alan's attributes.
Many things about Alan fill him with almost boundless admira-
tion. *That's* why she likes him: because he can read and write so
well. Furthermore, following an unpleasant remark of Vera's,
Russ has begun to entertain radical and sweeping doubts about the
size of his penis. Perhaps little Alan packs a whopper (after all, you
never know who'll get them)? All this Russ believes during his
dark nights of the soul, his skunk hours. Choirs of betrayal
serenade his every thought, and in the black night he broods on
revenge.

'Well at least *Alan* will be all right for a while,' I hear you
murmur. But he won't be. Alan thinks that other stuff was bad.

He thinks that other stuff was as bad as stuff could get. He's wrong. You wait.

～ ～ ～

'Do you want to go down first?' he asked her the next morning.

Mary turned over. Alan was sitting on the brink of the bed, his legs placed together, fully dressed. The night had changed him very little. All his facial colour appeared to have seeped into the whites of his eyes: the red they held was more brilliant than their blue. His mouth still rippled drily along its parting line. Mary sat up and Alan turned away quickly.

'Why should I want to do that?' said Mary.

'I don't know,' he said, and finally there was a tremor of furtive triumph in the contours of his face. 'I mean, do you want everyone to know?'

'Know what?'

'About us.'

'What about us?'

'I really love you, you know, Mary.'

'What does that mean exactly?'

'It – I'd die for you, on my mother's life I would.'

'I see. But you don't have to die for me, do you?'

'No, but I would.'

'But you don't have to.'

'No.'

'Then what does it mean?'

'I'd do anything for you,' he croaked, and took a tug at his hair. 'Look, I'll go down now so that they won't know.'

But they soon found out. They found out because all through that Sunday Alan was either staring palely into her face from close quarters or actually holding her hand (his hand was cold and wet, too, and he always kept *moving* it, either wiggling a finger or buffing her knuckle with his thumb). Mary was bewildered further by the immediate effect these attentions had on other people. An awful hushed twinkliness started emanating from Norman and Charlie, and a set-smiled, clear-eyed disdain from Wendy and Alfred. Ray and little Jeremy at least seemed quite indifferent to the matter; but there was a palpable coarseness and loss of distance in the looks and laughter of Vera and Paris. And Russ simply gazed at her all day with an expression of disgusted incredulity on his face.

Mary, feeling intensely confused, took her earliest opportunity to plead with Alan to forget whatever had happened and go back to how things had been before. Alan said he would do anything for her, apart from that. 'Go on – ask me. Anything,' he said. But Mary couldn't think of anything she wanted him to do for her, apart from that. He shed tears when she relented. Mary began to wonder what she had got herself into.

Take Wednesday evening.

With a blanket between herself and the moist grass, Mary was sitting in the late sun of the garden, reading a book. She was reading *Lady and Lapdog and Other Stories* and being told some curious things about women. It had been an averagely turbulent afternoon at the café. When Alan's back was turned Russ ran into his office and came dancing out again brandishing some secret pamphlets that Alan kept in a drawer. They were called things like *Hair Transplants: The Facts*, *How To Save Your Hair* and, more brutally, *Going Bald?* Alan was dizzy about it all afternoon. Later he said to her tremulously, with a bad-stomach grin on his face,

'Mary. You know Russ? Guess what. He can't even read and write.'

Alan suddenly didn't look as pleased as he thought he was going to be about imparting this information.

'Poor Russ,' said Mary.

Mary read on in the waning light. She turned a page. Every now and then her dark fringe was lifted by a stray salvo of wind. She leaned forward and scratched her bare ankle with a careless fingernail. She turned a page: the turning paper threw light on her eyes as she lifted her chin calmly to face the next oblong of print. Her eyes did not wander. But she knew Alan's face was watching her from behind the sitting-room window, a pale fish in its pond.

Now. Mary knew that Alan would soon make his bid to join her. She knew he knew he shouldn't try it: clearly she didn't want him there, and he would just subtly augment her pity and her weariness. But he would have to try it, his mind made up by love. If he didn't do it quickly, then Russ would do it instead. By some random dispensation, Russ seemed to be able to do more or less as he pleased with Mary, in public too, without the slightest forethought or constraint. Twice now she had spent whole evenings on his lap. It was comfortable there, she had to admit, and Alan didn't appear to mind. He looked the other way and concentrated on his hair. He never said anything about it.

Through the corner of her eye, where the eye joins the brain and its radar, Mary saw Alan begin his wheel towards the garden steps. She turned the page. He reappeared on the shallow wooden balcony and looked up at the sky, as if simply savouring the shrewd evening air. He looked as though he might try to seal his nonchalance with a whistle. He did. God, what a bleat it was. She turned the page. His raised leg dangled above the top step – but then he heard the familiar jinking bustle behind him. Russ! The whistle was his great mistake! He moved aside and looked at the flowers while Russ jogged down the steps.

'There you are, my flower,' said Russ.

Mary put down her book. It was no use trying to read with Russ there. He liked playing instead, pinching and tickling mostly. They played for about twenty minutes. Mary laughed a lot as she rolled about with her legs in the air – Russ was very funny, she had to admit. Afterwards he led her by the hand up the steps. Alan was still on the balcony, watching the flowers. As Mary passed him he turned to her and audibly wrenched a fistful of hair from his head. He looked down in astonishment: an entire pigtail bristled in his palm. He looked up at Mary. They both thought: he can't do that many more times. He's only got about three or four of those left.

Mary followed Russ into the sitting-room. She felt very sorry for Alan and wished he could stop worrying about his hair.

After the staggered suppers, after the television had run its course and all the other people had dispersed in ones and twos, Russ, Mary and Alan stayed up late in the communal sitting-room.

Mary was on Russ's lap. She didn't really know what she was supposed to do about this or whether it mattered. Russ just took her and put her there. Alan had tried it once, but the experiment had not been a success. He put her on his legs rather than his lap, and almost immediately his knees started trembling with such violence that it made Mary's voice quaver when she spoke. She got up and went and sat on Russ's lap. It was more comfortable there. Russ worked you properly into the enclave of his body and fastened his arms securely round your waist.

'Why do you bother with that fucking little wreck?' Russ asked her, wagging his head towards Alan, who smiled.

Mary shrugged. There was nothing she could say. The evenings always ended like this now. It made her uneasy and she didn't know why. But the boys seemed to enjoy it. Russ kissed her ear with a pop. She put an arm round his shoulders, to be more comfortable.

'You me babe,' Russ whispered loudly, 'we could go to the stars. We could make sweet-sweet music. Mm-*hmm* . . . I mean, *look* at him.'

'Come on, Russ,' said Alan shyly.

'He's gunna be bald as an egg in about – half an hour. Hah! I got more air on me left armpit than he's got on his whole bonce! Look at the chest on me.' Russ breathed in deeply. Mary felt his chest for something to do. 'See? Now look at fuckin Alan!'

'Come on, Russ,' said Alan, shrugging modestly.

'*Look* at him . . . Did you ever see such a fuckin little spaz in all your life. What's he like inna cot, eh Mary? *Fuckin pathetic*, I bet. What's he do, eh? Eh? Shoe-horns it in, quick sneeze-job, then wipes it onna pillow? Eh? Eh? Hah! Now with *me*, what *I* do is, first I –'

'Come on, Mary,' said Alan.

He was standing before her with his arm outstretched. Mary took his hand – to stop it shaking, apart from anything else. She got up and went with him towards the door.

'Sweet dreams, Baldie. Stay in one piece, my love,' Russ called after them, and for a long time they could hear his bitter laughter skirling up the stairs.

Mary lay naked in her bed, waiting for Alan. He preferred to ready himself downstairs for the final stage of his daily ordeal. In a few minutes he would make his entrance. Then he would untie and slip off his oddly hirsute dressing-gown and come forward in a crouch to join her in between the sheets. Then he would do what he needed to do.

Clearly this was giving him no more pleasure than it gave her. Few aspects of life on earth made as little sense to Mary as all this did. She and Alan had tried the two things – sleeping apart and sleeping together – and neither was any good. Perhaps they could go back, or move on, to sleeping apart again. Perhaps, if she had to sleep with anyone, she could sleep with Russ, who looked as though he would mind doing it less. She had presented these alternatives to Alan, and he had seemed very much against them. He said he would do anything she asked of him but not those two things, although those two things were the only things she had ever asked of him. What she really wanted was to go back to the old way. She could then read a book at night and sleep far more comfortably. Russ would perhaps revert to how he was before, and she might lose this unwanted power she had over Alan, the power to make feel bad. Surely he couldn't bear this much longer. Surely he couldn't love her that much.

Alan came into the room. He tried to whisper a secretive 'Hi', but it just sounded like a parched gasp escaping from the back of his throat. With movements that were hurried and yet took quite a long time, he disentangled himself from his dressing-gown, seeming towards the end to be fighting off the hairy, clinging thing. He dropped it on the chair and crept low towards her through the dark.

His chest was damp but his mouth was completely dry. Alan was always getting things wrong like that. His body smelled of atrophied anti-perspirant, his mouth of toothpaste and the remains of a powerful, wide-spectrum mouthwash. There was an acrid sponginess about him at such moments, with his moist scalp and his shimmering hands. Poor ghost, thought Mary. She lay crucified as his clamped mouth kissed her lips. His hanging, creaturely part was just a soggy presence against her thigh, neither limp nor hard, sadly waiting. Sadness, that's what this is, thought Mary. He rose above her starfished body. Oh my God, he's dying, she thought, he's streaming everywhere, he's melting away.

It never lasted long and soon he slept, or he tried. He wasn't very good at that either. For many hours Mary lay awake and listened to his dream talk, the words not forming properly but managing to say quite a lot about his confusion and sadness at being alive among all these other people.

This was a turbulent and tiring time for Mary; but nothing really happened. She brought many feelings to bear on her night out with Prince, from defiance to numb surrender. But she didn't know what to do about it – except try to be good, and she was doing that, she *was* trying. The phantom of the past wasn't about to go away, so Mary just worked on getting used to it, getting not to mind about it so much. She lived the huff-and-puff step by step, along with everybody else. She was waiting. Time was waiting. Then one Sunday her next move became clear.

It was the day they went to the local swimming-pool: Mary, Alan, Russ, Ray, Paris, Vera, Alfred, Wendy and Jeremy. Mary was nervous about the scheme to begin with, particularly about what she should wear, but Wendy reassured her. Wendy had become a good friend to Mary, explaining to her, for instance, about contraception. Mary thought for some reason that only people in books had babies. But *Wendy* had a baby, didn't she? Mary thought about what she had risked – having a baby, Alan's baby. Ay! And to think that the act of pain or sadness was also the act that peopled the world.

'Can you swim, Mary?' asked Wendy as they splashed their way down the tunnel with Jeremy and Vera, heading for the booming echoes of the pool.

'I don't know,' said Mary, pleased with her hired costume. Mary looked good in black.

'What you mean, you don't know?' said Vera.

'I mean, I may have forgotten how,' said Mary in confusion, stepping out into the high arena.

'Come down the shallow end then,' said Wendy.

'I think I'll just sit down first,' said Mary.

Mary didn't know where to turn. Never had the brazen present thronged so mightily. Look, look, look, look at this, look at that, look at him, look at her, all in such liquid lucidity. The water sent out ribboned oceans along the high walls. The raw, tangled,

stinging forms thrashed and leapt in chaos, ignited by the light
. . . Black Ray flashed past, thumped both feet on the pool's corky
edge, and climbed in a failing arc through the air to topple as his
arms pierced the water. His face and shoulders shot up again and
he yelled at Paris, who bounded up the leaning gangplank,
clutched his knees to his chest, and scattered the water with his
atomic splash. Even Alan, looking no older than Jeremy in furry
grey trunks, ran past waving and dived with his legs spread into
the deep end. Jeremy himself stood tensed on the poolside, eight
fingers in his mouth, watching his father trying to drown his
mother. Wendy seemed to have plenty of appetite for the deed,
yodelling lasciviously after each fresh attempt, until Alfred tired
and flopped back gratefully into the shallows, where Paris now
strode about with Vera on his shoulders.

Do I dare go in? she thought, feeling a great eagerness tearing at
her. She watched Alan help lift a thrashing Jeremy into the shallow
end. Even Alan seemed at freedom in this glazed and glassy
element.

'Look at those mad coons.'

Russ sat dripping moodily at Mary's side. He pointed to Paris
and Ray, who were obviously destined to distinguish themselves
as the true heroes of the afternoon. At present they grappled on the
board; Paris hooked Ray's right leg out from beneath him and
together they twirled into the water. Vera and Wendy shouted
from the side, Wendy clapping her hands and Vera bouncing up
and down.

'They're like fucking kids,' said Russ.

'Look,' said Mary.

Ray was back on the board, standing on his head. He opened his
legs in a Y. Paris raced up the chute and dived between Ray's pink
quivering feet. Paris tumbled over backwards slightly when he hit
the water. Black people always did that when they dived, Mary
noted. They couldn't keep the lines of their vigour straight; their
bodies were always busy getting ready for the next thing.

'Big deal,' said Russ. 'So Paris can stand on his head. Brill.
"Paris". Hah! What kind of a name is that? *Paris*. Call that a
name? Call that a name?'

'It was Ray who stood on his head,' said Mary.

'Yeah?' said Russ boredly. 'Well what the fuck difference does it make. They all look alike to me.'

Mary had heard this said before. She agreed. They all looked relatively alike to her too. It was self-evident: it was like saying that their teeth all looked alike. The reason that they all looked so alike is that they all looked so alive, so well-made. They just have a better time with their bodies than we do, that's all, she thought. Whereas nothing could be more monstrously various, so traumatically patched and motley, as the pandemonium of pink dripping and bubbling before her eyes. A man whose swelling, disjointed belly and behind bore the same relation to each other as the Americas on a globe; a woman whose legs were all snakes and ladders; an old man constructed entirely of barbed wire and sheep fur. Even the young shouldered their differences. The business of breasts, for instance: Vera was thin and had big ones, which gave an immediate impression of sly bendiness and athleticism; Wendy, though, was fat and had small ones, a clear and hurtful injustice. Fat but no tits: thanks a lot. And this was before time got to work. Mary saw the work of time everywhere she looked. So *this* was time's work . . .

'Atta boy, atta monkey,' said Russ loudly. '. . . Bitch.'

Paris and Ray now had Vera hammocked between them. Alan stood near by, counting. They swung her once, twice, three times – and let go. Vera sailed up into the air, sailing on her scream, until her frantic body collapsed in the water. Paris dived in and surfaced near her like a giant tadpole wriggling up from the depths.

Later, while the others were having tea at the stall, Mary slipped off alone. She walked down the skiddy poolside to the shallow end. The pool was nearly empty now, but the water still slopped thirstily round its banks. Using the rails, Mary backed her body into the cold medium. Without hesitation she turned and pushed herself forward. Yes. She could do it. She could join in too. Her legs mirroring her arms, she shinnied smoothly through the water, which still lapped loosely, smacking its lips, eager for more. Her head erect and her face shining in the light, Mary made her way up into the deep end.

★

So when the message came that night she was ready for it. After all, it was a very simple message. She had probably heard it before and not quite recognized it. The message was on television.

Mary was used to television by now, its contests, its suspended worlds, its limitless present of vociferous catastrophes. No one came on (as Mary nightly expected someone to do) and explained what was wrong with Earth and why it was coming to the boil with crisis and rage in this way. Everyone on television seemed to be a little bit mad, which perhaps accounted for it. Mary imagined that the world contained a fizzing knot of flame and metal that wriggled ever outwards from its core. When the pressure became critical, parts of the world's vast distances would sprout fire in the form of liberty, terror and boredom. Fire chose hot places but the heat was spreading. Earth seemed to be sprouting fire all the time now. There seemed no stopping it now. Perhaps one day soon all the earth would be fire. How strange and lucky it was that she lived in a place where the fire showed only in tiny points that were soon extinguished. How lucky and strange to live on a quietly simmering island.

'And later on tonight,' said the television fondly, 'we'll also be hearing from Michael Shanc, who has just come back from Ethiopia with a two-part report.'

Mary looked up from her book. The screen was filled by the photograph of a smartly posed young man, his chin on his knuckles, gazing out at them with patient, serious eyes. Mary remembered what Prince had told her – the photographs in your old room, think about them. She thought about them, and then she heard Marge say in her mind: 'That's Michael. He's famous now of course . . . Such a thoughtful boy.'

15
By
Heart

———~~———

'Hello, can I speak to Michael Shane?'

'Moment please,' said a woman's voice.

Mary waited. She yawned. She had stayed up late the previous night to see Michael Shane on television. Heralded by a series of brooding guitar chords, the lights had found him nimbly seated on the edge of a squeaky black armchair. To his right, perched on childishly high stools, sat a white man, a black woman and a black man. Behind him was a large screen on which Michael proudly showed his recent exploits.

'Current Affairs,' said a male voice with quiet pleasure, as if Current Affairs were his name.

'Hello, can I speak to Michael Shane?'

'Ah. Just hang on one moment please.'

Michael's sun-helmeted adventures had taken place somewhere on fire in Africa. He had visited a coffee factory, a tin mine and a banana plantation. He had crouched in a helicopter. He had stumbled through slums. He had spoken to key black men, some of whose faces and names could not be revealed. Everyone had been very hot, scared and angry, what with all the fire about. And there was one authentically bad moment when Michael had had to go down on his knees while a black soldier approached, sternly unslinging his rifle. Overweight, T-shirted white friends of Michael's quickly appeared and the soldier had gone off looking very embarrassed. Mary thought that it was clever of Michael to go down on his knees like that.

'Hel*lo*,' said a female voice of almost asphyxiating warmth. 'This is Mr Shane's personal assistant. May I help you?'

'Hello, can I speak to Michael Shane?'

'*Ah*,' said the voice understandingly. 'Who's calling please?' she asked, clearly hoping to get this stray detail out of the way.

'Mary Lamb,' said Mary.

'*I* see,' she said. 'One moment please . . .'

Michael had then talked about his exploits to the people on the stools. They had got very angry too, with each other and with Michael, and Michael had got quite angry back. The programme ended before they did. You could see them still gesticulating intelligently at each other as the lights went down and the guitar chords started up. Mary thought that Michael acquitted himself exceptionally well throughout, considering the plain fact that he was only about twelve years old.

'Hello,' said the voice with fresh warmth. 'I'm afraid that Mr Shane is just going into conference at the moment. Would you like to tell me what it's about?'

'Yes. I want to talk to him about Amy Hide.'

'One moment please.'

'Hello?'

'Hello. Is that Michael Shane?'

'Speaking,' said Michael Shane.

Ah, so the world works, thought Mary, or parts of it do. The things that happened on television weren't all on the other side. Thin lines connected the two.

'Did you say Amy Hide?' he asked.

'Yes.'

'Who are you?'

'Mary Lamb. I'm a cousin of Amy Hide's. I want to talk about her.'

'Amy . . . I haven't thought about her for – for at least ten minutes. Well you've found the right guy. She's my pet topic, Amy Hide. When can we meet?'

'Next Sunday?'

'Now let's think. I'm going to Australia this afternoon,' he said calmly.

'*What?*' said Mary. 'I mean – are you?' That's that then, she thought.

'Mm. It's a drag, actually. If I'd known I'd have gone straight from L.A. I'm only going for a day or two – let's see. I want to stop over in Madras to catch an afternoon of the Test, and there'll probably be something in the Gulf to check out. Sorry about this, I'm just thinking aloud. Now I've got to go to Tokio *some* time next week. Boring boring boring. Carol! Is Tokio *after* Bogota? Right, right. No,' he said, 'Sunday'll be fine.'

'Are you sure?' said Mary.

'Yeah, I'll be here all day putting the lid on this Eritrea thing. The trouble is it's hard for me to get across town. Why don't you come here?'

Mary ran from the callbox to the café. Alan was covering for her at the sink (she had told him a lie about wanting to go to the chemist) and Antonio didn't see her, so everything was still all right. Sunday was six days away, six days tugged at by Russ and Alan, six days of walking to work when the sky looked like heaven and walking back when the sky looked like hell.

Mary went to Michael Shane. The building in which he sold his time was just over the river, not far from where the Bothams had lived before Mary broke Mr Botham's back. She wondered, as she often wondered, where they were now and whether she would ever see them again. The river's surface was goose-pimpled in the swiping wind. It looked like chainmail. Overhead, the clouds were having a hard time of it too. She knew now that clouds were dead – air, gas, spore – but these clouds resembled the ghosts of living things, the ghosts of pigs, perhaps. The weather was turning, no question; the air was full of change. Michael hopped from furnace to cauldron, from desert to volcano-mouth, but Mary's stretch of earth was getting colder. She looked again at the clouds nosing about above, their ears fringed with pink. The changing air reminded her of something, something transient in itself: stopping dead in a courtyard, frozen by the strange tang of the light. Times of year must take you back, she thought – if there are times for you to go back to. Everyone is getting older all the time; they all have big houses in their minds where they can hang around. I'm tired of my narrow stretch, this gangplank of time. I'm tired. I'm tired of these thin shallows, littered with spoons and dishes, where now pallid Alan paddles. I want to swim a little deeper now. I can't go on sucking each passing second dry . . . A mad gull with a terrible face, a rodent's face clenched with rage and panic, dropped down past her in search of leavings on the water. What is life like for that bone-nosed rat on wings? Mary hurried over the bridge. Ten yards from the other side the mad gull flew out of nothing and hurtled past her face, its eyes aware that it had been watched. It knows about me, thought Mary. She asked a tall old man the way. He bent down to tell her, resting one hand on his knee and pointing with the other, and staying that way for quite a while after she had gone.

Mary had somehow idly acquired the notion that Michael Shane would confront her in the shrill clarity of the studio – the guitar chords, the squeaky chair, the lean-browed questions. It wasn't like that. A polished, burnished girl was waiting for her when she came through the flashing segments of the revolving door. Mary was on time. Mary was always on time. The girl, who had transfixed brown hair and a good deal of knowingness of an elementary kind in her nerveless eyes, chose not to approach Mary immediately when she gave her name at the desk. She looked at Mary first, quickly, with coldness and relief. The look made Mary think about her clothes – the unseasonal sandals and insubstantial cotton dress, the cheap but flamboyant shirt that Paris had strongly urged her to buy in the market near the squat, Alan's brown cardigan, which she wore because it was too cold not to. (Mary had an overcoat, one of Sharon's. It had an orange check and was permanently damp. It lived in her wardrobe. Mary didn't like it, and it didn't like Mary much either.) It made Mary feel hot, thinking about her clothes. As she followed the girl along the corridor, Mary admired the rumpy convexities of her narrow black skirt, the dark veins of her stockings, the noisy shoes and their smug shine. How well did I know this man? wondered Mary. How well did he know me? They entered an empty room – the girl's room, clearly, with its splayed handbag on the desk, the cigarette packet and gold lighter, the overcoat nonchalantly at rest on its hanger. The room had an inner door. The girl opened the inner door and smiled at Mary with encouragement and triumph.

'You can go right in,' she said.

Michael sat behind a desk with his back to the door, a black telephone nestling like a kitten on the boxy material of his shoulder. He was murmuring affirmatively into the mouthpiece.

'Right, right. You're making a big Mustique, you know,' he

133

said and chuckled to himself. 'No, I hate that place. Give me Guadeloupe every time. Yeah, or St Lucia. Or Tobago, yeah, Barbados? *Barbados?*'

He swivelled and faced her. Mary needed all her courage to hold his gaze. At first she thought that his expression had not changed but before she could sigh she noticed an urgent thickening in his fleshy brow. He had stopped listening to what the telephone whispered.

'Stay where you are,' he said, looking straight at her. 'I'll get back to you.

'You're very like Amy,' he said then. 'Very like, very like.'

'People do say that,' said Mary.

He stood up. 'I'm sorry. My name is Michael Shane. And you're Mary Lamb. Ah – the hands are different. Amy had white hands, lazy hands. The eyes are different too. Colour's the same, but they're different.'

He sat down again. At his invitation Mary sat facing him across the shining plane of the desk. His open face gave off exceptional light – eyes, hair, teeth. She saw now that he wasn't twelve years old by any means, but at least seventeen or eighteen, possibly even older.

'Really?' she said.

'What side of the family are you from?'

'Oh, the mother's side,' said Mary, who had looked into all this a bit. Mary straightened her cardigan. She found she was trying to project herself differently, deceptively, to put herself forward in light disguise – quieter, milder, nicer. Saner.

'You look more like Baby, actually,' he said vaguely. 'What do you want to know, Mary?'

'I knew Amy as a child,' said Mary. 'Then I went and lived somewhere else. I never heard from her again until I –'

'Yes, that was a shaker, wasn't it. They're still not absolutely sure though, are they?'

'No, they're not,' said Mary. 'You see, I just want to know what she was like.'

He joined his hands together and flexed them. 'Would you like some *wine*?' he asked. 'I don't drink a great deal but what I do drink tends to be . . . rather good.' He produced a bottle and two glasses from the cupboard beneath his bookcase. There was a little refrigerator down there too, Mary noticed. 'It's a rather audacious Brouilly, whose initial tart piquancy soon subsides into optimism and warmth. And it won't fuck up the taste of your cheeseburgers.' He turned to her with an expectant smile. It had all the ingredients, all the material, of a good smile. But it wasn't a good smile.

Mary, who had no idea what he was talking about, smiled back.

Michael Shane wrenched out the cork and poured the wine. He sipped, sighed, and flexed his hands again. He gazed out of the window for a while. Mary knew as soon as he started to speak that he had said all this many times before, had let it all out many times, had used it all many times before.

'She was my first love,' he began. 'In every sense my first love. You'll always love your first love, they say. They don't lie. She broke my heart.'

'I'm sorry,' said Mary.

'It's all right. It's fixed now, I think,' he said, and smiled again. 'It was unforgettable too. I mean the good things were unforgettable too. She was tremendous to be near – funny, very exciting, very expressive. Wild as hell, of course. *Very* passionate.' Michael allowed himself a full ten seconds of sultry-eyed reverie at this point. It might have lasted even longer if the complicated telephone on his desk hadn't suddenly parped out.

'What?' he said. 'What? Borneo. I mean Winnipeg. Carol – no more calls, okay?'

'But what was bad about her?' Mary asked.

'Insecurity, I think. For all her brains and looks, I think she was really desperately insecure . . .'

. . . Big deal, thought Mary as Michael chatted contentedly on. Insecure. Is that all. Who isn't? What did people do and say about what they said and did before that kind of word came along?

'. . . and as soon as she started caring about someone, and I mean really caring like she did about me, a part of her turned against them – or against herself. She had to fuck it up, and by humiliating herself in some way.' He winced. 'She did some terrible things. Wow.' He whistled. 'Some terrible things.'

'What sort of things?'

'Oh you know. There aren't really many ways for people to behave badly. It's quite a limited field really. They can taunt you and fuck other people and get drunk and vicious and so on. She did all that a lot. She hit me once, quite hard too, while I was asleep. That takes some doing, I'd have thought.'

'Yes,' said Mary. She found herself sharply affected by this man and she couldn't tell why. At the moment, for instance, she was wondering just how much doing it would take to give Michael Shane a good punch while he lay there dreaming about himself. What's happening to me? she thought. And then she knew. She was remembering Michael Shane. But not with her mind – not with her mind.

'What was the worst thing she did?' asked Mary.

He leaned forward, examined her for a few worrying seconds, and said, 'I'll tell you' – as if this willingness singled him out for originality and nerve. Perhaps it did. Mary listened. She was feeling hot again. Michael had stopped looking at her, and a gleam of wretchedness showed in his young face. He didn't seem to have told this part of the story before. And now she could tell how old he really was.

'Have we time? Yes, we have time . . . I'd been writing a play, been writing it the whole year I'd been with her. About this guy who seems to have everything, but really he's – Anyway. It probably wasn't that good. It probably wasn't *any* good. We were alone in the country in this cottage I'd borrowed. I was reading my play through, correcting it – that was the idea. One day she locked herself in my study. I was banging on the door. I heard the sound of paper being thrashed about – there was an open fire in there. She whispered through the door that she was going to burn it. My play. Her voice was mad, not like her at all. She knew I had no copy. There was no reason for it or anything . . .'

'I'm sorry,' said Mary, without volition.

'I started pleading with her through the door. I could hear the fire crackling. By the way it's not what you think. This has a trick in its tail. She started reading bits out. Bad bits, in a terrible voice, my voice but . . . a mad voice. It lasted an hour. You know – "Now we come to Act II, Scene Two, when Billy says –", and she'd read out some phrases in the terrible voice. Smoke was pouring out underneath the door, even ashes. It lasted an hour. Then she let me in. The play was gone and the grate was overflowing. It was hell in there. I could hardly see. She was pointing at me and giggling.'

'I'm sorry,' said Mary. She delegated a part of her mind to concentrate on not saying sorry again.

'There's more. We had an incredible fistfight, with fists. The only time I've ever hit a woman. She gave pretty well as good as she got, by the way. That lasted about an hour too. When we were too bushed to hit each other any more and I was lying there sobbing and moaning, she said that she hadn't burnt the play after all. The play was in the other room. She'd been burning the blank paper. I'd never felt happier in my life. We got drunk and went to bed, ran around the house naked. Oh, man. Wonderful girl, intense girl, I thought – this is living. But it's not living. It's the other thing. Very soon afterwards I realized something. She must have known that play *by heart*. She must have hated it *by heart*. Can you imagine? A week later *I* burnt it. We ended about then. I thought I was going queer for about a year afterwards. After her, women look transparent. They *look* transparent. They aren't of course,' he said, and looked at Mary.

'So – so that was the worst thing Amy ever did?'

'To me, yeah. Mind you, this was *way* back. This was before all her really heavy numbers. This was kid's stuff. She was nineteen. Ah, Carol. Yes, no, bring him in.'

Mary stood up. She noted incuriously that something had happened to her legs; they were numb and tingly, especially in the calves, not legs at all, just a vanity of legs.

'I wasn't surprised by what happened to her,' he added conversationally. 'I don't think she was either, not by then. Thank you,' he said to Carol and got to his feet.

Mary turned. Carol came forward, tentatively offering a sheath of pink paper. Behind her in the doorway a tall young man bobbed about.

'Ah, this is the dope on the Eritrean thing, right?' said Michael. 'You'll never guess what these jokers are trying to do now. Hi, Jamie,' he called as he started reading.

'Hi,' Jamie called back. 'Hey, *Mike* . . .'

'Well goodbye, Mary,' said Michael. He shook her hand. 'It's been nice talking to you.' His eyes returned to the pink paper. He said, without looking up, 'Carol, I'll need you on this. Jamie. Why don't you see Mary out?'

～ ～ ～

Before we go any further, let's just clear up two rather crucial inaccuracies in Michael's dramatic tale – two telling distortions that probably result from imperfect memory, *amour propre* or simple disbelief.

The first point is this. Michael says: 'I thought I was going queer for about a year afterwards.' Now that's misleadingly put. Actually, Michael was right. He did go queer – and he stayed there too. He never went back to not being queer, not really. He sought shelter from the lunar tempest, and never went out to face the wind and the rain. From my own dealings with her, I'd say that this was what Amy was probing for in Michael Shane.

The second point concerns that play of his. Its title, incidentally, was *The Man Who Had Everything* – and it wasn't *that* awful, just very conscientious and very mediocre. Michael says: 'A week later *I* burnt it.' This isn't strictly true either. Doesn't he remember? Is he still blinded by smoke and his own ball-broken tears? He burnt it, but she made him. He didn't want to, but she made him. She did. Oh, she did.

～ ～ ～

Mary followed Jamie through the outer room. He closed the door after them and turned to face it with his hands on his hips. 'Scumbag,' he said with finality.

Mary watched. Jamie started talking to the door as if it were a person and he wanted a fight with it. She had seen this writhing, sidling style in public houses, just before trouble broke out.

'Oh, Mike, you fucking cocksucker. Well I got news for you, man, cos I'm fucking fuckin out! Cos I don't *fuckin need it, man!*' He turned to Mary with a wriggle. She started moving down the deserted passage and he came after her. 'You know what he makes me do?' he said shakily. 'Makes me go to fucking *Sketchley's* to pick up his safari suits! The little scumbag's safari suits! He treats me like *shit*. I don't need this! I got *stacks* of dough.'

'I'm sorry,' said Mary, 'I'll go out by myself.'

'Oh it's nothing to do with *you*,' he said, halting and turning to her with aghast kindness. He was long, thin and slightly twisted, like his hair. The skin on his narrow face was girlish pale. He had hot blue eyes, hot eyes, and lips that trembled with some imminent defeat or triumph. 'I'll see you out. I *want* to see you out.' They walked on. 'What do I care? What do I care? Oh that fuckpig,' he said thickly, and Mary thought he was going to start crying at last. 'I'm cracking up.'

He paused and ran a thin hand across his forehead. 'Christ! I really *am* cracking up . . . I suppose it's quite a relief in a way.' He clasped his hands together and looked up at the light with his hot eyes. 'Pray, oh pray, pal,' he said.

'Don't crack up,' said Mary.

'What?'

'Don't break.'

'Who are you anyway?' They walked on. He was looking at her with great interest, his face clear now. 'What were you doing with that little scumbag?'

'I came to ask him about a friend of mine.'

'And why do you wear these shitty *clothes*?' he asked with concern. 'I mean, you talk all right and everything.'

'They're all I've got and I haven't enough money to buy new ones.'

'I've got lots of money,' he said with pleased surprise.

'Well done,' said Mary.

'Do you want some?'

'Yes please.'

'Here.' He took a damp matted wad from the back pocket of his jeans. 'How much do you – here, take this lot.'

'Thanks,' said Mary.

'Your eyes,' he said. 'Something's happened to you, hasn't it.'

'I'd better go now,' said Mary. They were in the empty hall.

'No don't. Okay then – fuck off! No don't! Don't you want to see me ever again?'

'Well I would like to, yes.'

139

'Here, give me your number then.'

He offered her a pen, and paper, and Mary wrote down Norman's number. 'Bitch,' he whispered as she did so.

'Goodbye then,' said Mary.

'Goodbye. Hey look, this is a bit embarrassing – but could you lend me some money? For a cab?'

Mary took the money from her bag. He had given her a great deal, she now realized – two or three times what she earned in a week. 'Are you sure you want to give me all this?' she said.

'Oh yeah. Just lend me – a couple of quid'll do. I'll pay you back. What's money anyway? It's only time, after all, as they keep telling me here.'

'Goodbye then.'

'Goodbye. Think of me,' he said. 'And don't break.'

16
Second
Chances

————⁓————

Mary never knew how poor she was. Poor Mary, she never knew.

She has grown used to cheap chafing skirts, their imposture exposed by all natural light. Her complexion, it pains me to say, shows signs of submission to the ravages of unvarying fried food, and her hair has to fight to hold its brilliance in the kitchen mists. She still has the quality, the expectancy, the light; but it's getting to her, all this, of course it is. She has grown used to the poverty of Alan's smell, and to the poverty of his mind. Poor Alan, poor thing; but then they are all poor things where Mary lives.

Now she knows. She thought that life itself was poor. Now she knows it needn't be – not poor, not poor in that way. She thought that money only happened in books. Now all day she feels that sense of exclusion and tearing eagerness she felt as she sat at the poolside: she too wanted to swim and play, and knew she could if she only dared. Little Jeremy's report-card said 'very poor'. Already! thought Mary. Poor little Jeremy, poor little thing.

Life is interesting, life has a lot to be said for it, but life can be terribly poor. Mary knows that now. She has seen enough of the well-kept people, scowling in shops and cars. She doesn't want their money; she only wants their time. And the changing light is telling her something about the poor and winter.

⁓   ⁓   ⁓

Mary waited for Alan in her bed. This was the only time she had ever had to herself. That wasn't much, was it? That wasn't much time? She heard his steps on the stairs and shook her head. She had made up her mind.

Alan opened the door. As usual, he seemed to want to say something, but he didn't or he didn't dare. He moved sideways-on to the foot of the bed and began to slither from the clutches of his dressing-gown, not knowing quite where to look. The moon and the window framed him in their square of light: his churned porridgy hair, the unstable eyes darting downwards, the suddenly revealed defencelessness of his white shoulders.

'Alan,' said Mary from her bed. Alan dropped the dressing-gown to the floor, his arms at his side, his head bowed – he was ready.

'I can't have you up here at night any more. I can't have you in my bed any more. I can't. I hope you understand.'

He did two things at once. It didn't at all help that he was naked. The first thing he did was to start to cry – or at least that was what Mary supposed he had started doing. With utmost desolation he clenched shut his mouth and his eyes, and his white chest began to rock or pulse, all in silence. The second thing he did was even stranger: slowly and with shame, but not in concealment so much as in a gesture of protection, to keep it warm or out of harm's way, he cupped both hands over the creaturely pith of his body.

All this Mary watched from her lair.

At last he turned towards the window. He hadn't looked at her yet. The moon did pale things to his face and to the queue of tears that lay like ice on his cheeks. He exhaled, then breathed in heavily. He looked very far away but proportionately the same, as if he were weakening into another medium of air and flesh. But when he spoke Mary was surprised by the steadiness, the relief, in his voice.

'I never really thought it would go on anyway,' he said, telling the window something that only the window needed to hear. 'I hoped it would go on, but I never really thought it would. I know I'm not . . . I know, I know. Oh I don't know. I'm glad it happened,' he said, and his head gave a sudden nod. 'I mean, I wouldn't have had it not happen. I've never, you're the only thing of . . . *beauty* . . . that's ever happened to me in my life.'

'Thank you. I'm sorry.'

'Will you promise me one thing?'

'*Yes*,' she said.

'You won't start – you know, with Russ.'

'Yes, I promise.'

'Do you swear on your mother's life?'

'. . . I can't do that,' said Mary.

Alan sniffed. He picked up his dressing-gown and started trying to get into it. He sniffed again, more wetly. When other people cry, it is always much worse if they are trying to do something else at the same time. He hugged the material to him and gave an absent-minded tug at his hair.

'I'm sorry,' said Mary.

He turned to her and spread his hands. He looked away again. 'Goodbye, Mary,' he said.

The next day was Sunday and the squat slept late. Competent Norman, swathed in floppy jeans, prepared his civilized breakfast of boiled egg and spinach-juice and took it out on a tray to the garden; he had a ladylike self-absorption at such moments, as if he lived alone and all these other people were the remains of friendly dreams that had come and gone in the night without bothering him. Perhaps some men turn into women too. Perhaps some men have to suffer the Change. Ray and Alfred sat about with newspapers on their laps, reading out football scores in murmurs cadenced to resignation or impressed surprise. From upstairs came the melancholy sound of Paris's clarinet. With a wincing expression on his face, old Charlie cleaned the chrome entrails of his motor-bike, pausing every now and then to watch the children play. 'Good morning, my lovely,' he said when Mary took a cup of tea out on to the steps. Mary smiled at him and he turned back to his bike, shaking his head and muttering to himself. No Alan.

Mary watched the children play, listening to them more alertly than she usually did. They played quite sleepily, without competition and its shape. What was it they were saying, what was it that they said more often than they said anything else? 'Watch! . . . Look! Watch this! . . . Look at me!' That's what they said more often than they said anything else. It occurred to Mary that perhaps that was what some people went on saying throughout their lives on earth. Watch this! Look at *me*!

Amy had said that a lot, Mary guessed. Mary betted that Amy had said that a lot. Amy: what was Mary to do about it all? Amy had been bad, Amy had been mad. Did this matter, and, if so, how much? Well, one thing was clear: being mad didn't matter. Being

143

mad didn't matter. If being mad mattered, then nearly everyone was obviously in terrible trouble. Most people were mad, and it was okay. (Was Prince mad? No, probably not. Prince was probably un-mad. He could probably call his thoughts his own.) And how about bad, how bad was that, how serious? Who minded? The law did, and other people. The law did, but the law was quite hard. You had to be pretty bad to break it, whatever Prince said that time. The law wasn't as delicate as other people and their bits and pieces. The law wasn't as delicate as Trev's mouth or Trudy's nose or Mr Botham's back or Alan's spirit or Michael's heart, or the heart of Mrs Hide, all of which had got broken at some time. The law was hard to break. But God, I hate her, thought Mary.

'Mary?'

She turned. It was Ray. 'Some guy for you on the blower,' he said.

Mary went into Norman's room. She feared the worst.

'Hello, it's me, Jamie. Do you know the man I mean?'

'Yes. Hello,' said Mary.

'How are you feeling?'

'Quite bad. How are you feeling?'

'Terrible. I've got this incredible hangover. Still it's better than nothing, I suppose. I rang to ask you if you'd like to come to lunch?'

Mary said yes. She was pleased, she had to admit. It would be nice to get out of the house and, besides, the change of air would do her good.

Mary went upstairs again. She hesitated in the noiselessness outside Alan's room, but decided against it.

She sat on her bed. For the first time she thought seriously about clothes. Apart from warmth, protection and propriety, what was the idea of clothes exactly? Why had Jamie said that about hers? Patently the idea was to express something through the medium of shape and colour. But express what? Were clothes just saying 'Look!'? Money and sex seemed to be the main commodities on offer here. Clothes could deny or affirm either of these. Mary speculated what her own clothes might have to say on the topics of money and sex. Could clothes express a lack of one and a simple bafflement about the other? Yes, but that wasn't what clothes were in business to do; that wasn't clothes' line; that wasn't what clothes were keen on expressing. Clothes were interested in the other things, in abundance and expertise. Obliquely and perhaps inadvertently, clothes also did a third thing: they told other people about the soul they encased by dramatizing your attempted lies about money and sex . . . Mary had a bath next door to Alan's room, which was still in silence. Alan used to spend a lot of time in here, Mary reflected, especially before coming to her bed. What occult ablutions, what bleak rethinks, took place among all this lino and iron? Wrapped in a towel she returned to her room. She brushed her hair and heightened the colours of her face. She put on white pants, tugging them up into the tight nexus of her body; then she put on red shoes and a white sweater and a white skirt, all things she had bought with Jamie's money . . . As Mary came down her stairs she saw Russ emerging from Alan's room. He said nothing. He looked at her in a new way, with challenge but also with respect or fear. Mary's eyes faced his; but she knew his look said he thought her clothes lied.

Mary walked. She had consulted Norman's book of graphs about how the city lay and memorized her route, which took her through the great park. It was nice of whoever could stop you doing this to let you go on doing it. The day was clear and equipped with wind; there was a stretched splintery brightness in the lines of the sky, and in the distance important clouds had gathered. The people were outside in numbers. Those who were alone seemed to stick together with a newspaper each, lolling by the park's exits and entrances or walking briskly from one to the other. People with families or just with lovers of their own ventured further afield. Mary kept an eye on the couples and wondered what it would be like to be part of one. It looked pretty good to her. It was obviously a matter of the confidences they shared. The best couple was circling the water that was the park's heart. They gave each other pleasure by four simple expedients: by being there and not being anywhere else, and by being themselves and not someone else instead. Mary had never felt part of a couple, a part of anything, when she was with Alan. They had just done the thing, in pain. They had never lightened each other's load. God, she hoped he would be all right.

In the end she let her mental notes blur and asked other people the way: if you had time, it was an infallible method of getting to other places. The place where Jamie lived was improbably vast, but then lots of other people probably lived there too. She pressed the right buzzer and, almost immediately, the heavy half-glass door responded by giving a buzz of its own. Mary stood back, hoping that this wasn't going to prove serious. The door went on buzzing for several seconds in mounting impatience, then broke off exasperatedly. She heard footsteps. A girl with a baby slung over her shoulder appeared in the passage and pulled at the door with a frown.

The door opened. 'Has it gone wrong again?' asked the girl. The baby looked at Mary with open astonishment.

'I hope not,' said Mary.

'Are you coming to lunch?'

'If that's all right,' said Mary.

The girl turned neutrally and preceded Mary along the passage, the baby's consternated face bobbing over her shoulder. They shunned the caged lift and climbed the stairs. Mary thought it was a shame that Jamie had a family already. No wonder the baby looked at her with such puzzlement. Halfway up the stairs, Mary heard the sounds of many voices through the open door above. She remembered her memory of the time when as someone young she had prepared to enter a room containing other people – and the intimate pink of the dress slipping past her eyes. In some ways other people had worried and excited Mary more then than they did now. So much was already impossible; she knew there was no true limelight you could step into. Mary was aware, and had been aware from the start, that other people spent hardly any time thinking about other people.

Mary followed the girl and the baby down a long passage to the brink of a tall room full of people and light. And full of couples, Mary quickly sensed. But before the room could confront or absorb her, Jamie's head appeared through a nearby doorway and he wiggled a finger at her to come inside.

'Hi,' he whispered, and closed the door behind them. They

were in a big kitchen, bigger even than the one at work. And it was clean and light, not kippered and sallowed with that coating of damp dust on everything you touched. Jamie's fine hair was in disarray, and his eyes contained much agitation and heat. 'Do you want a Bloody Mary?' he asked.

'What's a Bloody?'

'It's – God you're strange. You don't know shit, do you? Here. There's only one cure for a hangover.'

'What's that?'

'Getting drunk. But Bulgakov says spice helps too, and I believe everything I read. That's why it's so spicy. Don't you *like* it?' he asked in an offended voice.

'No, I do.'

He walked to the circular white table in the centre of the room. Mary noticed that he had a limp. His legs were equally long but one was a lot stiffer than the other and he used it more carefully.

'It's a summer-thunder one, my hangover. They're a classy kind to have. I don't feel ill, just mad. I bet berks don't feel mad at all, just incredibly ill. And now I've got all this horrific *food* to deal with. Can you cook and everything?'

'No.'

'At all?'

'At all.'

'*What?* You're a *girl*, aren't you?'

Mary nodded.

'Then what do you think is the point of you if you can't cook? You must have a pretty high opinion of yourself, young lady. Wait a minute.' He straightened a trembling finger at her. 'Can you make beds?'

'Yes.'

'And do you pee sitting down?'

'Yes.'

'Well,' he said, considerably mollified, 'I suppose two out of three isn't bad. Come on, you can give me a hand with this stuff, can't you. Come on, be a pal.'

The food that Jamie was unzipping and slapping about was elementary but expensive-looking. It was the kind of food Mary had only seen through glass, looking too artful to eat behind its pitying sheen. Mary helped him as best she could, and her hands were naturally much steadier than his.

'I'm surprised you've got a baby,' she said.

'What? A *baby*?' He shook his head. 'That's not mine, pal. It's hers. Babies! . . . babies?' he muttered, rather in the way that the boys had muttered '*Books*.' 'Not me, pal. I haven't got no baby. Can't you tell?'

'No. How can you tell?' she asked. This was just the sort of thing she had always hoped she would one day be able to tell about other people.

'I'm childish. Childless people always are. Terrifying, isn't it. Life is full of terrifying tricks like that. I'm getting more and more respect for it.' He looked up. He came towards her, holding a knife. He put his hands on her shoulders. 'You know, you look *really* good.' He looked down at the red shoes, the white skirt and sweater. '*Really* good.'

It worked, thought Mary.

'I look terrible,' he said. 'Don't think I don't know it. You should see what I look like from my end. I look really bad.'

'No you don't,' said Mary. 'You look good.'

He placed the side of his cold face on her bare throat and made several strange noises – grateful sobs, they might have been. As if prompted by memory, Mary felt the impulse to put her arms round his shoulders. It was an option. It was one of the things you could do at such moments. But she didn't do it, and, anyway, he soon moved back to where he was before and started taking lunch more seriously.

For the next hour Jamie was busy serving food and encouraging people to eat it. Mary sat alone near the window with a plate on her lap. Only one of the people there said anything to her during this time, a billowing, leather-faced man with the loudest voice Mary had ever heard. He stood above her, one leg wriggling or palpitating inside his trousers.

'Are you a great pal of Jamie's?' he shouted.

'Yes,' said Mary.

'Curious set-up he's got here. What's he like?'

'I don't know,' said Mary. And that was that. But Mary didn't mind. She had the couples to watch, and it was all very interesting.

There were fourteen people in the room not including the baby, who was called Carlos. They arranged themselves easefully within the generous ventricles of light. In sudden bursts clockwork Carlos shinnied along the floor on palms and sore kneecaps, the theme of delighted speculation wherever he went. If anything caught his eye he tried to snatch it. All it had to be was a thing, for Carlos to want to snatch it. At several points he came near Mary and stared up with awe. She tried to talk to him but he didn't respond. He just couldn't work Mary out.

The room contained six couples. It took Mary quite a while to make the right connections. Some were easy. One couple held hands practically all the time, even when they were eating. Another couple seemed to pool their nervous intimacy in everything they did; there was a flexible yet constant avenue of collusion between their eyes: Mary could tell that they hadn't been a couple for very long. The billowing man who had talked to Mary was older than everyone else by the same amount that Carlos was younger; the wild-haired girl he formed a couple with seldom looked his way, and then only to refresh her contempt: Mary could tell that they weren't going to be a couple for much longer. Other people there often seemed unaligned or mis-attached; but then their lovers loomed up on them inexorably, and they once again submitted to the bitter pact. Jamie didn't appear to be a part of a couple, but then you never really knew.

And the room, the flat, the labyrinth: it was like the house of Mr and Mrs Hide, airy and blank with its own superfluity, full of spaces between things. This is different all right, thought Mary. This is new, this is more. All the people here have been specially differentiated; they are all together freely, and seldom have to do things that they aren't already quite keen on doing. Although varying in many of the ways that people vary, the people here enjoy a brash unanimity about money and time. And they think that this is all right.

Only scurrying Jamie, and clockwork Carlos, and of course Mary herself, continued to operate on their own uncertainty principles.

'Look at all these people,' said Jamie excitedly, crouching down on the floor beside her. Mary looked at them all. He coughed and said, 'I'm drunk again now, thank God, so don't be surprised by the general lowering of my tone . . . Look at them all. You know what they've all got in common?'

'What?' said Mary.

'They've all done it to each other,' he said, as if referring to a mysterious and distasteful habit of theirs. 'Everyone I know has done it to everyone I know. You haven't done it to anyone here, have you?'

'No,' said Mary, who was fairly sure she hadn't.

'That's a relief. Actually that's one of the things I like about you.' He started to make a regular bobbing motion, originating from somewhere in the region of his bony waist. 'All the girls here – they've all been there. They've all done it like that, and then round from the back, and then on their sides with one leg up, and then bent triple with their knees hooked under their elbows. Why do they do it? Women aren't in it for *sex*. They used to do it because everyone else did it and they didn't want to miss out. Now they're all pushing thirty and terrified because they want husbands and kids same as anybody else. They all want second chances. They all pretend they haven't been doing it now, though they all keep on doing it. They all think they're all virgins now. But who wants them all now, eh? Who wants the old fuckbags?'

Mary decided to try something. She leaned forward and said, 'I've lost my memory.'

'Oh, don't even talk about it,' he said, flinching with a hand on his cheek. 'I get that *all the time*. And I'm only twenty-nine! I do things twice – I mean letters and things like that. Like an *old* fuck. I –'

'No. I mean I can't remember any of the things I've done.'

'Me too! I wake up, and for a moment the night before is all there. Then a black hand just swipes it from my head. And it's all gone for ever. You get somes clues sometimes. Like if your stomach hurts you know you must have been laughing a lot. Things like that. I –'

'You don't understand. I mean – I don't know who I am. I might be someone else.'

'Right! Right! I mean, half the time I could be *anyone* as far as

I'm concerned. Anyone at all – *I* don't mind. There's just a great blackness about me. I'm just . . . wide open. I –'

'Is everyone here like that?'

'Yeah! Well. No. No, *they're* not. This lot, they're just out of their fucking minds, that's all.'

'I see,' said Mary, and turned away to hide her disappointment.

Now people started to leave. Mary thought at first that they were just going out somewhere; but then it became clear that they were going home, that they lived in other places . . . In confusion Mary announced that she was going home too. Jamie nodded abstractedly and said he might walk with her some of the way if he felt up to it. He would walk with her as far as he could.

Mary went to the lavatory. She felt strange, slipped, dangling. The flat was shadowy and vast, possibly endless. The high corridor had no light at the end, so any distances might be covered by the granulated air: anything might be happening down those distances. She went where she had been told to go. People were still leaving but by now she couldn't hear them. She had been heading for the fourth door on her right for quite a long time and still had a fair way to go. What was overwhelming her? At last she reached the door. She knew at once there was someone inside.

'It's open,' said a girl's voice.

Mary opened the door and stepped forward cautiously. It was a long room, and thickly carpeted – not a bathroom so much as a room with a bath in it. At the far end stood the small muscular girl who belonged to the tall billowing man. She stood in front of the mirror, shaking her electric red hair.

'I'll only be a minute,' she said to Mary's image in the glass.

Mary came closer. The girl was busy in the mirror, muting the freckled kaleidoscopes of her cheeks and the mulberry aura on the outward edges of her mouth. Mary folded her arms and waited. The girl dropped two canisters into her handbag – a black clam with its jaws open. Suddenly the girl turned her wild face. Mary stepped back startled by the fear and hatred in her eyes.

'You're Amy Hide, aren't you.'

Mary felt intimate heat come over her. 'What if I am?' she said, but with the opposite of challenge in her voice.

The girl edged past her towards the door. She was clutching her bag tensely, as if Mary were ready to snatch it from her hands. 'Nothing. But just don't think I don't know.'

'Don't tell anyone. Please . . . Goodbye.' Mary stood blinking in the rush of air from the slammmed door. She got on with the next thing. She lifted the lid and sat on the cold seat. A hand passed upwards across her face. She looked quite old there for a moment, with the knees pressed together under the brim of her skirt, the white pants limply frilling her ankles, the red shoes on tiptoe. 'You've got to stop minding about all that,' she said. 'It'll never go away. You've just got to stop minding about all that, that's all.'

17
Absent
Links

———⁓———

Jamie walked her half way home, as far as the park's misty heart.

'Do you mind if we hold hands?' he asked. He was calm again now.

'No,' said Mary.

'You can cope? It's not too embarrassing?'

'No.'

'Oh good. I like it. It's one of the few things I can still do with girls that doesn't embarrass me.'

'Why?'

'I don't know. It makes me feel innocent, I suppose,' he said. 'But you're upset and I'm hungover again and there's no need to talk.'

They walked on. Holding hands with Jamie bore no resemblance to holding hands with Alan. Mary wondered why. True, Jamie's hand was warm, dry and supple, which made a change from cold, twitchy and damp; but there was more to it than that. Perhaps, like so much else, it was all a question of age. Alan was twenty-one, Jamie was twenty-nine, Mary was somewhere in between. With Alan she always felt that she was leading or being led, as if she were the mother and he were the child, alternately lagging or pressing on ahead. But Jamie moved at the right pace, the even pace, despite or maybe because of his poor stiff leg . . . Other people soon noticed the difference. Not so many of them looked at her and those that did looked at her in better ways. Men looked at her covertly, with ruefulness rather than hostile levity. Women apparently didn't need to look at her at all now, except at her clothes, and again in semi-professional scrutiny rather than in challenge or triumph. As for the old, they beheld her with outright benignity, evidently cheered, bucked, braced by her very existence. What had she done to deserve all this? One particularly old old man came to a faltering musing halt in front of them and stood there becalmed, his motors idling, as they walked past. Through his clamped smile came a woozy tremolo, a high nasal wobble, like a forgotten hum.

Jamie laughed.

Mary said lightly, 'You'll be like that in time.'

'That's why I'm laughing now,' he said. 'I won't be laughing then. If I make it, that is. Where do you live?'

'In a squat,' she said.

'Mm, I thought so, something like that. It's not much, is it? Not much? Listen, there's plenty of room where I am. People are always staying there. This isn't a number or anything I'm giving you,' he said, writing out a number on a piece of paper and giving it to her. 'I mean it's not a pass or anything,' he said, passing it to her. 'I'm past all that. I'm just saying you can come and stay at my place any time.'

'I understand.'

'Do you want some more money?'

'No, I've got enough.'

'Sure? Okay then.'

They parted at the pondside. Jamie seemed to have no more idea than Mary about how people in their position should say goodbye. Eventually he just squeezed her arm and walked off. She looked round once and saw his long hunched figure, hands in pockets, about to move beyond her sight. Then he looked round too and gave a sharp wave, walking backwards.

The grass was getting darker. Traffic moved with Sunday freedom down the straight road beyond the distant railings that girded the park. Obedient to the remote lunar action and its silent tempests of light, the days were closing in, the days were huddling up. Mary had already heard talk of winter. On cold evenings people spoke of it with resignation and sometimes a stoical dread. There was no fixed date for its arrival and everyone had different theories about when it would come. Mary wasn't too worried. Winter was sure to be very interesting.

Mary was starting to feel better about Alan already. She speculated. It could be that the point of love was to surround all people on earth with a circle, a circle which was often broken in places but constantly tried to be complete. She would always be one of the people who joined arms to protect Alan, and she hoped he would always be one of the people out on the line surrounding her – imperfect though it would always be, with broken chains and absent links everywhere, and many hands with no hands to hold. That had to be right. She resolved to go up to his room straight away and tell Alan this, to see if he would say yes.

In the play street only a few children lingered now. Hardly visible, they called and beckoned to each other like receding ghosts. Soon they would be safe and having tea behind other people's windows. Mary hurried up the steps, suddenly cold in her white sweater and skirt.

She came into Alan's room without pausing to knock. It was silent and empty in the dusk. 'Alan?' she said. On the table in front of the window some papers shimmered listlessly in the last of the light. As Mary turned to leave she saw Alan standing in the corner with his face to the wall. Why would he be doing that? 'Alan, I've–', she began, moving towards him. Then she saw that it wasn't Alan. How could it be? It was someone much taller than Alan. She hesitated. Perhaps Alan was standing on something. Why would he be doing that? She moved closer. Was he standing on his bed, or on that chair? The bed was too far away and the chair had fallen over. Mary reached up and touched Alan's shoulder. He turned. But not in the way that people usually turn. Round his neck was the cord of his dressing-gown.

Alan had left a note on the table. It was all about his *hair*.

⌢ ⌢ ⌢

Poor Alan. Poor ghost.

Suicide is what everyone young thinks they'll do before they get old. But they hardly ever get round to it. They just don't want to commit themselves in that way. When you're young and you look ahead, time ends in mist at twenty-five. 'Old won't happen to me,' you say. But old does. Oh, old does. Old always gets you in the end.

How often does suicide cross your mind? Every day? Once a week? Hardly at all any more? It probably depends on how old you are. Old takes nerve but suicide takes far more. It's a very risky business. Young Alan must have had a lot of nerve up there that afternoon. He was lucky he was young. He wouldn't have managed it otherwise.

Old is when you see that life is poor but it's all there is. Death is derisory; it only lasts a second; it's gone before you know it, so far as we know.

I've considered suicide, naturally. Yes, I've considered it. Some days I consider nothing else. Of course I can't consider it seriously until I've settled my score with Mary. And besides, I'm getting too old for it now. It's already too romantic a notion for me; I mean, it isn't very *realistic*, is it, suicide?'

People are doing it younger and younger – eighteen, fifteen, ten. They gag on life early now. When you're young: that's the time for it. Do I wish I'd done it then, back in the good old days when I was young? No, not really. Life is poor but it's all there is, so far as we know.

~ ~ ~

The first thing Mary had to do about Alan's suicide was make a statement about it, too.

'It's just a formality,' said the shabby policeman whose Sunday they had spoilt, moving hushedly round the room. 'Course, you're not *obliged* to say anything at all, but in my experience . . . it's usually . . . Actually, this isn't really my province at all, really.'

Mary sat and stared across the table at Russ's dipped, soaking face. She had no idea what she was going to say.

'Now, now let's see . . .' said the policeman, tugging on his ear. At first he proposed to transcribe a verbal narrative from each inhabitant of the squat. With a pimpled tongue sticking out of the corner of his mouth, he wrote very slowly as Paris and Ray successively drawled and stuttered identical accounts of Alan's discovery. The policeman looked at his watch. 'Perhaps I should . . . It's a pity, really, that there's so many of you here.' Then, flusteredly, and trying to ignore Russ's great wet sniffs (sniffs that managed to drain whole sinusfuls of grief into his reddened throat), he began to deal out scraps of paper and a sprig of biros silently provided by Norman. Mary sat at the long table with Russ, Ray, Paris, Vera, Charlie, Alfred, Wendy and Norman, and with much scratching of heads and flexing of shoulders they hunched down like schoolchildren to their task.

What could Mary possibly say? She was sorry she had broken Alan's neck; she had never meant to. She wondered whether Alan's hair was responsible, as he had claimed. But it didn't seem very likely that your hair could break your neck. It must have been Mary again. *I'm sorry*, she wrote in her fair hand. *I didn't mean to. I'll try not to do it again.*

But then two old men in uniform came downstairs with a lumpy stretcher. Russ stood up and cracked his pen down on the table. He looked across at Mary with his childish, dismal face.

'What am I doing?' he said. '*I* can't *write*.' He pointed with a finger. 'You did it, didn't you! He was only twenty-one. You did it, and you don't even *care*. Christ!'

Mary went on a journey, a journey that took several days. She rode the tubes, to and fro and round and round in the city's fuming entrails. She rode the Circle Line until, on this new scale of time and distance, the Circle made her head reel. And it never got her anywhere. She walked the clotted concrete of Piccadilly and Leicester Square. She slept in a room full of other people and the gurgles and gases of bad food. She leaned against a wall where other girls were leaning. Two different men came up and asked her if she was free; she shook her head both times and they went away again. For a while, time turned into a series of boxes. She rode in a van to a place where you had to empty your pockets and your bag and submit to the far-flung presence. They shut her in for the night with a girl who kept weeping and getting up to pee drillingly into the pot beneath her bunk. In the morning they made her undress and a woman examined her: by what right, Mary didn't know. She rode in a van again. She slept in a white row of other women who yelled and yodelled through the night. 'O you are hard!' the woman next to Mary kept saying. 'O you are . . . oh so unkind.' Mary knew that already; the woman didn't have to keep on telling her. They gave her her possessions in a brown envelope and some yellow pills that made the present recede some distance. You could walk in a garden or sit in a green room where lights and faces incessantly flickered. Mary did these things for quite a time.

Then Prince came and got her out. They had to let him in, of course. They had to let him in and let him get her out.

'I've got your style at last, Mary,' he told her in his office. 'Oh, so you're smoking now, are you? That's another new accomplishment of yours?'

Mary puffed on her cigarette. She had perfected this skill over the past few days, under the intent tutelage of various mad men and women. They said it would do her good, especially her nerves. Mary didn't know about that, but she liked having something to occupy her hands and her mouth – particularly her mouth. She said,

'I'm sorry.'

'. . . Brilliant,' he said. 'Now everything's fine.'

'I tried to be good.'

'And now you've stopped trying? That's the way a child talks.'

Mary said nothing.

'I've got some news for you,' he said more quietly. 'Mr Wrong – he's recanted.'

'Mr Wrong?'

'The author of the confession to your murder. He's taken it back. He says he didn't do it now.'

'What does that mean?'

'Well it's hardly a staggering move from his point of view. He was informed that you were alive and well. So he recanted. Wouldn't you?'

Mary said nothing.

'I've got to hand it to him. It took quite a time before he was convinced. He was sticking to his story. You don't often get that.'

'Don't you?' said Mary. He was waiting for her to look up. She looked up.

'No. You don't. He said he'd done it all right. He said you asked him to. So he did.'

Tears lined up in Mary's eyes. She didn't try to staunch them when they came. Some fell on her lap. One even landed on her cigarette. She heard Prince sigh and stand up. He came towards her waving his white handkerchief.

'Don't worry,' he said. 'He's not out and about yet – he's still got time to do. That's why we waited. We wanted to get him on some

other shit . . . What now then, Mary? What's left? The job's gone.
The squat's gone too, by the way.'

'Where? Why has it?'

'Any trouble at a place like that . . .' He flapped his hand
limply. 'No, Mary, there's nowhere you can go now. It looks like
you've used up all your good luck.'

'There is. There is somewhere I can go.' She showed him the
piece of paper.

'Oh you made that connection, did you,' he said, nodding.

'He told me I could just ring up and go there any time.'

Prince picked up one of the telephones on his desk and banged it
down in front of her. 'So ring him up.'

Mary called Jamie and Jamie was there. She wasn't surprised by
the relaxed way he said, 'Yes, sure. Come over.' Whatever other
people had done to Mary, they hadn't lied to her. As with so much
else, they kept most of that for themselves. There was only one
person, Mary felt, who was really in the business of lies; and he
was sitting opposite her now.

'But wait,' said Jamie. 'What about all your shit?'

Mary blushed. 'What?'

'All your stuff. Can you get it all in a cab or something?'

'Oh. No, I haven't got any stuff any more.'

Prince didn't look up when Mary finished. He was writing
something with a steel pen. 'All fixed?' he said.

'Yes.' Mary looked at him, and with hatred. What did he ever
do but tell her lies and make her cry? 'He's rich,' she said
randomly.

'Oh good.'

'I'm going now,' she said.

'That's right.' He didn't look up. He said, 'Remember, Mary.
Beware your own power. No one is powerless.'

'I'm going now, and I hope I never see you again until my dying
day,' said Mary, and walked out of the room.

18
No
Need

—~~—

'Now the first thing we've got to do,' said Jamie sternly, 'is get you drinking and smoking properly. Right. How much do you drink?'

'You mean alcohol?'

'Of course I mean alcohol. You mean there's other stuff?'

'Once a week,' said Mary.

'*What?* Well, we'll soon fix that, young lady. Have a drink. We'll start you on this. The trick is to drink very heavily every lunchtime. It saves a lot of effort in the early evening.'

'I feel terrible all day if I drink at lunchtime,' said Jo, who also lived where Jamie lived.

'So?' said Jamie.

'I don't like feeling terrible all day.'

'None of us *likes* it. That's not the point. You're not supposed to *like* it. Now Mary. What about your smoking.'

'Three or four a day?' said Mary hopefully.

But Jamie looked at her for a long time and then shook his head sadly. 'No. That won't do at all, I'm afraid.' He turned away, his eyes slightly hooded, and said breezily, 'I'm up to three-and-a-half packs a day . . .'

'Really?' said Mary.

'Yup. Oh, it was hell at first, I admit. Working your way from two packs to three – that's what takes real balls. After that it's quite easy. Now we'll set you a realistic target, say twenty a day, and then you can build up slowly from there. Okay? It's simply a question of willpower, that's all. The thing is: if you want to enough, you can. Believe me. It's possible Mary!'

'What's so clever about killing yourself,' said Augusta, who also lived where Jamie lived.

'Now don't *you* start. Oh I get it. I've got your number. Well check you out. You want to live, don't you. You want to *live*.'

Mary sipped her drink and stubbed out her cigarette. At once

Jamie rebrimmed her glass and offered her a fresh cigarette, which he lit.

'That's it. *You* can do it. Mary. Now just eat a lot of rich food and don't take any exercise, and you should pull through this thing okay.'

'You're quite manic, Jamie. It's not funny, you know,' said Lily, who also lived where Jamie lived.

'How would *you* know whether it's funny?'

'It doesn't make me laugh.'

'But you're a woman! Women don't laugh when things are *funny*. They laugh when they're *feeling* well.'

'Yawn yawn yawn,' said Lily.

'Oh what crap,' said Jo.

'Give him a Valium, somebody,' said Augusta.

'It's true! Why should you mind? It's just *different* for you . . .' He turned to Mary with his bowed head and hot eyes. 'Well. I just think, since none of us does anything, and is never going to do anything, we might as well do the other stuff, that's all.'

'Oh Mary,' said Lily. 'Are you all right for sheets and towels and everything?'

'Why, has the little man been?' said Jo.

'Did he bring back my shirt?' said Augusta.

'Which one?'

'They lost it. You know, the grey silk one with the –'

'I think,' said Jamie, climbing unevenly to his feet, 'I think I might just manage to tear myself away from this conversation.' He hesitated in the middle of the room. His eyes were burning with boyish eagerness and shame. 'I, it's just . . .'

Don't, thought Mary. It's all right. There's no need.

'That stuff about women not laughing,' he said, and at once the girls started to sigh and mumble and turn away. 'If I'd said *most* women, you'd have all agreed and had a laugh on your sisters. But I mean *you*, because you never read a book or *do* anything. That's why you only laugh when you like someone or *feel* well.'

'Boring,' said Augusta.

'Boring? Oh, it's boring, is it. Well in that case, man, I'm just fucking fuckin out. Gimme *shelter*,' he said, and stumbled from the room.

'Don't listen to him,' Lily told Mary. 'He's impossible when he's drunk.'

'That man hates women,' said Augusta with her eyes closed.

Jo shook her head. 'No, he just needs to get out and do something.'

It was true that no one in the flat did anything. Well, they did things, but they didn't do anything. They didn't do nothing, but they didn't do anything either. Mary soon worked out why: there was no need to. There was no need.

Mary recognized all three girls from the Sunday when she had come to lunch. She wasn't surprised to find them living here. She wasn't surprised to find that someone else was living here too, someone who didn't do anything either: little Carlos.

In a sense, Carlos was what Lily did. Carlos demanded and received almost full-time priming; he needed Lily's time all the time there was, and she gave it to him. Carlos was learning to walk, or waiting to walk. His burly, milk-flossed head bore an ever-changing patchwork of angry red bruises; Carlos got these by falling over a lot, especially in the bathroom, where he fell over most. You could hear him moving about in there, chirruping or gurgling interestedly: then there would be a sudden thump or crash, a shocked silence as Carlos marshalled his grief and outrage, and finally his forceful, hacking wail that sent Lily running in, hoping he hadn't broken anything. Carlos cried about other things too. He always cried to good effect: it always got him what he wanted. When you thought about it, Carlos was really pretty popular, had won quite a few admirers, for somebody who was only one year old. Just think how many friends and followers he would have when he was fifty – or seventy-five!

'What exactly's the schedule on Carlos?' Jamie asked Lily. Jamie spent quite a lot of time playing with Carlos, or just watching him play. 'He thinks you're God until he's three. Then he thinks he wants to climb into the sack with you until he's twelve. Then he thinks you're a scumbag until he's twenty. Then he goes queer or whatever and feels guilty about you until he's sixty and as old and fucked up as you are. That's the schedule, isn't it?'

'Don't talk like that,' said Lily, and gathered Carlos in her arms.

Something in Lily's eyes reminded Mary of the Hostel and its ruined girls. Lily had once been in trouble, but now she was out of it, out of trouble. She had tangled, wispy, weightless fair hair, sad lips, and no challenge in her presence. She also had a man called Bartholomé who worked in the North Sea. Lily thought about Carlos all the time, even when Carlos was asleep or jabbering contentedly in the next room. Lily didn't do anything, but this was all right. Carlos was what she did.

Jo didn't do anything but Jo did lots of things. Mary had never met or heard of anyone who did as many things as Jo did. She had 'money of her own', which perhaps explained it (everyone else there, including Mary, had money of Jamie's). She also had shoulders like the back of a sofa, short bobbing brown hair, and a kind of war-hero's jaw-line, with ferociously good teeth. She was always doing things, tennis, squash, riding, golf, and driving off to remote, virtually unreachable places at the wheel of her fat and powerful car. In the early evening she roared out hymns under the scalding shower, then marched through in chunky sweater and chunky jeans to superintend dinner with Lily. Later she watched television, knitting at the same time, or threading fish-hooks, or re-stringing tennis rackets, or oiling guns. Then at eleven-thirty sharp she stood up, stretched, said 'Well!' and strode off to bed. Occasionally she went out with her man. Very occasionally her man came round there. Her man was unbelievable, like someone on television. It was Jamie's often-expressed belief that Jo was really a man herself.

'She's a fucking *man*, that girl,' he said. 'Don't let her fool you – she's fucked up too. All that scuba-diving and mountaineering and pot-holing and hang-gliding – she just wants to fill the days and not think about anything. Do you think she likes going out with that fucking robot?'

One Sunday night the fuses went. While Mary and Lily held candles, Jamie peered fearfully at the fuse box, which glinted in triumphant recalcitrance from its cave. Jamie kept extending his trembling fingers and snatching them back again at the last moment. Jo marched into the flat with a gun and three dead pheasants swinging from her belt. She shouldered Jamie out of the way and restored light with a single swipe of her hand. Jamie fell over. Lily helped him up. Blinking, and dusting himself down, Jamie said petulantly.

'Christ, you're not a girl at all, are you. You're a bloke! Christ . . . Why don't you put an *e* on the end of your name and go the whole hog.'

But Jo just laughed and tramped off to her room. Soon after that she went out again. She had other things to do.

Augusta didn't do anything either, anything at all, but her life remained a throbbing epic of victories, reverses, strategies, setbacks, affronts, betrayals, campaigns and conspiracies. A social life was the kind of life Augusta had. And a sex life too. She had spiky black hair but her face was dramatically pale, paler even than her teeth, which were themselves very white. Mary saw her naked quite a lot, since she often sat with Augusta in her opulent brothel of a bedroom. Augusta was the same height and weight as Mary; yet she was not only slimmer than Mary but fuller too. Her body had an extraordinary jouncy, gymnastic look, with the narrow muscular back and voluptuous behind, and those conical breasts riding high on the frail ribcage. Augusta also had lots of men.

She rose late, later even than Jamie. By her bed she always had an enormous mug of water with a picture of the Queen of England on its webbed enamel surface. Before doing anything else Augusta drained her mug in one go. Then she got up and made herself coffee, quietly, with forbidding calm. She was always quiet and forbidding then, haughty too, almost regal – despite her startling pallor and her quivering hands. She looked especially quiet and forbidding if a man had stayed the night with her, and even more especially if the man hadn't stayed the night with her before. Augusta's men . . . Mary heard her clattering in late with them, and often saw them sneaking out in the morning – or sprinting out half-dressed, with Augusta appearing naked to shout them on their way. On such days she looked especially high-minded and dignified. She looked as if she were reassembling the bits of her that the previous day had dispersed – that disappointing and unworthy day, which just hadn't been good enough for Augusta. *Bad* day, to fall so short like that.

Jamie had similar theories about Augusta. 'She's a fucking *man*, that girl – when it comes to men, anyway. I know she's a tremendous sack-artist and everything. She says it's good for her figure. But look at her eyes. She's got . . . fucked-out eyes.'

After drinks and lunch, Augusta reliably started growing in beauty, and she didn't stop growing all day.

'You amaze me,' Jamie would say to her conversationally. 'You get up in the morning, you look like fucking shit. By the middle of the afternoon, you could be a virgin again.'

These were not riskless things to say to Augusta, who was justly famed for her touchiness and tantrums. Mary used to wonder how Augusta could be bothered to get as bothered as she frequently did. But it was no bother to Augusta, as Mary soon saw: her anger was part of something limitless inside her. There was plenty of Amy in Augusta all right. Oh, plenty, plenty. But by the time she started getting dressed for the evening, Augusta looked blindingly, unchallengeably good. She always went out, unless something had gone wrong. A car or a taxi or a man came, and Augusta walked off to present herself to the expectantly waiting night. And when something had gone wrong and she stayed in, she looked more dignified and forbidding than ever.

On such evenings Augusta would get drunk, talk a lot and laugh fiercely at her own jokes. Jamie jeered at her then, if he thought it was safe.

'Boffed and betrayed again, eh Augusta? Dorked and dumped. I bet someone's going to get it in the neck tomorrow. Whew! She's a terror.'

And Augusta would laugh at that too. But Jamie never said anything in the mornings, when Augusta looked so high-minded. For instance, he never said anything that day when Augusta had a black eye and could be heard vomiting noisily in the bathroom. No one said anything, she looked so high-minded about it.

Mary would lie in bed at night in her small room at the end of the corridor, fielding the unwelcome thoughts that always came to her then. Jamie was right in a way: Augusta and Jo *were* like men. They had the power, the power of imposing, of imposing fear – they had formidability. Formidability! . . . How shameful, really, that when women tried to be free of men and strong in themselves, they just watched the way men were strong and copied that. Was there no second way to be strong, no female way? Mary was sure there must be. But perhaps not, or not any more, or not yet. Perhaps women would never be both strong and female. Perhaps women would never have the strength for that.

Where was pallid Alan now? He never had any, any formidability. Where was he, in heaven or in hell? If he was in heaven, he would perhaps be diving into a nebulous swimming-pool – but diving perfectly this time, with his legs taut and straight; or maybe he just lolled on a cloud all day, teasing his thick good hair. If it was hell that had him, then it would be a pale and humble one with fake flames like those on the Bothams' golden fire, and all very quiet with not much going on. Most probably, though, Alan had simply stopped, stopped dead. His life had been subtracted, cancelled out. That was the most likely thing, Mary was afraid. She didn't believe in life after death. She just believed in death.

She'll get over it.

. . . Well, Mary seems to have fallen on her feet again, and without breaking. Of course, women love men who have lots of money, don't they? Oh, come on. They do. If I were a woman I'd love them too. Why do you think men fritter their lives away trying to earn the stuff? Men used to vie for women with fists and clubs and teeth. Now they use money. That sounds like an improvement to me.

Mind you, Jamie didn't earn his money. He had it all along. It was always there, waiting to be his. The rich have special terrors, inhabiting the land where there is no need. Here things swim too slowly, and the rich have special terrors. It serves them right, but they do. Mary will have to watch herself here. Disaster will sneak up the other way.

Have you ever stayed in a place where you wanted someone who didn't want you? Well don't – never do. Get out. Don't stay in a place where you want someone who doesn't want you. Get out as quickly as you can and don't come back. That's all I can say. That's all you can do.

166

One morning as she lay in bed Mary remembered how as some-one young she had sat down and wept on the grey concrete of a school playground, had wept inconsolably, and with no one to console her.

She had been excluded from something – they wouldn't let her join in and play. Everyone expected her to stop crying when playtime was over. She expected this too. But she didn't stop. The tearing, the rending, it wouldn't go away, ow, ow, it hurt, it hurt. She sat at her desk in class with her head in her hands and her shoulders shaking. The mistress was not unkind. She led her to the corner and stood her on a chair, opening a window to help her breathe. This didn't stop the rending either. She stared out at the booming afternoon and listened to herself for a long time, as surprised as anyone by the depth and harshness of her sobs.

. . . Mary sat naked on the edge of her bed. She was crying again. No more of this, she thought. She couldn't go on being alone. It wasn't just *Jamie* – she knew what was wrong with *Jamie*. But only he could stop the rawness and the rending, the needing, the tearing eagerness. And everyone needed someone to make them feel halfway whole.

19
Opposite
Number

———— ∼∼ ————

Jamie didn't do anything. Jamie didn't do anything either. Anything. Of course, he used to do jobs, like the one he did for Michael Shane, but –

'But I'm just fucking fuckin out,' he said in his rocky voice. 'I just don't fuckin need it, man. Who needs it? I don't.'

Jamie just read all day. Mary would sometimes pick up the books that he had finished or abandoned. They tended to be American, and about poor kids making good. Mary soon discovered that many of the things Jamie said – phrases, entire paragraphs, stoutly held view-points – and many of his mannerisms and stylish quirks of appearance were in fact stolen from the books he read. Was it all right to steal things from books and not give them back? Mary supposed it was, in this place anyway. Books didn't seem to mind and, besides, everything was all right in this place.

Mary read too, but books were no help. She found herself reading for clues and not for anything else. 'Nothing is so cheerless as the company of a woman who is not desired,' she read somewhere. She tried not to be cheerless. But was she not desired? How did you tell? She read somewhere else: 'A woman's solitary thoughts are almost exclusively romantic' . . . but men weren't like that. But *women* weren't like that, not any longer. She found a few cuboid paperbacks with pictures of women like Augusta on their covers and the word *Love* in their titles. Mary read them all. In these books the women who wanted men simply took all their clothes off and said things like 'Make me' or 'Take me' or, in one extraordinary case, 'Fill me with your children'. Mary didn't see herself saying that to Jamie, somehow. 'Jamie? Fill me with your children.' No, Mary didn't see herself saying that. The women also dressed up in special ways: there was a lacy, minimal black outfit that had had the desired effect, had told the right lies, to a man who had been behaving much as Jamie was behaving now; and sometimes the girls just turned up naked except for a fur coat. Then the men fucked the women, usually giving them a slap or two in the face on top of everything else. That wasn't what Mary wanted. She had to admit, however, that the men and women seemed to have quite a good time when they did it, in their embarrassing and vaguely hateful way. But the men were all racing-drivers or business moguls or gangsters or film stars. And Jamie wasn't like that. What was Jamie like? Was Jamie queer, perhaps, like Gavin? Mary didn't think so.

And suddenly she realized: books *were* about the living world, the world of power, boredom and desire, the burning world. These books were just more candid about it than the others; but they all fawned and fed on the buyable present. What had she felt before? She felt that books were about the ideal world, where nothing was ideal but everything had ideality and the chance of moral spaciousness. And it wasn't so. She ran her eyes along the shelves with mordant pride. Books weren't special. Books were just like everything else.

Later that day Mary went into the bathroom and locked the door behind her. Slowly, before the long mirror, she took off all her clothes. Standing back and shaking her hair, she gazed at the malleable slopes of her body . . . She looked posed, she looked awkward (by no means herself), but – yes, she looked good. Her solidly sculpted hair dropped down to the tips of her breasts, curving past the glowing throat. Were these breasts of hers good breasts? The shape and texture seemed pleasant enough – round and giving, without any sensation of fat – and there was something sore and meticulous about the nipples which she could imagine other people getting fond of. More or less exactly halfway between the shadowed undercurves of her breasts and the second line of hair lay the puckered and babyish eyelid of the navel, itself the central point of the shallow convexity that now flattened out on to the hinges of the hips, where the skin was weak, and tender veins were disclosed . . . And then came this other crucial point, whose role in life was so much-discussed, so much-in-the-news, so revered, so prized. Protected by hair and a protuberance of bone, it too was made up of flesh and resilience. Feeling decidedly uneasy now, Mary looked closer. Yes, this was new all right, this was more. The skin was pink, intimate pink. There were various other creaturely things going on down there. Frankly, it didn't look too good down there to Mary. To tell you the truth, it looked pretty bad to Mary down there. But at least it wasn't permanently on view, which was more than you could say for its opposite number. And then the gleaming thighs swept off along their true lines. It's good, it's good, she thought, it must be good: it's all I've got. She slipped back into her clothes and unlocked the door. Jamie was walking past.

'Hi, Mary,' he said, and walked on.

What's wrong with me? she thought.

Mary asked the other girls.

She asked Lily.

'Nothing's wrong with *you*,' shouted Lily over Carlos's steady wail. Carlos wasn't crying, just testing the power and gurgliness of his screams. 'Quiet, darling, there's an angel. It seems that he's just . . . he's *had* all that. Oh Carlos, please stop it, please stop.'

It turned out that Lily and Jamie had been a couple, a long time ago.

'Why did you stop being one?' Mary asked.

'I wanted a baby and he didn't.'

'Oh I see.'

She asked Jo.

'What? With him? Yes, and if pigs had wings,' said Jo. Jo was unstrapping an explorer's outfit in favour of her tennis gear. 'He's just a little *wank*er, that's all. Could you pass those gyms?'

It turned out that Jo and Jamie had been a couple, a long time ago.

'Why did you stop being one?' Mary asked.

'Because he wasn't man enough to *work* at it. We had a massive construction-job to do on our relationship, and he just wasn't up to it.'

'Oh I see.'

She asked Augusta.

'Come in. Close the door. I'm glad you asked me about this. There are some things I think you ought to know,' said Augusta.

For a long time they sat and talked on Augusta's glossy bed. The conversation was maddeningly jangled because Augusta kept taunting and conciliating various men on her battered telephone. She hadn't gone out much since the morning of the black eye. It was fading now through its spectrum of reds, but she still looked very high-minded about it. She drank vodka from a bottle dunked in a plastic bucket full of ice.

'Basically,' said Augusta, 'he's homosexual. And he's impotent. Narcissists always are.'

'Really?' said Mary.

'He hates women. He's terrified of them.'

'Then why does he have us all living here?'

'To oppress us. To oppress us with his sneers. Answer that, would you. Find out who it is first. Mm – yes all right.'

'. . . But he lets us do what we like,' resumed Mary, 'and gives us all the money we need.'

'*That's* how he oppresses us.'

'But if he hates and fears us, why does he bother to oppress us?'

'I'm telling you the *truth* Mary,' said Augusta, with a glare of such baleful rectitude that Mary nodded quickly and turned away. 'Of course I suppose you know he masturbates? Oh answer that, would you. Ask who it is . . . Oh all *right*.'

It turned out that Augusta and Jamie had been a couple, a long time ago.

'Why did you stop being one?' Mary asked.

'Over one stupid little fight! Can you believe it? I went to see him *every day* for three weeks at the clinic, and when he came out he said' – and here she let her mouth go floppy and lugubrious –, '"I'm fuckin fucking out". Can you believe it? Answer that. Ask . . . No! Oh all *right*.'

'. . . Oh I see,' said Mary.

'From the first moment I saw him,' said Augusta, snapping a finger. 'I knew he'd lost his nerve. Like all men he's basically a pornographer. What do they *know*? What do they *feel*? I mean *really* feel? Nothing! Oh, they're just – Who?' Augusta reached out high-mindedly for the receiver and then whispered into it for a very long time.

For a while they talked about other things. They talked about the large farm in which Augusta would one day dwell, and the eight or nine children she would raise there.

Much later, Augusta said, 'I knew you . . . before.'

'Really?' said Mary.

'What was your name . . . ?'

'Was it Amy?'

'Yes.'

Mary wasn't too alarmed. Perhaps Augusta was two girls too. After all, Jamie had told Mary that Augusta wasn't Augusta's real name either. Augusta's real name was Janice.

'We talked all night, and then we had scrambled eggs. You were strange.'

'I don't remember,' said Mary.

'Well I was quite drunk myself. But I'll *always* remember something you said. I've forgotten it now.'

'I see.'

'You were doing some strange things. With heavy men and ethnic guys and things like that. Then you'd ring up your parents.'

'What?'

'When you were with these ethnic guys.'

'Why?'

'Because you hated them.'

'Who?'

'Your parents. But really you had this one guy. This strange guy. For years and years. You said you'd never leave him. You . . . I liked you more then.'

'Did you?'

'Yes.'

'Why?'

'Yes. You were more . . . real.'

'Really?'

'Yes. I remember now what you said. You said you loved him so much you wouldn't mind if he killed you. Something like that. I'll never forget that.'

Augusta received two more telephone calls and finished the

vodka. They talked about other things. They talked for a long time about the poems that Augusta very occasionally wrote late at night when she was especially drunk.

Mary walked through into the sitting-room. Augusta had fallen asleep in an unlikely posture and couldn't be moved. Jamie was asleep too, in front of the blankly buzzing television, with a book on his lap.

'Oh, man,' he said when Mary woke him.

'Are you all right?'

'Well I wouldn't go that far. Oh, *man*,' he said, slowly rubbing his face with his hands. 'Whew. Well I'll – whoops. I'll just – ah! My . . . *ow*. Holy *shit*. Well I'll, I'll . . . Night!'

Mary watched him wheel and stumble from the room.

What's wrong with him? she thought.

～ ⌒ ⌐

Try this.

Policemen look suspicious to normal murderers. To the mature paedophile, a child's incurious glance is a leer of predatory salacity. In more or less the same way, live people are as good as dead to active necrophiles.

It is often extra affectionate to leave people you care about alone. Anyone who has ever walked into a lamppost knows that all speeds above nought miles per hour are really pretty fast, thanks.

Some people look at the sunset and can see only blood in the vampiric sky. And when at evening they see an airborne crucifix bearing down on them from the west, they just sigh and are thankful that another plane has escaped from hell.

If you don't feel a little mad sometimes, then I think you must be out of your mind. All clichés are true. No one knows what to do. Everything depends on your point of view.

～ ⌒ ⌐

I'm depressed,' said Jamie the next morning.

Mary believed him. He was also cruelly hungover. He had drunk too much the night before. Mary speculated that people would never drink that much unless they were quite drunk already. Gulping tightly, and with the occasional twitch of his damp white cheeks, Jamie picked up a book and started to read. Mary watched him. After a few minutes Jamie laughed out loud. The laughter went to his head, and it hurt.

'Ow,' he said. 'God, that's really funny. God that's so *good*.' He reread the passage and began laughing again. '*Ow*,' he said.

'Let me see,' said Mary. She went over and sat on the arm of his chair.

'That bit. From there to there,' he said, pointing. 'This guy really wants to fuck the daughter,' he murmured thickly, 'but he's got to fuck the mother instead.'

Mary narrowed her eyes.

And so I tom-peeped across the hedges of years, into wan little windows. And when, by means of pitifully ardent naïvely lascivious caresses, she of the noble nipple and massive thigh prepared me for the performance of my nightly duty, it was still a nymphet's scent that in despair I tried to pick up, as I cantered through the undergrowth of dark decaying forests.

Mary read it but she didn't laugh or smile. She could see it was funny, she could see all its delight. But she didn't laugh or smile. She turned to Jamie, invigorated by the expressionlessness of her own face.

He frowned and straightened up. Hurt showed in his hot eyes. 'I suppose you have to read the whole thing,' he said, and looked away.

Mary went to her room. In a sense she was appalled by what she had done. But it was no help being appalled. She would do the same thing again. What helped? Something did: the knowledge that she had a power. She decided she had better use it, since it was the only power at her disposal. And of course it was the power to make feel bad.

That day Mary could feel life losing its edge, and she was pleased. She looked at life and urged it to interest her, to perform some convulsion that would render it interesting. But of course life stayed inert, and she thought the less of it for that. She knew why, but this was no help, not to women. She was a woman and it was no help. She knew that it was no help, for instance, to know that she went a little mad for five days every month. She still went a little mad, five days, every month. She knew when it was she went a little mad, and knew when to expect it. But, boy, she didn't know she was a little mad while she was a little mad. Just think: if you're a woman you go a little mad for several years when the real age comes. Will I know it then? she wondered. Oh man . . . *Women* are the other people, yes we are. We're deep-divers, every one. You face the surface tempest where you can thrash and shout, but we swim underwater all our lives.

Mary made Jamie feel bad by feeling bad herself. She concentrated on this feeling and it struck her with its purity. After a few days it seemed obvious, just, even admirable. God, Mary feels bad. Do you see how bad she's feeling? Mary condensed the world and its present into a settled haze above her head. She glowed with it, her new power. It was true, it was true; how could something be as intense as this and also false? If Jamie addressed a casual remark to her, she stared at him for several seconds and then turned away, her disdain so palpable and definitive that there was no need to disclose it with her eyes. If they crossed in the passage, Mary would halt and stand her ground, daring him to travel through her force field. One day as she left the sitting-room she heard Jamie say to Lily,

'*Christ*. What the fuck's the matter with *Mary*?'

Mary felt a rush of exultation at this open tribute to her power. She went back and stood in the doorway.

'Is she having her *period* or something?' he said. He looked up and saw her, with terror.

'*What* did you say?'

'Nothing, nothing,' he said, writhing on the sofa and waving his hands in the air.

Mary went back to her room and sat on the bed staring at a point of air midway between the wall and herself for several hours without blinking. That was good too, and she started doing it on a regular basis. Her sorties into the sitting-room became unpredictable and dramatic. She liked to sit near Jamie and send her aura out to probe his peace. The girls avoided talking to her. Even Augusta stayed upwind of Mary now: Augusta knew that the diadem had been wrested from her hands. Jamie began going out in the evenings, something she knew he hated doing. That was good, good. She would still be here tracking him, beaming him with her power.

One Saturday night Mary and Jamie were alone together in the flat. Mary was having a good session of making Jamie feel bad by sitting on the sofa and staring palely out of the window, careful not to blink. Repeatedly she hugged her bathrobe to her as if she was cold. She wasn't cold. Jamie churned about with a book in the armchair opposite. By this stage in the evening it hardly occurred to Mary what she was feeling bad about or what feeling bad about it would achieve. Feeling bad was the main thing. So it gave her an uneasy jolt when Jamie threw down his book, drank deeply from his glass, and turned her way with his arms folded.

'Okay, Mary. What is all this shit?'

'All what?' she said simply, her face quite open.

'All this tragedy-queen stuff. It's like Tristan und Isolde here every fucking night. What's going on?'

'I have no idea what you're talking about,' she said, remembering herself.

Jamie sighed and closed his eyes. Feebly he drummed his shoes on the floor. He stood up and walked sidlingly across the room towards her. He sat down on the cushion's edge.

'Now don't play dumb. You walk around here with a face like a kicked butt, trying to heavy me over all the time, as if it's all my fault. It's only you vain, good-looking types who ever try this sort of stuff. If you were some poor dog with frizzy hair and spots, d'you think you'd be working this one on me? I just don't need it.'

'Why? What's *wrong* with you?'

'Forget it. I know the type, I know the type.' He looked away, squeezing his forehead as if in pain.

'. . . Have you got a headache?'

'Of course I've got a headache! So what? Everyone's got a headache.'

Mary took his hand. 'I'm sorry,' she said.

'Listen . . . Darling. I'm just – *out* of it. I'm not in that line any more. I'm not in futures any more. I'm not up to you heavy dames. I'm just wide open. You'll chomp me up and poop me out before I know it.' He turned to face her. 'Now what are you looking so pleased about? You don't understand what I'm saying, do you? Let me put it this way.'

'Kiss my breasts,' said Mary.

'What? Hey now look . . .'

'Oh *please*, kiss my breasts.'

'. . . I'm no good at all this, I warn you,' he mumbled after a few moments. But she could hardly hear him now.

'Quiet,' she said. 'Oh thank God. Quiet, quiet.'

Mary woke up slowly. Before she opened her eyes a memory had time to settle and slip past. Memories happened to her quite a lot these days, but always as analogies of mood rather than deliveries of hard information; and they all seemed to antedate the crucial things in her life. Mary remembered what it was like to wake up as a schoolgirl on weekend mornings, when you coped with the subtle luxury of drowsing in bed while teasing all the time that was suddenly yours.

She opened her eyes. Yes, the eagerness, the rending had gone. She turned her head. She had never felt more radiant with generosity and relief. What she saw made her close her eyes again. What she saw wasn't much, just Jamie, naked under his trench-coat, smoking an early cigarette and staring at the completely grey, the emphatically neutral wash of the window-pane, his face quite numb with remorse.

20

Deeper
Water

———~~———

Now the tranquillized days came and Mary needed them.

The weather turned. 'It's turned. I knew it would,' Jamie said to
her that morning. The weather turned bad, as a matter of mere
faceless routine; and it was determined to stay that way.

The balcony puddles pinged with their space invaders from the
sky, helplessly reflecting this new war of the worlds. The row of
damp-plug houses opposite provided good radar for the rain: you
could always see how much was falling and at what angle. It was
not the voluptuous rain of the hot months. It was thin needling
rain, white-mouthed and unsmiling in its task. And it went on for
days without getting tired and without wanting to do anything else
instead. Jamie would stand seriously in front of the window for
long stretches now, holding a drink and a cigarette, while behind
him Carlos beat the floor with his palms and Lily and Mary gazed
at the walls or at their men. 'It's insulting, this weather,' he said.
'That's what it is. It's a fucking insult. It's like a kick in the arse.
You . . . it makes you keep on having to wish it *away*.'

Mary went out in it, past the porous houses, stalwart and dreary
in the wet, to the rained-under commerce of the junctions and
shops. You could say one thing for rain: unlike so much else these
days, it was clearly in endless supply. They were never going to
run out of it. People shopped with wintry panic, buying anything
they could get a hand to. They shouldered and snatched among the
stalls, at the drenched vegetables and the sopping, sobbing fruit.
Like the holds of ships in tempest, the shop floors swilled with the
wellington-wet detritus of the streets, each chime of the door
bringing deeper water, umbrellas working like pistons, squelch-
ing galoshes and sweating polythene, all under the gaze of the
looted shelves. Things were running out, everything was running
out, things to buy and money to buy them with. But the rain would
not run out. It was part of the air now, long-established in its

element. Rain would never dry up. Mary went out in it for a long time and came back as soaked as grass. They made her change her clothes and have a hot bath. Even Carlos was shocked.

At night she lay in bed for hours waiting for Jamie to stumble in. He would sink naked on to the sheets and kiss her good night with a final decorous grunt. But it never was good night. To begin with he used to ask her whether she was asleep or not. But now he never bothered, because now he knew. He embraced her with elderly formality or lay like a plank in the far twilight zone of the bed. Mary didn't mind which. She simply waited until he was about to go to sleep and then started crying. Every night. Crying was a good idea, as Carlos knew: it always got you what you wanted. And she cried beautifully – not too loud, and with a sweetly harrowing catch at the end of each breath, like the soft yelp at the peak of a sneeze, bringing to the weeper's tragedy a pang of the sneezer's comedy. Mary was good at crying. It always worked when she did it.

'Oh don't, please don't,' he would say.

Jamie rolled over with a moan and started kissing her face. As he did so Mary imagined that her face must be rather delicious, with all that salt and wet on her hot cheeks. The taste inside her mouth was better than the taste inside his, at least to begin with. But after a while the taste inside their mouths was the same . . . It all went in stages. It wasn't a fight or a single act, a single convulsion, in the way that Trev and Alan had performed it. It felt like a process of allaying, of shoring up something – against what, Mary didn't know. Just time, perhaps.

He had the talent, or the memory of a talent – for talent was surely what it was. He remembered quite a lot about how you did this dance of extremity, this stretched dance. He could chug and bob and glide, he could advance and sustain. Mary would sometimes open her eyes and see his dipped head or his tautened throat; there was something flexed and askance about Jamie at such moments, as if a disobedient motion within him secretly churned to soundless music. And afterwards he smoked cigarettes in silence and stared at the dark ceiling for a long time. He could remember what you did, but he couldn't remember what you did it for. And Mary couldn't remember either.

Afterwards the rain intensified, like nails being hammered into the roof, and the seven winds started up. The seven winds swooped round the shuttered house, in frantic quest of an opening, a way to the inside. You could hear them trying window after window, throwing their combined force against any weakness. And when a wind found a window it would call the others and they would all charge screaming through the gap to bullock and plunder round the high rooms until someone got up and locked them out again. Then they went and tried somewhere else. Last thing, just before dawn, you could often hear thunder, high in the heavens at first, then in crazed asteroids across the rooftops, until finally it split through the lower air and crackled like an ambulance along the empty streets.

Prince telephoned.

'How are you?' he asked.

Mary raised her chin a few inches. 'I'm very happy,' she said.

'Oh you're very happy, are you. You're very happy. I'm glad to hear that. You sound terrible.'

Mary closed her eyes. Prince wasn't about to worry her.

'Anyway, it's happened,' he went on. 'He's out.'

'Who is?'

'Mr Wrong. He's out and about. He's done his time. Even as I speak, he's lumbering hungrily through the streets.'

'Is he,' said Mary. This wasn't interesting. This wasn't about to worry her.

'He said something about coming to *get* you, whatever that means. But I can tell you're not finding this very gripping. Don't worry, we'll be keeping an eye on him. I'll see you soon no doubt . . . Goodbye, Mary.'

Mary dropped the receiver into place and moved towards the window. She lit a cigarette.

'Who was that?' asked Jamie.

'Prince,' she said.

'The Prince of what?'

'Nothing. He's a policeman.'

'A pig? Really?' said Jamie, pleased. 'You know a pig?'

'I knew him a long time ago. He just keeps in touch.'

'Well check you out. A pig called Prince. I thought only berks' dogs were called Prince. Pigs' dogs too, I suppose. Pigdogs. No, I suppose it makes sense. Do you want a drink or anything?'

'Yes please.'

Raindrops fell to their deaths against the window-pane, tirelessly, in endless series. Mary saw her face in the beaded glass, and the other face, quietly waiting.

⁓ ⁓

These are the Seven Deadly Sins: Avarice, Envy, Pride, Gluttony, Lust, Anger, Sloth.

These are the seven deadly sins: venality, paranoia, insecurity, excess, carnality, contempt, boredom.

⁓ ⁓

Soon Jamie and Mary would be alone.

Christmas was coming, and there were things to do. Christmas was coming, and everyone else was getting out of the way.

Jo went to Switzerland to ski with her man. Two grinning rakehells came to take Augusta off to a country house – Augusta, still very high-minded about the yellowing badge on her eye. Lily and Carlos were going to stay with Bartholomé, up in the North Sea. Jamie and Mary put them into a taxi and waved goodbye. When they got back inside the flat, alone together at last, Mary immediately felt different about everything. She had expected the flat to seem larger, but in fact it seemed smaller. She was glad to see them go, she had to admit. Now she would have Jamie all to herself. Without really thinking about what she was doing, Mary cut the cord of the telephone, just to make sure.

'Now you'll have to cope with all the shit,' said Jamie later, lifting himself off the sofa and working his hands into his pockets for all the crushed notes he kept there. 'Take lots of money.' He looked out of the window, where of course it was still raining patiently. 'God, it's so lucky that we've got all this money. I mean, where would we *be* if I didn't have all this money?'

'I know,' said Mary.

'Don't worry about what food you get. I don't care what I eat, really. Christ, Christmas scares me. I'm not one of these people who hate Christmas. Christmas hates me. Everyone drinks a lot then, though, and that's what I'm going to do.'

'How long will it last?'

'Ten days . . . Mary?'

'Yes?'

'You must promise not to cry too much, while we're alone like this. Okay?'

'I promise.'

'I mean, you can cry a reasonable amount, of course. But not too much. Okay?'

'I promise,' said Mary.

Mary shopped among the blood-boltered marble, inspecting murdered chickens. She walked the terraces of the vegetable stalls, watched by the scarred toothless louts who swung like lewd monkeys from their wooden supports. She presided over the icy offal of the fishmongers' slabs, where the bug-eyed prawns all faced the same direction, as imploring as the Faithful. She started finding playing-cards in the street. She started collecting them. Today she found the Ace of Hearts.

Often she made Jamie come too by feeling bad at him until he said yes. But he wheeled around between the sloping stalls or stood outside shops theatrically tapping his foot, in an agony of hate and boredom. He purchased clanking bagfuls of drink and snarled in the wet wind. How dare he, thought Mary.

'They're all fucking mad out there,' he said sorrowfully when they returned. But Mary wasn't listening. Mary was wondering about the flat. How small it had become. And it used to be so large.

The compact kitchen was her new world. Her face shone in the steel rings of heat. She put a murdered chicken in the oven and watched its wizened skin until it went as brown as the chicken Lily made. She took it out. It was warm enough to eat. Jamie sat slumped over the table as she served it up. Jamie stared at the chicken for a long time.

'It's like Keats's last cough,' he murmured.

'*What?*' said Mary.

'I mean, chicken isn't usually like this. Is it. I mean, is it. I don't know what the exact difference is, but it's not usually like this. It doesn't usually have all these . . . red guys in it, now does it. Does it . . . It's no use you looking at me like that,' he said.

But it was. It was quite a lot of use. He ate nearly all of it. Mary watched him with satisfaction and pride as she munched mechanically on. Pretty purple juice ran down her chin.

Together they endeavoured to abolish the idea of diurnal time, time as a way of keeping life distinct, time as a device to stop night and day happening at the same time. Noon would find Jamie and Mary, refreshed by several hours of hard drinking, about to settle down to their midday meal. When Jamie had eaten as much as he could, which wasn't very much any more, Mary would urge him into the shadows of the dark and helpless bedroom, over the tundra of paper tissues from all the crying she needed to do, and in between the sheets, where she fondly prepared him for the performance of his daily duty. Then they slept, deeply, often for as much as six to seven hours, a whole night's rest filtered through the hours of the dangling afternoon. At evening they rose like ghosts, like weary vampires, to begin the long night's work. The nights were long, but not too long for Mary and Jamie. They were always up to them. They were always still there when dawn arrived, heavy, slow, but still there, ready for the morning haul. During their first few nights, Mary waited until Jamie was fuddled by drink and drugs and then talked to him for hours about why he had never done anything with his life and about the fact that he was secretly queer and mad. But they didn't talk much any more. They didn't need to. They were so close.

At midnight Mary worked in the chaotic kitchen. The tiny room had a hot yellow glare like the blaze of ripe butter. She cooked in colours. One meal consisted of haddock, chicken-skin (astutely preserved by Mary from the previous day), and swede darkened with the blood of beetroots; another of liver, grapes, kidney-beans and the outer leaves of artichokes. She cooked everything until it was the right colour. She cooked with her bare hands, hands stained with juice and blood and the liquid-like patches of burn-scars as multi-wrinkled as Chinese cabbage. She thought it amazing how competent she was in here, how firm in all her decisions, considering how little practice she had had and how cramped the kitchen and the flat had suddenly become.

She stopped washing things. She stopped washing dishes, surfaces, clothes, even those cusped parts of herself that seemed to need washing more often than the other parts did. She took grim pleasure from the salty exhalations, the damp-dry textures of her body. She smelled wholesomely of the food she cooked; she could identify the smell of several different meals issuing from her all at once. She would never run out of clothes because Augusta, Jo and Lily had left lots of theirs behind in case she needed them. She made Jamie wear a dress of Augusta's. He didn't want to at first – but the dress was quite comfortable, he had to admit. She turned up the heat, and made sure all the windows stayed closed. Jamie sometimes hovered hopefully by the balcony; but Mary shook her head with a firm but gentle smile, and he shrugged and moved away. One night she was sitting by the fire eating an apple. She noticed a squirt of blood on the ridgy white pulp. She went over to where Jamie was lying slackly on the sofa. She kissed him on the lips. He resisted at first, but he didn't have enough strength to struggle for long. She worked her mouth into his, knowing that this would bring them even closer together than before. And of course she prized the malty, creaturely tang that issued from between her legs. That was him too, after all, his tissue, his sacrament, his fault. And when the lunar blood came she let it flow.

In the dead of night Mary's face glowed above the red circles of heat. It was their last meal and she was determined that his food should be the right colour. She cooked him brains and tripe, and veal heated just a little so as not to spoil its light tan. She was *determined* that his food should be the right colour. She bore the tray into the sitting-room. Jamie got up from the floor and sat down facing her on the armchair. The flat was so small now that they were forced to eat like this, with their plates on their laps and their knees touching. It didn't matter: they were so close. Mary ate quickly, unstoppably. As she chewed she told him her story – everything, about her death, her new life, her murderer, and her redeemer who would be coming to get her one day soon. When she had finished Jamie lowered himself to the floor again. And he hadn't touched his food! Mary stood over him for a long time. She could not control her face or the extraordinary sounds that came from her mouth. These sounds would have frightened her very much if it hadn't been Mary who was making them. It was lucky Mary was making them. She wouldn't want to have to deal with anyone who could make sounds like these. Some time later she was in the bathroom, standing before the mirror in thick darkness, listening to laughter. The instant she threw the switch a face reared out of the glass, in exultation, in relief, in terror. She had done it. She had torn through the glass and come back from the other side. She had found her again. She was herself at last.

Part Three

21
Without
Fear

———~~———

Finally the weather started to turn again.

For several days now a tunnel of piercing blue had been visible here and there in the lumpy grey canopy of the sky. It changed its position from time to time, widened invitingly and then narrowed out, went away entirely for a whole afternoon, until one morning it replaced the sky itself with a spotless dome of pure ringing distance. You thought: So it's been like that up there all the time. It's just the clouds that get in the way. Now only aeroplanes lanced the spicy sky, beaming out of the cold sun-haze in the morning and, at dusk, trailing salt as they headed without fear into the mild hell-flames of the west.

Amy Hide stood in the square garden. She wore wellingtons, jeans and a man's blue sweater. She was watching rubbish burn. She folded her arms and glanced down the walled path towards the road. The kitchen door creaked; she turned to see David, the neighbours' cat, sliding nonchalantly into the house. She looked up at the sky. She began to hum vaguely as the fire crackled out its leaning tower of smoke.

'It won't last, Amy,' said a voice. 'It won't hold.'

Amy turned, smiling and shielding her eyes.

'You mark my words.'

'But Mrs Smythe. You always say that. How do you know it won't last?'

Mrs Smythe was leaning heavily on the scalloped fence that separated the two gardens. Only her large formless face was visible, and her two dangling, suppliant hands.

'They said,' said Mrs Smythe. 'On the TV. There's a cold front coming.'

'Why do you believe them now? You didn't believe them when they said there was a warm front coming.'

'Well you just mark my words, young Amy. Take a bit of advice from someone older and wiser than yourself.'

'Well, we'll see. How's Mr Smythe?'

'Oh, mustn't complain. He has his good days and his bad days, let's put it like that.'

'God, what's the time?' said Amy. 'I'd better hurry or they'll be shut. Is there anything I can get you, Mrs Smythe?'

'You are good, Amy. But I've been down myself today . . . He's very punctual, isn't he?'

'Yes,' said Amy, 'he is.'

'You must worry about him sometimes though.'

'Yes,' said Amy, 'I do.'

An hour later Amy surveyed the ordinary sitting-room. Reflexively she started tidying up, not that there was much to be kept tidy. She put the daily newspaper into the wooden wallet of the magazine rack, and bent down to remove a squiggle of thread from the grey hair-cord carpet. She made herself comfortable on the sofa, tucking her legs up in the way she had come to like. Every now and then she glanced up from her book, and out across the quiet road at the toytown houses opposite. When she heard the car she looked away and went on reading. She didn't want him to think that she spent the whole day waiting for his return. Nor did she ever.

The door opened and Prince strolled into the room. He dropped his briefcase on the armchair and quickly unbuttoned his overcoat.

'Hi,' he said. 'How was your day?'

'Hi. Very nice. How was yours?'

'Oh, usual stuff. City Hall. But there was some good human interest in the afternoon.'

'Do you want a drink? What happened?'

'You bet. The way people . . .' He stretched, yawning vigorously. 'The ways people can think up of behaving badly. They're like bloody artists, some of them. How was your day?'

'Nice. Very nice. The weather . . .'

'Tell me about it in incredible detail.'

So she told him about it, in detail. She did this every evening. She used to wonder how the routine rhythms and quotidian readjustments of her new life could hold any interest for Prince – Prince, who came home hot and tousled from the hard human action. But she enjoyed telling him about it all and he seemed to enjoy hearing it too. He never let her leave anything out.

'How are you feeling these days?' he then asked her.

She blushed, but her voice was steady. 'I'm very grateful. I can't stay for ever though, can I. You'll tell me when it's time for me to go.'

'No, stay!' he said. He stood up and turned his back on her. 'Stick around,' he said more quietly, running his eyes along the banked shelf of records. 'It's nice to have a woman in the house, as they say. Now who would we like to hear from?'

Amy said, 'I thought I'd make an omelette or something later on.'

'Good thinking,' said Prince.

At eleven o'clock Amy said good night and went upstairs. She stood before the mirror in the sane bathroom. With cleansing lotion and cotton wool she removed the light arrangements of rouge and mascara from her face. She looked good: she looked both older and younger than before, more substantial. Now she gazed into her own eyes without fear; she knew who she was, and didn't mind much more than other people minded. Her right temple and the soft chin still bore the tenacious discolorations of bruising. Amy didn't blame Jo for them. Amy didn't blame Jo for the skilful and virile beating she had given her – in the flat, on New Year's Day. It was an intelligible thing to have done. Jamie was going to be all right. He was in an expensive clinic called The Hermitage. She wanted to see him but no one thought this was a good idea. No one thought this was good thinking. Amy knew she would see him one day, and would tell him she was sorry without giving fear. She brushed her teeth, then went across the landing to her room.

Amy's room contained a bed, a table, a chair, and not much else. Prince of course had a bigger and more complicated room, next door to hers. In many ways Amy's room resembled her attic at the squat, and she liked it very much. But she liked it in an appropriate way. She knew that it was in no sense hers. The window neatly framed the black sky and its hunter's moon. Looking out, she could hear the faint creaking of the young trees and the discreet surge of an occasional car in the neighbouring streets. That was all. But she saw and heard all that she longed to see and hear. She took off her clothes and put on her white nightdress. She wrote in her diary for a few minutes, then said her prayers – yes she did, down on her knees at the side of the bed.

22
Old
Flame

She lived in a remote arcadia, a pleasant, fallen world. Dogs and cats moved among the people on terms of perfect equality; the slow cars veered for them in the right-angled streets. The place was called a dormitory town. It had baubelled hedges, and grass was shared out scrupulously, often in patches no bigger than paving-stones. This was where the earners of London came back exhaustedly to sleep in lines, while on the far side of the planet other people rose like a crew to man the workings of the world. Prince had shown her round the thought-out precincts, the considered mezzanines. There was one of everything. You wouldn't ever need to go further than this – though of course they sometimes did, like other people everywhere.

He gave her a certain amount of money each week, for housekeeping, and Amy had always liked testing money against the buyable world. Money, of course, was still in everyone's bad books; in shops and coffee-bars people talked bitterly about money and its misdeeds. But Amy had a lot of time for money and thought that people seriously undervalued it. Money was more versatile than people let on. Money could spend and money could buy. Also you could save money while you spent it. Finally, it was nice spending money and it was nice not spending it – and of how many things could you say that? Money seemed to work out much better here than it did before, when she had had so little and when she had had so much.

Prince got up at seven every morning without fail. Amy got up then too, partly for his company and partly for her share of the delicious breakfasts he made. Prince was always pleasantly irascible in the mornings; his vague anger was a rhetorical style directed outwards at the world. With calm relish he read out extracts from the newspaper that the boy brought – accounts of greed, spite and folly – and commented on them in that complicitous way he had of making the good seem bad and the bad seem good. Then he drove off just as it was getting light, to join the queue for London. Amy did the washing-up and readied herself to deal with the day.

In the evenings they sat and read and listened to music. Amy did most of the reading and Prince did most of the listening. Prince listened to music with his green eyes closed, the formidable, gourdlike face thickened out towards the jaws. Sometimes they watched television together. 'Let's watch television for a while,' he would say. He never wanted to watch anything in particular. 'When I want to watch television,' he said, 'I just want to watch television.' Occasionally they watched Michael Shane, who was still out there, still out on the burning zones, in jeeps, helicopters, canoes, in sweltering prison-yards, adobe huts, bullet-sizzled bunkers – in all the places where the world was on fire.

One night Amy hesitated and said, 'He's an old flame of mine, you know.'

'Mm, I know,' said Prince coolly. 'Hard to believe, isn't it. That little wimp?' He turned to her and nodded several times in amused appraisal. 'Boy, I bet old Amy made short work of him. I bet she didn't waste much time feeding his . . . feeding him through the wringer.'

Amy laughed shamefacedly and said, 'He told me that after Amy he thought he was going queer – that's what he said.'

'Actually he was right. He did go queer and never went – Whoops,' said Prince as his glass nearly skidded from his hand. 'I nearly spilt it,' he said.

'What were you going to say?'

He shook his head. 'Nothing. Talking of old flames, your Mr Wrong seems to be keeping a low profile these days,' he said, returning his gaze to the screen.

'Really?' said Amy.

'Perhaps he's gone straight.'

'Not before time.'

He turned to her with his knowing smile, the smile that knew things.

'I'm not afraid,' she said. 'I think I'd know what to do this time round.'

'Good for you, Amy,' he said.

That night she went to bed a little too early. As she got undressed and looked out of the window she heard from downstairs the deceptively brash opening of a piano concerto which she had grown particularly attached to over the past weeks. Hurriedly she put on her nightdress. She felt sure that Prince wouldn't mind if she came and listened with him for a while. The music settled as she walked barefoot down the padded staircase and opened the door. She saw Prince before he saw her. He stood in front of the window, his head erect, his arms tensed and raised, conducting the night air.

He turned suddenly, almost losing his balance. For a moment he seemed without bearings, unformidable, his hands still stretched out in supplication, or helplessness.

'I'm sorry,' said Amy.

'No that's all right,' he said, steadying himself. He smiled foolishly and held her eye. He's in awe of me too, she realized suddenly. She walked into the room and sat on the sofa with her legs tucked up. He stood before the fire. She closed her eyes and he closed his, head solemnly bowed, and they listened to the music together.

Later Amy got up from her knees and climbed into bed. Through the window she could see the moon, perched alone on the very tip of the night. The silvered tinge against the navy-blue sky contained tiny particles of rose among its inaudible storms of light. If tenderness had a colour, then that was the colour of tenderness. With her cheek on the pillow, Amy's thoughts began to loosen. She felt a gentle impatience for each successive moment, not the tearing eagerness but the half-anxious certainty of a mother at the school gates, waiting for her child to emerge from the crowd. She felt that Prince was watching her. She felt what it was like to be young. She felt that the moon and her own prayers and thoughts were living things that shared her room and carefully presided over the contours of her sleep. She wasn't sure whether this was love. She thought that everyone's heart must hurt slightly when they began to feel all right about themselves.

23
Last
Things

———～～———

'I'm going away for a while,' he said to her at breakfast the next day.

Amy wasn't alarmed or even surprised. In a way she was pleased. She knew that this was a salute to something in her, and that she wouldn't disappoint him.

'You'll be all right, won't you?'

'Of course I'll be all right,' she said.

They finished breakfast in silence. She walked out with him to the car.

'Something will happen while I'm gone,' he said. 'Something pleasant.'

'What kind of thing?'

'You wait. Something nice. And don't worry about Mr Wrong. I'll be keeping an eye on him.'

'A green eye,' she said.

She gave him her hand. He raised it to his lips, then pressed it against his cheek.

'I'll call you from time to time,' he said. 'Take care.'

Unterrified, she lived her life, waiting for Prince and waiting for the thing to happen while he was gone. She was glad to have all this time to experiment with her happiness alone. He telephoned quite regularly, checking in from the mysterious human action he attended. He asked whether the thing had happened yet, and Amy said it hadn't.

Then something did happen. Amy wasn't sure whether it was the thing Prince meant. She thought not, on the whole, because it wasn't pleasant, it wasn't nice. Late on Sunday afternoon Amy was browsing over the bookcase in the sitting-room. Now what would he like me to read? she wondered. There were some hefty textbooks on the top shelf, among them *The Anatomy of Melancholy*.

She worked the book out by its spine. It was heavier than she expected, and the dead weight made her hand drop down through the air. The pages windmilled, and something slipped out and wafted like a leaf to the floor.

It was an old photograph, oddly moist and limp to the touch; and the scene it showed immediately disturbed the eye. Seven men stood on a raised platform. The five men on the right were pale, top-hatted, with the sanctified air of aldermen or city fathers. Their faces were minutely averted from the camera's gaze; they looked clogged, qualmish, as if they were secretly trying not to be sick. The seventh man, on the far left, wore a black hood. The angled noose in his gloved hand hovered like a halo above the head of the sixth man, who alone held the camera's eye. His thin face was taut and unshaven, and there was something desperate and triumphant in his stare, almost a snigger of complicity in this terrible act he had goaded the world into. It was as if he were the punisher and they the punished – the nauseous city fathers and the hooded man who did not dare to show his face. Amy looked into the murderer's eyes. Poor bored idiot, she thought. She was about to replace the photograph and the book when she saw that something had been written on the back, just two words. They said: 'You wait'. Prince had written them. This saddened her and she didn't know why. She got to her feet and the doorbell rang.

Amy walked dazedly into the hall. She saw the shape waiting behind the rippled glass. She decided not to hesitate. She opened the door. Instantly her heart seemed everywhere at once; and then the two women embraced.

'I can't believe it,' said Baby a few minutes later. She blew her nose. 'You look so young, Amy. You look younger than *me*.'

'Oh I don't.'

'I thought you were dead.'

'Don't say that. I'll start again.'

'Oh don't. Oh God. This is ridiculous . . . What happened? Do you know now?'

'No. I still – I can't remember anything for certain.'

'But you're alive. And you're different. You were awful, Amy.'

'I know.'

'You were a cunt. I'm sorry. You were . . . No, you haven't changed. You've just gone back to how you were before, when you were sixteen. Before you met *him* and changed like that. It's the eyes that make you look so young. They've completely lost their . . .'

'What?'

'That sullen, challenging look. That bored look.'

Amy said, 'How's father?'

'Dad? Oh all right. He's completely blind now, you know. Marge and George are wonderful. I haven't told them about – you know.'

'Yes, I think that's best.'

'Perhaps soon. Who knows?'

'Yes.'

'God! You know I've got a baby?'

'*No.*'

'*Yes.* She's *sweet.*'

'And you're married?'

'Of course I'm married! You know me. That's why I can't stay long. I didn't think you'd be here anyway. I couldn't believe it.'

'He rang you, did he?'

'Mr Prince? No, he came round. Is he your man?'

'Yes,' said Amy. 'He is.'

'Is it serious?'

'– Yeah,' she said, surprised. 'He saved my life really.'

'Yes, he seemed very nice. He cares about you a lot, I could tell. Oh God, I *have* to go. And I thought I'd never see you again.'

'But you will now.'

'Yes I will. Come on, see me out.'

The sisters stood together by Baby's car. Amy was the taller by a couple of inches, but they looked the same age out there. A schoolgirl cycled past, one hand resting forgetfully on her lap.

'It's his,' said Baby, tapping the roof of the car. 'Not bad, is it?'

'No. What's it like?'

'Being married? Oh it's fine. It's just – inevitable. It's just the next thing, like leaving home. You have to do it eventually. You wait.'

'What's your daughter called?'

'Not Amy, I'm afraid. I'll call the next one Amy if she's a girl. She's called Mary.'

'How strange.'

'Well it's a very common name.'

'What's his name? What's *your* name?'

'Bunting, worse luck. I've gone back to Lucinda. Baby Bunting. To hell with that. Give us your number then. I'll call you. Write it here. You must come over with your man and meet your niece. And your brother-in-law. God, it's so nice having a sister again.'

They embraced. Baby opened the car door. She paused. She turned and looked at Amy with great meaning. She said,

'"How do I know I am me?"'

'. . . "Why? Are we twins?"' said Amy.

'"No, but I love thee."'

'"And I thee."'

'See? You wait,' said Baby. 'It'll all come back to you in time.' The car pulled off. Amy watched it vanish in the evening haze.

To steady herself, and to see if she could be of any good there, Amy went next door and spent two hours with Mr and Mrs Smythe. It was impossible to go to this house without being forced to consume a great deal of tea and cake. Red-faced Mr Smythe smoked gurglingly on his pipe, a sly wood demon in the corner of the room. He didn't say or do much any more. On the carpet of the exhaustively beautified sitting-room, David licked his flossy stomach, one leg up like a shouldered rifle. Mrs Smythe served tea and talked, not for the first time, of those two sons of hers, Henry, the bachelor headmaster of a vast school in the North, and young Timothy, who had been killed by a drunken military policeman during his third year of voluntary service overseas – Timmy, who had always been a thinker, a poet, a seeker. In one of her tremulous reveries Mrs Smythe made the prediction that, were Henry ever to wed and have a son of his own, then Timothy would be reborn in the soul of the small child. Henry was fifty-four. Amy drank more tea. She wanted to tell Mrs Smythe about her sister and her sister's baby, but felt this might dash her. She asked if there was anything she could do for them both, and she meant it.

She would have done anything they asked. But they said they were all right, so she finished her tea and went home.

The telephone was ringing when she got there, ringing with a kind of dogged petulance, its arms prissily folded. Amy was about to pick up the receiver when a perverse thought struck her. If she let it ring five more times it would not be Mr Wrong. She let it ring five more times. It was Prince. His voice said,

'Hi, it's me. Where have you *been*? I was going out of my *mind* here . . . Oh. I see. Has it happened yet? . . . And was it nice? . . . Good, good. I'm glad. Listen, I've got some last things to do. I'll be back tonight – I hope . . . I won't be able to ring again but – wait up for me, will you? . . . You wait. Soon then. Goodbye, Amy.'

Midnight passed.

Amy wasn't worried – no, not at all. How could she be in danger if Prince could leave her alone like this? Yet there was a restlessness in her. It had to do with the tone of his voice the last time he called – something reconciled, almost melancholy, but with a new kind of concern. He would come. And why should she fear?

There was nothing to do but wait. One o'clock tiptoed by. Amy had two books beside her on the sofa – she was reading them concurrently, as was her habit. Now she tried to become absorbed by each in turn, but her head couldn't hold the curlicued print and the lines trooped past her eyes without meaning. She put the book aside; she felt that this couldn't be good for either of them. Briefly she experimented with the gramophone, playing the early movement of the piano concerto that she especially liked. But there was something open-ended in its plangency, just as there had been something exclusive about the ideal order that the books had passively hinted at, the order of words. Amy was not yet quite whole, and she would have to fill up the time herself, waste the time, kill it.

The minute-hand completed its slow lob between two and three. The time was not now and the time was not now. Amy fetched her diary. She described her day, she described Baby. She reread some earlier passages, but they too seemed nugatory, pitiable; it wasn't much, was it, not much to make up a past? 'How do I know that I am me?' . . . She made a last effort to send herself back in time. She had been a child with Baby once; she had grown older; she had got bored, met the man, gone bad; she had been cruel to her mother and father, and to many others; the man had nearly killed her; she had wanted him to and he nearly had; he *thought* he had, but he hadn't quite. Then she had woken up again and memory began.

No, she couldn't remember. She only remembered entering a room full of other people, waking early on a weekend morning, stopping dead in a courtyard frozen by the light, weeping on a chair at school, wanting to shine a light into other people's houses when the boys had all gone home. She listened to the seconds race. Dawn came, but Prince did not come.

Amy didn't mind, Amy wasn't worried. Light brought the present back. She stood in the garden, dew moistening her hair, and watched the morning star go out. She made some coffee and gave David his illicit breakfast, which he ate unconcernedly. David had nine lives. She wished he knew how good this one was: four meals a day and more or less ceaseless stroking. Other cats had much harder lives; but it was one of cats' privileges to be indifferent to the fates of other cats.

She walked out into the waking dormitory town. Now stretched by time, her perceptions had lost much of their doleful sharpness, but it was still interesting all this, still interesting, interesting; and she watched everyone in their human lights, their human traffic. A certain unwanted lucidity remained. When she saw other people, she kept seeing how they would look when they were old and how they had looked when they were young. This was poignant, but tiring. As she walked she smiled at the very young and at the very old. Her affection for things seemed congruent: her affection for a sparrow was a small affection, perhaps the same size as the bird. She felt no desire to go home. He wouldn't mind, he wouldn't worry. He could always come and find her.

She sat on a bench in the flat park. An old man came up and perfunctorily bothered her; but he couldn't be bothered to do it for long . . . She sat quite still, without blinking. As the day began to turn on its axis, colour bled from the grass. Slowly criss-crossed by parkies and prams under the blank sheet of the sky, the green stretch turned milky and alkaline, like a lake, in the neutral afternoon. She closed her eyes and opened them again. Something was happening to her, something endless and ecstatic. Everything in the named world was pressing for admittance to her heart; at the same time she knew that all these things, the trees, the distant rooftops, the skies, had nothing to do with her. Their being was separate from hers, and that was their beauty. Only a little of life is to do with you, she thought, with relief, with rapture. She felt – she felt dead. They're wrong when they say that life's too short. Life isn't: it's too long. I've lived enough. He can come for me now.

Prince sat down on the bench beside her. He was breathing fast and rhythmically. After a while he said,

'I'm very sorry.'

'It's all right now,' she said. 'Everything's all right now.'

He moved nearer. The sleepless moons of Amy's face shored up pallor against the darkness of her brows and hairline; and yet her skin glowed with the tranquil advance of fever. His breath came closer, sweet and distempered like her own.

24
Time

It was still dark when she woke up. The pleasant, rusty tang of exhaustion in her throat told her that she hadn't slept for long. She was in Prince's room, of course, and in his bed.

He was sitting there naked with his feet on the floor, shoulders bunched, looking at her sideways. She could see by the set of his forehead that he had been looking at her for a long time.

'How are you feeling?' he asked.

'I'm so happy, I think I must be going to die.'

He looked away.

Amy said, 'I am. Aren't I. Going to die.'

'No, that's not strictly the case,' he said and stood up. He took her hand. 'Come on, Amy. It's time, I'm afraid.'

After a moment he turned and walked across the room. Amy pulled off the sheet and sat up, her arms crossed in front of her.

'There's just one last thing to do,' he said, shaking out his clothes. 'It's – we've got to go and see someone.'

'Mr Wrong.'

He nodded. 'Right,' he said, 'that's right.'

'How bad will it be?'

'No worse and no better than this. You won't be alone. I won't ever leave you, I promise. Ever.'

'Ever? . . . I must wash.'

'Yes.'

'What's he like?' asked Amy as they drove up into black empty London. She felt like a child being taken on holiday or to hospital at an impossible hour, submitting to the grown-up machines. There was mist lying low in the dark defiles, thin and salty in places, then as thick and fat as collapsed cloud.

Prince shrugged. 'Oh I think you'll like him. After all, you always did before.'

'Why are you doing this to me?'

'You know,' he went on, and his voice had the pressing, driving quality she had heard once before. 'I think you liked him for the same reason you like me. The policeman, the murderer. We're both – outside.'

Amy turned away from him. The mist cleared briefly at the open vault of the river. The water was stretched and taut, as if being tugged at from either end. It shone like scratched armour. She glimpsed the plumed factory, sensed the aloof mass of the warehouses, saw black grass and its elliptical pond.

'You know why we're doing this?' he asked. 'You do really, don't you.'

'I think so.'

'You can't have a new life without . . .'

'I know,' she said. 'I never really thought you could.'

They came back to the river – or another river, perhaps. Whoever had been holding it tight had let go again. The water writhed now, lunar and millennial beneath the turbid mist. He stopped the car in the same place. There were no people there any more, and the rat-like, threadbare dogs owned the land.

'Why aren't there any people? There were before.'

'It's all dead here now,' said Prince, leading the way. 'Condemned.'

He ducked in through the same door, using his own keys. The vegetable damp had entered the building with its moist osmosis. The air was hard to breathe; something in the lungs shut it out. Prince paused on the stairs, listening.

They climbed out into the wide room. He helped her through the trapdoor. She was glad she was so tired; it would make this easier to bear. A bottle clinked suddenly and there was a frantic patter across the floor.

'Only rats,' he said.

He pulled a cord and a lone bare purple bulb winked into life. Prince started out across the smudged boards; they were damp and gave slightly underfoot. He guided her into the deeper shadows, where the door was.

'Now we go behind the door.'

She turned to him. 'I'm – I'm tired,' she said.

'I know.'

He kissed her forehead. Moving behind her, he turned the handle and urged her forward through the door.

As soon as she heard the door close behind her she knew that Prince was no longer there. She turned quickly. She was right. She tried the handle. It wouldn't give. She heard his footsteps somewhere. She straightened herself. Nothing mattered.

A red glow came from behind thin veils or curtains suspended from the roof. She heard the distant creak of someone shifting his weight in a chair. The room was unexpectedly long and narrow, more like a tunnel than a room.

'Amy?' he called. 'Come closer. Is it really you?'

She walked under the veil; it slid slowly over her head, seeming to linger in her hair, like a hand or the trail of a bird, or like a known dress with its intimate pink.

'Does this take you back?' he said.

Amy stared. The man was a long way away. She could see that he wore some kind of hood or cowl. He began to move towards her. There was time for her to run but she did not run. Perhaps there was no time, either, not really. She knew who the man was now.

'Do you remember?'

'Yes, I remember,' she said.

'Look what you've done to me. Look what I've done to you . . .'

'Are you – will you kill me now?'

'Again? How can I? You're already dead – can't you see? Life is hell, life is murder, but then death is very lifelike. Death is terribly easy to believe.'

He had been coming forward for some time now and still had quite a way to go. She started to move towards him, to make the next thing happen sooner, to save time.

'You know who I am?'

'Yes.'

'And now you know I can never leave you. I am the policeman, I am the murderer. Try again, take care, be good. Your life was too poor not to last for ever. Get it right this time. Come, I'll be very quick.'

His arms enfolded her. She felt a sensation of speed so intense that her nose caught the tang of smouldering air. She saw a red beach bubbled with sandpools under a furious and unstable sun. She felt she was streaming, she felt she was undoing everywhere. Oh, father, she thought, my mouth is full of *stars*. Please put them out and take me home to bed.

The sensation of speed returned for a moment, then nothing did.

⌣ ⌣ ⌣

Her first feeling, as she smelled the air, was one of intense and helpless gratitude. I'm all right, she thought with a gasp. Time – it's starting again. She tried to blink away all the water in her eyes, but there was too much to deal with and she soon shut them tight.

'Are you all right now, Amy?' her mother asked.

'Yes.'

'You're yourself again? Are you sure?'

Amy opened her eyes. She was lying on her bed. 'I'm sorry,' she said.

'I don't know what comes over you sometimes. You just *have* to have your own way, don't you. Oh well. Off you go then, this time.'

'Thank you. I'm sorry.'

'Be good now.'

Her mother left the room. Amy sat up. She must have been crying for a long time. It was a relief to be able to stop, and to rejoin things again. She wiped her tears away in front of the mirror and hurriedly brushed her hair.

She ran down the stairs. Her father stood with his back turned in the hall. He was winding the grandfather clock. She walked up to him and put her hand on his shoulder, her face full of gentle insistence.

'Amy,' he said, and turned slowly. 'Back in the land of the living, are you?'

'Forgiven?'

He took her hand and kissed it. 'Forgiven. Now take care.'

Amy opened the door and stepped out into the afternoon.

Epilogue

This is a promise. I won't do anything to her if she doesn't want me to. I won't do anything to her unless she *asks* for it. And that's not very likely, is it, at her age? That's not very *realistic*? Still, at least she's legal – just about, I'm pretty sure.

Here she comes, shutting the front door behind her and walking quickly down the path. I'm standing in the deep shade on the other side of the street. Even at this distance I can tell by the brightness in her eyes that she's been crying. Poor baby . . . Oh man, what is that girl doing to me? She's doing something. I'll find out in time. Time . . . I feel as though I've done these things before, and am glazedly compelled to do them again. But perhaps all things like this feel like that. I'm – I'm tired. I'm not in control any more, not this time. Oh hell. Let's get it over with.

Any moment now I'll step out into the street. I can see her coming to the end of the path and hesitating as she reaches the road, looking this way and that, wondering which way to go.

BY THE SAME AUTHOR

Success

A candid study of sex and class, sparkling with wit and insight. 'Beautifully constructed to make a coherent, powerful and still fairly unusual statement about changing English society' – *Evening Standard*. 'A terrifying, painfully funny Swiftian exercise in moral disgust' – *Observer*

The Rachel Papers

Winner of the Somerset Maugham Award. Charles Highway, a precociously intelligent and highly sexed teenager, is determined to Sleep With an Older Woman before he turns twenty. 'Extravagantly sexual . . . highly enjoyable' – *Evening Standard*. 'Very funny indeed' – *Spectator*

Dead Babies

A dazzling satire on the seventies – toxic, tasteless, funny and ferocious. 'It's transfixing . . . At first it's funny. It teases, exaggerates, deliberates. Then it becomes ferocious, stricken, moving . . .' *The Times*. 'Very funny, extremely clever' – *Guardian*. 'Viciously funny, at once a hilarious joke and a technical triumph' – *Financial Times*

Money

'Terribly, terminally funny: laughter in the dark, if ever I heard it' – *Guardian*. 'An astonishing achievement. The work of an artist of rare talent' – *Scotsman*. 'One of the key books of the decade' – *London Review of Books*. 'A book that should rank with *Lolita*' – *Literary Review*

Einstein's Monsters

'In five cataclysmic short stories Amis creates perplexing visions of a post-nuclear-holocaust world, highlighting schizophrenia, rape, brutality and suppurating despair' – *Daily Mail*. 'A provocative and highly accomplished collection' – *The Times Literary Supplement*.